RECKLESS CREED

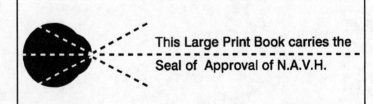

This Large Print Book carries the
Seal of Approval of N.A.V.H.

RECKLESS CREED

ALEX KAVA

THORNDIKE PRESS
A part of Gale, Cengage Learning

GALE
CENGAGE Learning·

Farmington Hills, Mich • San Francisco • New York • Waterville, Maine
Meriden, Conn • Mason, Ohio • Chicago

GALE
CENGAGE Learning®

LIBRARY OF CONGRESS CATALOGING-IN-PUBLICATION DATA

Names: Kava, Alex, author.
Title: Reckless creed / Alex Kava.
Description: Large print edition. | Waterville, Maine : Thorndike Press Large Print, 2016. | Series: Thorndike press large print basic
Identifiers: LCCN 2016036046 | ISBN 9781410484796 (hardback) | ISBN 1410484793 (hardcover)
Subjects: LCSH: Search dogs—Fiction. | O'Dell, Maggie (Fictitious character)—Fiction. | Dog trainers—Fiction. | Search and rescue operations—Fiction. | Veterans—United States—Fiction. | Criminal profilers—Fiction. | Conspiracies—Fiction. | Large type books. | BISAC: FICTION / Suspense. | GSAFD: Mystery fiction. | Suspense fiction.
Classification: LCC PS3561.A8682 R43 2016b | DDC 813/.54—dc23
LC record available at https://lccn.loc.gov/2016036046

Published in 2016 by arrangement with G. P. Putnam's Sons, an imprint of Penguin Publishing Group, a division of Penguin Random House LLC

Printed in the United States of America
1 2 3 4 5 6 7 20 19 18 17 16

In Memory of
Patricia R. Kava
July 17, 1933–February 17, 2016

And again for my boy, Scout.
(March 18, 1998–May 8, 2014)
This whole series is dedicated to you,
buddy.

1

CHICAGO

Tony Briggs coughed up blood, then wiped his mouth with his shirtsleeve. *This was bad.* Although it was nothing he couldn't handle. He'd been through worse. Lots worse. But still, they didn't tell him he'd get this sick. He was beginning to think the bastards had double-crossed him.

He tapped out "fine mess I got myself into" on his cell phone and hit Send before he changed his mind.

The text message wasn't part of his instructions. Not part of the deal. He didn't care. So what if the watchers found out. What could they do to him now? He already felt like crap. They couldn't make him feel much worse.

He tossed the phone into the garbage can along with the few brochures he'd picked up throughout the day. His itinerary read like a sightseeing family vacation. Or in his case, something presented by one of those make-a-wish charities — one final trip, all expenses paid.

He laughed at that and ended up in a coughing fit. Blood sprayed the flat-screen TV and even the wall behind. He didn't like leaving the mess for the hotel housekeeping staff. But it was a little too late for that. Especially since his instructions included touching everything he could throughout the day. The list rattled in his head: light switches, elevator buttons, restaurant menus, remote controls, and escalator handrails.

Earlier that morning at the McDonald's — before the cough, just before the fever spiked and he still had a bit of bravado along with an appetite — he'd felt his first tinge of apprehension. He'd taken his tray and stopped at the condiment counter.

Touch as many surfaces as possible.

He'd been told to do just that. Germs could live on a hard surface for up to eighteen hours. He might have screwed up a lot of things in his life, but he could still follow instructions.

That was what he'd been thinking when he felt a tap on his elbow.

"Hey, mister, could you please hand me two straws?"

The kid was six, maybe seven, with nerdy

glasses, the thick black frames way too big for his face. He kept shoving at them, the motion second nature. The kid reminded Tony immediately of his best friend, Jason. They had grown up together since they were six years old. Same schools. Same football team. Joined the army together. Even came back from Afghanistan, both screwed up in one way or another. Tony was the athlete. Jason was the brains. Smart and pushy even at six. But always following Tony around.

Old four-eyes.

"Whadya doing now?" was Jason's favorite catchphrase.

In grade school they went through a period where Jason mimicked everything Tony did. In high school the kid bulked up just so he could be on the football team, right alongside Tony. In the back of his mind he knew Jason probably joined the army only because Tony wanted to. And look where it got them.

Tony shoved at the guilt. And suddenly at that moment he found himself hoping that Jason never found out what a coward he really was.

"Mister." The kid waited with his hand outstretched.

Tony caught himself reaching for the damned straw dispenser, then stopped

9

short, fingertips inches away.

"Get your own damned straws," he told the kid. "You're not crippled."

Then he turned and left without even getting his own straw or napkin. Without touching a single thing on the whole frickin' condiment counter. In fact, he took his tray and walked out, shouldering the door open so he wouldn't have to touch it either. He dumped the tray and food in a nearby trash can. The kid had unnerved him so much it took him almost an hour to move on.

Now back in his hotel room, sweat trickled down his face. He wiped at his forehead with the same sleeve he'd used on his mouth.

The fever was something he'd expected. The blurred vision was a surprise.

No, it was more than blurred vision. The last hour or so he knew he'd been having hallucinations. He thought he saw one of his old drill sergeants in the lobby of the John Hancock building. But he'd been too nauseated from the observatory to check it out. Still, he remembered to touch every single button before he got out of the elevator. Nauseated and weak-kneed.

And he was embarrassed.

His mind might not be what it once was thanks to what the doctors called traumatic brain injury, but he was proud that he'd kept his body lean and strong when so many of his buddies had come back without limbs. Now the muscle fatigue set in and it actually hurt to breathe.

Just then Tony heard a click in the hotel room. It came from somewhere behind him. It sounded like the door.

The room's entrance had a small alcove for the minibar and coffeemaker. He couldn't see the door without crossing the room.

"Is anybody there?" he asked as he stood up out of the chair.

Was he hallucinating again or had a shadow moved?

Suddenly everything swirled and tipped to the right. He leaned against the room service cart. He'd ordered it just like his watchers had instructed him to do when he got back to his room. Never mind that he hadn't been able to eat a thing. Even the scent of fresh strawberries made his stomach roil.

No one was there.

Maybe the fever was making him paranoid. It certainly made him feel like he was burning up from the inside. He needed to cool down. Get some fresh air.

Tony opened the patio door and immediately shivered. The small cement balcony had a cast-iron railing, probably one of the original fixtures that the hotel had decided to keep when renovating — something quaint and historic.

The air felt good. Cold against his sweat-drenched body, but good. Made him feel alive. And he smiled at that. Funny how being this sick could make him feel so alive. He'd come close to being killed in Afghanistan several times, knew the exhilaration afterward.

He stepped out into the night. His head was still three pounds too heavy, but the swirling sensation had eased a bit. And he could breathe finally without hacking up blood.

Listening to the rumble and buzz of the city below, he realized if he wanted to, there'd be nothing to this. He had contemplated his own death many times since coming home, but never once had he imagined this.

Suddenly he realized it'd be just like stepping out of a C-130.

Only without a parachute.

Nineteen stories made everything look like a miniature world below. Matchbox cars. The kind he and Jason had played with. Fought over. Traded. Shared.

And that was when the second wave of nausea hit him.

Maybe he didn't have to finish this. He didn't even care anymore whether they paid him. Maybe it wasn't too late to get to an emergency room. They could probably give him something. Then he'd just go home. There were easier ways to make a few bucks.

But as he started to turn around he felt a shove. Not the wind. Strong hands. A shadow. His arms flailed trying to restore his balance.

Another shove.

His fingers grabbed for the railing but his body was already tipping. The metal dug into the small of his back. His vision blurred with streaks of light. His ears filled with the echo of a wind tunnel. The cold air surrounded him.

No second chances. He was already falling.

2

Ryder Creed's T-shirt stuck to his back. His hiking boots felt like cement blocks, caked with red clay. The air grew heavier, wet and stifling. The scent of pine mixed with the gamy smell of exertion from both man and dog. This deep in the woods even the birds were different, the drilling of the red-cockaded woodpecker the only sound to interrupt the continuous buzz of mosquitoes.

He was grateful for the long-sleeved shirt and the kerchief around his neck as well as the one around Grace's. The fabric had been soaked in a special concoction that his business partner, Hannah, had mixed up, guaranteed to repel bugs. Hannah joked that one more ingredient and maybe it'd even keep them safe from vampires.

In a few hours it would be nighttime in the forest, and deep in the sticks, as they called it, on the border of Alabama and

14

Florida, there were enough reasons to drive a man to believe in vampires. The kudzu climbed and twisted up the trees, so thick it looked like green netting. There were places the sunlight couldn't squeeze down through the branches.

Their original path was quickly becoming overgrown. Thorny vines grabbed at Creed's pant legs, and he worried they were ripping into Grace's short legs. He was already second-guessing bringing the Jack Russell terrier instead of one of his bigger dogs, but Grace was the best air-scent dog he had in a pack of dozens. And she was scampering along enjoying the adventure, making her way easily through the tall longleaf pines that grew so close Creed had to sidestep in spots.

They had less than an hour until sunset, and yet the federal agent from Atlanta was still questioning Creed.

"You don't think you need more than the one dog?"

Agent Lawrence Tabor had already remarked several times about how small Grace was, and that she was "kind of scrawny." Creed had heard him whisper to Sheriff Wylie that he was "pretty sure Labs or German shepherds were the best trackers."

Creed was used to it. He knew that neither he nor his dogs were what most law enforcement officers expected. He'd been training and handling dogs for over seven years. His business, K9 CrimeScents, had a waiting list for his dogs. Yet people expected him to be older, and his dogs to be bigger.

Grace was actually one of his smallest dogs, a scrappy brown-and-white Jack Russell terrier. Creed had discovered her abandoned at the end of his long driveway. When he found her she was skin and bones but sagging where she had recently been nursing puppies. Locals had gotten into the habit of leaving their unwanted dogs at the end of Creed's fifty-acre property. It wasn't the first time he had seen a female dog dumped and punished when the owner was simply too cheap to get her spayed.

Hannah didn't like that people took advantage of Creed's soft heart. But what no one — not even Hannah — understood was that the dogs Creed rescued were some of his best air-scent trackers. Skill was only a part of the training. Bonding with the trainer was another. His rescued dogs trusted him unconditionally and were loyal beyond measure. They were eager to learn and anxious to please. And Grace was one of his best.

"Working multiple dogs at the same time can present problems," he finally told the agent. "Competition between the dogs. False alerts. Overlapping grids. Believe me, one dog will be more than sufficient."

Creed kept his tone matter-of-fact for Grace's sake. Emotion runs down the leash. Dogs could detect their handler's mood, so Creed always tried to keep his temper in check even when guys like Agent Tabor started to piss him off.

He couldn't help wonder why Tabor was here, but he kept it to himself. Creed wasn't law enforcement. He was hired to do a job and had no interest in questioning jurisdiction or getting involved in the pissing contests that local and federal officials often got into.

"I can't think she'd run off this far," Sheriff Wylie said.

He was talking about the young woman they were looking for. The reason they were out here searching. But now Creed realized the sheriff was starting to question his judgment, too, even though the two of them had worked together plenty of times.

Creed ignored both men as best he could and concentrated on Grace. He could hear her breathing getting more rapid. She started to hold her nose higher, and he tightened his grip on the leash. She had definitely entered a scent cone, but Creed had no idea if it was secondary or primary. All he could smell was the river, but that wasn't what had Grace's attention.

"How long has she been gone?" Creed asked Sheriff Wylie.

"Since the night before last."

Creed had been told that Izzy Donner was nineteen, a recovering drug addict who was getting her life back on track. She had enrolled in college part-time and was even looking forward to a trip to Atlanta she had planned with friends. Creed still wasn't quite sure why her family had panicked. A couple nights out of touch didn't seem out of the ordinary for a teenager.

"Tell me again why you think she ran off into the forest. Are you sure she wasn't taken against her will?"

Seemed like a logical reason that a federal agent might be involved if the girl had been taken. The two men exchanged a glance. Creed suspected they were withholding information from him.

"Why would it matter?" Tabor finally asked. "If your dog is any good, it should still be able to find her, right?"

"It would matter because there'd be another person's scent."

"We had a tip called in," Wylie admitted, but Tabor shot him a look and cut him off from saying anything else.

Before Creed could push for more, Grace started tugging for him to hurry. Her breathing had increased, her nose and whiskers twitched. He knew she was headed for the river.

"Slow down a bit, Grace," he told her.

"Slow down" was something a handler didn't like telling his dog. But sometimes the drive could take over and send a dog barreling through dangerous terrain. He'd heard of working dogs scraping their pads raw, so focused and excited about finding the scent that would reward them.

Grace kept pulling. Creed's long legs were moving fast to keep up. The tangle of vines threatened to trip him while Grace skipped between them, jumping over fallen branches and straining at the end of her leash. He focused on keeping up with her and not letting go.

Only now did Creed notice that Agent Tabor and Sheriff Wylie were trailing farther behind. He didn't glance back but could hear their voices becoming more muffled, interspersed with some curses as they tried to navigate the prickly underbrush.

Finally Grace slowed down. Then she

stopped. But the little dog was still frantically sniffing the air. Creed could see and hear the river five feet away. He watched Grace and waited. Suddenly the dog looked up to find his eyes and stared at him.

This was their signal. Creed knew the dog wasn't trying to determine what direction to go next, nor was she looking to him for instructions. Grace was telling him she had found their target. That she knew exactly where it was but she didn't want to go any closer.

Something was wrong.

"What is it?" Sheriff Wylie asked while he and Tabor approached, trying to catch their breath and keep a safe distance.

"I think she's in the water," Creed said.

"What do you mean she's in the water?" Tabor asked.

But Wylie understood. "Oh crap."

"Grace, stay," Creed told the dog, and dropped the leash.

He knew he didn't need the command. The dog was spooked, and it made Creed's stomach start to knot up.

He maneuvered his way over the muddy clay of the riverbank, holding on to tree branches to keep from sliding. He didn't know that Wylie was close behind until he heard the older man's breath catch at the same time that Creed saw the girl's body.

Her eyes stared up as if she were watching the clouds. The girl's Windbreaker was still zipped up and had ballooned out, causing her upper body to float while the rest of her lay on the sandy bottom. This part of the Blackwater River was only about three feet deep. Though tea-colored, the water was clear. And even in the fading sunlight Creed could see that the girl's pockets were weighted down.

"Son of a bitch," he heard Wylie say from behind. "Looks like she loaded up her pockets with rocks and walked right into the river."

3

Creed kept Grace on her leash, although he exchanged the working one for a retractable that allowed her more freedom. He'd backed her off to a clearing along the river, about ten feet away, where she could enjoy her reward. She chomped down on the pink toy elephant, making it squeak repeatedly, the sound foreign out there amid the buzz of insects and the gentle churn of the water.

From where he stood he could still see the body downstream. Creed's job was to help find whatever they were looking for, but he wasn't a part of the investigation. Once the search was over, he took his dog and stayed out of the way until and unless there was something else that needed to be found.

A Marine and K9 unit handler, Creed had remained a certified trainer and handler after leaving the military. Hannah managed the business and Creed trained the dogs. In seven years, their facility in the Florida Panhandle had become a multimillion-dollar business. They'd earned a national reputation for their quality training and the success rates of their air-scent dogs. And they did it by rescuing abandoned and discarded dogs and turning them into heroes.

As he watched Grace fling her toy up into the air and jump to retrieve it, he couldn't imagine how anyone would abandon such a smart and spirited animal. But then, Creed had seen firsthand enough depravity to last a lifetime.

He looked back at the young woman's body. Whether or not he was a part of the investigation, he couldn't help but wonder what had happened. Bobbing in the water, she looked small, almost childlike despite the ballooning jacket.

Sheriff Wylie had said earlier that her family claimed she might have gotten lost. Did she really intend to go for a walk alone in the forest, then just lose her way? Not impossible. People got lost. It happened all the time, and Creed and his dogs were often called in at such times.

The Conecuh National Forest covered eighty-four thousand acres between Andalusia, Alabama, and the Florida state line. The

Conecuh Trail was twenty-two miles, a trek popular with hikers during the winter and early spring months. But the trail was up in the northeast part of the forest, nowhere near here. In fact, they hadn't seen anything that resembled a trail for quite some time.

If Izzy Donner went for a walk in the forest, why did she stray so far off the trail? Did she actually put rocks in her pockets and walk into the river?

Creed watched Sheriff Wylie and Agent Tabor. Both men were on their cell phones. They stood on the riverbank. Neither attempted to get closer to the body. The sheriff was animated as he talked, waving his arms, pushing his hat back, then jerking the brim back down low over his brow. Agent Tabor, on the other hand, looked calm and appeared to be doing more listening than talking.

They were losing sunlight. The moss-draped branches hung over the area, creating long shadows. Creed pulled out his GPS tracker and saved the coordinates. It would make it easier for the recovery team to find this spot whether they came by foot or by boat.

He reached around into his daypack for Grace's collapsible bowl and grabbed his flashlight, too. He clipped it onto his belt, then poured water for Grace. She came to the sound, sat, and placed her toy beside her, waiting patiently for a drink. He squatted down to make sure there were no fire ants nearby, then placed the bowl for her. Before he stood back up, Creed noticed a flash of reddish brown under a scrawny cypress bush about five feet away.

He left Grace to investigate. The shadows made it difficult to see under the brush. He switched on his Maglite as he planted one knee on pine needles a couple feet from the cypress.

It was a dead bird. The robin lay belly up — its red breast was what had caught Creed's attention. He couldn't see any marks from a predator. It looked untouched. He heard the crunch of branches behind him and turned to see Grace. She was prancing and wagging, proud to be bringing him something. She offered it to him, and that was when Creed's stomach dropped to his knees.

It was another dead robin.

"Give it to me, Grace." He kept the emotion from his voice as he put his hand out. She released the robin, dropping it into his palm.

"I thought your dogs weren't supposed to put dead stuff in their mouths."

Sheriff Wylie had made his way over to the clearing and stood with strings of kudzu trailing from his pant legs while he swatted mosquitoes on his face. He looked like a comedic character from an old movie, slapping himself and leaving red welts from his own hand.

"They know the difference," Creed told him, "between dead animals and dead humans. I don't train them to track dead animal scent, so it's not off limits. She saw I was interested in this one and brought me another."

Creed pulled out two plastic Ziploc bags from his daypack and gathered the robins, one in each bag. He stayed calm and kept his movements casual. He didn't want to punish Grace for doing something that was second nature to her, but he also didn't want her to see his concern.

Truth was, he had a bad feeling about these dead birds, and he hated that Grace had taken one in her mouth.

■ ■ ■ ■

TWO DAYS LATER

MONDAY

■ ■ ■ ■

4

CHICAGO

By the time FBI agent Maggie O'Dell's flight started its descent, a light dusting of snow covered the runway at O'Hare International Airport. She'd left Washington, D.C., in sunny skies. Sun or snow, it didn't matter. O'Dell hated flying. But if she had to land in snow, thank goodness it was at an airport that was used to it. Where better than Chicago?

As the plane taxied, O'Dell watched the ground crew, some in jackets and no headgear, caught off guard by the unexpected March snow as though it were winter's last hurrah. She hadn't just left sunny skies but warm weather as well. The East Coast had been enjoying springlike conditions for weeks now.

Looking out the window, O'Dell suddenly felt a chill. She pulled up the zipper of her sweater, but she knew it had nothing to do with the weather. It was this assignment.

Months ago it had already become a cold case. There had been no leads, no trails, no digital footprints. *Nothing.*

It was almost as if the subject, Dr. Clare Shaw, had vanished. As if she had been buried in the North Carolina mudslide that had taken out the research facility where she'd served as director. It was the last place the scientist had been seen. Yet they had good reason to believe that not only had Dr. Shaw evaded death, but, quite possibly, she had murdered several people in order to cover up her own escape.

O'Dell had been tasked with finding Shaw. After five months it was beginning to feel like she was hunting a ghost.

Until now.

Detective Lexington Jacks had arranged to meet O'Dell at baggage claim. O'Dell picked out the detective from across the terminal — the woman was the only one in the crowd without a handbag or suitcase. Plus she looked like a cop, dressed in a trench coat and trousers with her legs spread and arms at her side. Her eyes were inspecting everything and everyone and still they skimmed over O'Dell, dismissing her.

Then Jacks backtracked and found her. She made eye contact but waited to be sure.

When O'Dell nodded, Jacks started making her way through the crowd.

The detective was tall with a confident gait. Her hair was pulled back, emphasizing smooth brown skin flawed only by a faint white scar on her upper left cheek. Up close, O'Dell could see that the woman was older than her, most likely well into her forties. Crow's-feet danced at the corners of her eyes.

"Detective Jacks." O'Dell met her halfway.

"Agent O'Dell, call me Lexi. Do you have more baggage?" she asked as she hitched a thumb over her shoulder, pointing to the carousel behind her.

"This is it."

"No coat?"

"In my carry-on."

"You're gonna need it." Jacks stopped and crossed her arms as if expecting O'Dell to open up her roller bag right there and dig out the coat. O'Dell almost smiled. She couldn't remember the last time a law enforcement officer was concerned about her well-being.

When O'Dell didn't make a move, Jacks said, "Okay, suit yourself. We need to hit the ground running. They're ready to process the room. It's my understanding they're waiting for you." Jacks stuffed her hands in

31

her pockets and turned to lead the way.

"How much containment were you able to get before CDC arrived?" O'Dell asked, walking beside the detective and trying to keep up with the woman's long strides.

"The hotel's management had the good sense to close off the room as soon as they discovered the victim was one of their guests."

"Housekeeping hasn't been in?"

"Hotel management says no."

"No cops?"

"We already had a body on the sidewalk. Of course, we taped off the room, but with a jumper there's usually no hurry. Good thing, because our techs would not have suspected the place might be hot."

By "hot," she meant contaminated by a possible deadly virus. It was the medical examiner who had discovered during the autopsy that the man's organs had begun hemorrhaging days before his body hit the sidewalk.

Jacks led O'Dell through the crowd and to the front exit. O'Dell followed her out into the cold. They didn't need to walk far. An airport security guard stood alongside a dark blue sedan. When he saw Jacks he opened the door on the passenger side for O'Dell as he took her roller bag and placed it in the trunk.

"Thanks, Carl." Jacks rewarded him with a wide, toothy smile, then ducked into the car.

As soon as the sedan left from under the awning, large wet snowflakes decorated the windshield.

"Did anyone see him jump?" O'Dell asked.

"No, but several people saw him hit the sidewalk. We don't think anyone touched him." Jacks reached over and hit a button, blasting hot air. "Nineteen stories, flat on his face," she said. "Ever see a person after a fall like that?"

O'Dell had seen bodies in many stages of decay, pulled out from underwater and underground, as well as bodies that had been tortured and dismembered, but no, she hadn't seen one after a fall like that. She shook her head.

"Actually didn't look too bad," Jacks told her. "On the outside. I don't know what I was expecting. ME said there was a lot of hemorrhaging inside. The lungs were a bloody mess."

"What kind of protective gear was the ME wearing?"

Jacks winced as she said, "Evidently it wasn't enough. CDC has him in isolation."

5

No one paid attention as Agent O'Dell and Detective Jacks walked through the hotel's huge, luxurious lobby. Lines of travelers waited to check in. Bellhops pushed loaded carts. Small groups of men and women in business attire huddled together, making plans. Other than the police officer walking the perimeter, there were no indications that anything was wrong. The four-star hotel on Michigan Avenue was a curious choice for a man to end his life.

Jacks had explained that the entire nineteenth floor had been evacuated and isolated. The only access was by elevator with a special keycard. When the elevator doors opened, one of Jacks's officers nodded at them from his post. Detective Jacks led O'Dell to a staging area right around the corner. Each hallway had been barricaded with crime scene tape. Three feet beyond, a thick plastic sheet hung from the high ceiling to the floor.

A stainless steel cart held boxes of latex gloves and surgical masks. A stack of Tyvek coveralls were folded and sealed individually in plastic bags. On the bottom shelf were hoods with plastic shielded faceplates.

The sight of the gear made O'Dell hesitate. A few years ago she had found herself in an isolation ward at Fort Detrick on the other side of a hazmat suit. After being exposed to the Ebola virus, she'd landed in the slammer. It had been a claustrophobic nightmare. Now, as she stared at the hoods and coveralls, she realized being inside that gear could trigger those feelings all over again.

"You okay?" Jacks asked.

O'Dell held back a grimace. She hated the fact that her discomfort was obvious even to this stranger.

"I'm fine," she told the detective. She thumbed through the stack of plastic-sealed Tyvek coveralls, pretending they might be the objects of her discontent. "They never realize that one size does not fit all."

Jacks smiled at that while she pulled out a cell phone.

"I'll text them that you're here."

"You're not joining us?"

"Not allowed. You know how the CDC is.

Always secretive. Special invitation only. Even though we locals might need to actually know what the hell's going on."

O'Dell felt the detective's eyes watching for her reaction. Though she doubted that Jacks cared whether she might be out of line. She continued, "We're providing officers to secure the scene, help set up a staging area, and stand guard. You know, make sure the CDC's presence is a well-kept secret."

"Don't want to start a public panic."

Again, Jacks eyed her suspiciously.

"Heaven forbid the public know they're in danger," O'Dell added.

The corner of Jacks's lip curved up as she recognized O'Dell's sarcasm.

"They didn't even want to tell us what was going on. Made it sound like it was some routine check."

"But the ME had already told you."

"That's right."

"Hey, Maggie," a hooded figure called to her from down the hallway.

She was expecting Roger Bix, the CDC director who had requested her presence. But before the man pushed back the faceplate, O'Dell had already recognized Colonel Benjamin Platt from his voice.

"Ben?"

Platt was not a part of the CDC. He was the director of USAMRIID, the U.S. Army Medical Research Institute of Infectious Diseases. He was the doctor who had quarantined her in the slammer at Fort Detrick after her Ebola exposure. The two had since become friends . . . more than friends. Right now she wasn't sure if she was upset because he hadn't told her he was here or because his presence meant this was a much more serious incident.

"Assistant Director Kunze didn't mention that you were going to be here."

Assistant Director Raymond Kunze was O'Dell's boss at the FBI.

Instead of answering, Platt smiled at Detective Jacks and said, "Thanks for making sure Agent O'Dell arrived safely."

Jacks glanced from Platt to O'Dell, recognizing that she was being dismissed. She handed O'Dell a business card and said, "Call me if there's anything else I can help with or any questions I can answer."

"I'd like to see the autopsy report," O'Dell told her.

Jacks's eyes darted to the colonel, and it was Platt who answered. "I can get you a copy."

The two women exchanged a look that echoed their earlier frustration with government bureaucrats. Ironically, Jacks saw O'Dell as an ally despite her federal badge. She could see that the detective knew exactly what Platt was doing, shutting her out yet again even though he and the CDC were all too willing to use her department's resources and have the Chicago police provide a cover and protection for them to work in secret.

O'Dell wanted to remind him that it only made things more difficult in the long run. She had worked with enough local law enforcement officials to know that pulling rank and flexing your federal muscles only ruffled feathers and sometimes put you in danger if you needed them to watch your back.

Jacks gave O'Dell a smile and nodded at Platt as she turned and left. He watched, waiting for Jacks to be gone and the elevator doors to fully close.

"I think we may have found her," Platt finally said.

Without asking, O'Dell knew he meant Dr. Clare Shaw, the scientist-slash-madwoman whom O'Dell had been trying to track down for months.

Dread knotted in her stomach. When the scientist disappeared they believed she had confiscated and taken with her a lockbox from her research facility. An insulated lock-box that most likely contained at least three deadly viruses.

"Bix is examining the blood labs himself. That's why he asked me to help you process the room."

Roger Bix was the infectious-control director at the CDC. He and Platt had worked together many times on cases that had been as dangerous as they were frightening. One of those had been her own exposure to Ebola.

"Even if this jumper was infected with one of the viruses Shaw stole, how can you be certain it came from her? Surely there are other ways he may have come in contact with it." She started putting on the gear, doing her best to hide her hesitation.

"I know this isn't easy for you, Maggie."

She glanced up at him. The bureaucrat who had rudely sent Detective Jacks away was gone. Soft brown eyes found and held hers. He had removed the hood, and tufts of his short hair stood on end. This was the man who had won her friendship and even a piece of her heart.

"You don't have to do this," he continued. "I know Shaw is your case, but AD Kunze could send someone else to do this part."

"No, it's okay." She reached for one of the

hoods and a pair of gloves. "Besides, I'm already here, so let's do this."

She felt his eyes still studying her. "You didn't answer my question," she said as she rolled up the cuffs of the Tyvek suit, then wrapped and secured the Velcro straps tightly around her ankles, then around her wrists. "How can you know that the virus in this jumper has anything to do with Dr. Clare Shaw?"

"From the samples that the medical examiner provided the CDC. Bix has already determined that the young man was infected with the bird flu. He's double-checking his findings and rerunning some tests, but he sounds quite certain it's a new strain of the virus. One we've never seen before."

"And Dr. Shaw?"

"We know she was working on it before her research facility was destroyed in the mudslide."

"Wait a minute. If it's never been seen before, how was she working on it?"

"She helped create it."

6

"What's so special about a goddamned dog?"

The old man ambushed Creed and Jason as soon as they brought the dogs through the security door to the senior care facility. Creed recognized the man from the last time he had visited. The old guy had grilled Creed on how he'd gotten into the place. Creed had pointed to the door but failed to mention he knew the security code.

"They keep that door locked," he'd told Creed at the time, and he only seemed to become more agitated by Creed's casual attitude.

At first Creed believed the man was concerned about safety, fearing that someone could easily breach security and come in. But then he told Creed, "Let me know when you're leaving, so I can get the hell out of here with you."

That incident had stuck with Creed. He

couldn't imagine being held someplace against his will and everyone around him telling him it was his new home. He almost hadn't come back today except for Hannah's pestering and nagging. Somehow — as always — she'd convinced him this was a valuable training opportunity for their dogs.

So he'd brought Jason with him. But already Creed could see that the old man had rattled Jason as well. The kid was tense. Jason had told Creed on their drive that his grandfather had been moved to this place recently. He admitted he hadn't been to see him, but it didn't look like guilt that had Jason shifting his weight from one foot to another.

As soon as the old guy left, Jason confessed in almost a whisper, "I'm just not comfortable around old people."

"Why?" Creed asked, and that one-word question seemed to startle Jason. Sort of like the kid didn't think he'd ever need to explain it any further than making the statement.

"What do you mean, why?"

"What is it about old people that makes you uncomfortable?"

Jason thought about it.

"For one thing, they get away with saying stupid things. Stating the obvious. It's like they get a pass for being rude or embarrassing. Just because they're old. Ten bucks says we're not in there fifteen minutes and one of them points at me and says something like, 'Oh look, that guy's missing half his arm.'"

"No different than kids. Maybe that's how you need to look at them — like they're kids again."

"Yeah, well, one of those kids taught me how to ride a bike. Picked me up and carried me when I wiped out. Hard to think of him as a kid. I looked up to him."

Creed didn't have an answer. The only grandparent he'd ever known died when he was a teenager, shortly after his sister Brodie disappeared. He always figured not knowing what had happened to Brodie had probably killed his grandmother. Years later Creed knew it was what drove his father to commit suicide. In one way or another, Brodie's disappearance had killed a piece of all of them.

Now, as Creed and Jason waited for the director, Creed squatted down on his haunches so he was eye level with the dogs. Grace didn't need his reassurance. She was a pro, anxious to get to work. Her nose was already working the air. But this was Molly's first time outside their training facility, and Creed wanted it to be a positive experience for her.

He scratched behind her ears and told her what a good girl she was. She was watching Jason's foot tapping. Her tail was down.

Creed glanced up at Jason, disappointed to find his trainee's eyes darting around the community area and checking the hallways to the rooms. His eyes were everywhere except the one place they needed to be — on his dog. He was so caught up in his own discomfort that he wasn't paying attention to Molly.

With one hand Creed continued to pet Molly. With his other hand he covered the toe of Jason's shoe. Then he leaned down hard, putting as much weight as he could on the top of Jason's foot, pinning it to the floor.

The tapping stopped.

7

Creed glanced up. He could see Jason holding back a grimace of pain.

"Emotion runs down the leash," he reminded the kid before taking his hand off Jason's foot.

The kid nodded. Shifted his weight and his attention. He tightened his grip on Molly's lead.

This was supposed to be a training session for Jason as well as the dog. Jason had started working with Creed and the dogs about seven months ago. When Jason wasn't so focused on himself, Creed saw signs that he would make a good dog handler. He seemed to genuinely enjoy the dogs, and the dogs were eager to please him when they trained together.

Creed was trying to cut the kid some slack. A year ago Jason was still in Afghanistan when his life turned upside down. An IED explosion took off Jason's lower right arm. It was a lot for any twenty-one-year-old to deal with. But being a good K9 handler meant constantly putting yourself in situations outside your comfort zone and all the while still thinking about your dog first — above and beyond anyone or anything else. Jason still had a chip on his shoulder and Creed wasn't sure what it would take to change his attitude.

This senior care center was outside Creed's comfort zone, too. As was the topic of their search. Hannah had recently convinced Creed that they needed to include infections and diseases in their repertoire of scent detection. Several years ago she had added natural-disaster searches along with drugs and explosives. All of those were things Creed understood, although he was never crazy about searching for explosives. Like Jason, Creed had experienced an explosion in Afghanistan, too, while he was a Marine K9 handler. The one time he didn't listen to his dog, it had almost gotten both of them killed. He'd learned the hard way the importance of putting his dog and the dog's instincts first.

But Creed respected Hannah's instincts, too. He'd discovered early on that his business partner had a nose of her own for what was right, not just for the business and the dogs, but for him as well. So if Hannah believed they needed to add infections and diseases to their list, Creed added them.

The process was basically the same. He knew the dogs were capable of sniffing out almost anything as long as Creed could figure out a way to communicate with them. He used a variety of techniques that included different words or phrases. "Fish" meant drugs. So he could tell his dog to "go find fish" in the middle of a crowded airport and not have drug dealers or mules running for the exits.

He also changed up collars, harnesses, and vests so his multitask dogs knew what they were searching for from the minute he put on their gear. This medical stuff required a new level of creativity for him to come up with words and phrases that wouldn't alarm patients and residents. After all, he couldn't just tell the dog to "go find cancer."

This care facility had agreed to let them come in and test their dogs. It was a great on-the-job opportunity for both the dogs and the trainers. Yet as Creed patted Molly and Grace while he stood up, he could see that Jason still looked uncomfortable.

"We've been through the drill," Creed told him, eyes boring into him now as he tried to hold the kid's attention. "It's not that much different from our other searches."

"I'm good," Jason said, but his face told a different story.

"The dogs can smell that you are not good."

This time surprise registered on Jason's face. He hadn't thought about that. He looked at the dogs, then reached down, giving them his hand to sniff before he scratched them behind the ears, one at a time.

"But so far, the dogs have only sniffed samples in containers." Jason glanced around the facility again. "Not people."

Creed followed the kid's eyes. Several residents sat on the sofa at the far corner of the room. They were watching the dogs and not the big-screen TV. A couple of old men played cards on the other side of the large area. A staff member smiled as she kept pace alongside an old woman using a walker. Creed decided no one was close enough to listen.

"We walk Grace and Molly around."

"Into their rooms?"

"No. Not unless they invite us. As far as the residents are concerned, they're therapy dogs. They're used to them coming in."

"Like the old guy that met us at the door?"

"He has other motives," Creed said as he

looked over his shoulder to see the man still hanging around the door. "This is Molly's first time out, so I expect her to just observe. But Grace knows what we're here for."

"Because of the collar?"

"Right. She'll sniff the surrounding air, but she should be able to tell if there's a resident with *C. diff* and if so, let us know exactly which person it is. If she does detect it, she'll alert by lying down in front of the infected person, or in the doorway to his or her room."

"You've seen her do this?"

"Twice last week."

"And both people had *C. diff*?"

Creed nodded.

Clostridium difficile was a bacterium picked up from contaminated surfaces and usually spread from health care providers. From Creed's own research, it was particularly nasty because symptoms didn't show up in the beginning. Toxins released by the bacterium attacked the lining of the intestines. The resulting infection could be fatal if not detected early, especially in people with compromised immune systems. Diagnostic tests could be expensive and slow. In the test studies Creed read about, dogs were able to detect *C. diff* with one hundred percent sensitivity and ninety-six percent specificity. And they were able to do so in the very early stages, sooner than any of the available lab tests. The same was true for several cancers.

"I get how dogs sniff out dead stuff and drugs," Jason said, now keeping his voice low and quiet as more residents wandered closer. "Even explosives. They're all very different smells. But infections? Cancer — all that stuff — seems like it would smell similar."

"You mean like a sick person just smells like a sick person."

Jason met Creed's eyes as if checking to see if he was making fun of him. Creed wasn't.

"Remember that dogs can differentiate between smells. Consider beef stew on the stovetop. You smell beef stew. Dogs have the ability to layer scent. They smell the beef, carrots, potatoes, onion . . . every ingredient. They can separate each of those scents. So to Grace — and hopefully Molly — diabetes smells different than cancer, and lung cancer smells different than prostate cancer, because each of those conditions triggers different reactions in the body. The immune system releases different mechanisms to fight or compensate."

"Dead bodies seem easier."

"But even they smell different at various stages of decomposition."

"Okay, I get it," Jason said. "It just seems . . ."

"Too incredible?"

"A little bit."

"But for dogs, it's second nature. A dog's whole world is based on scent. It's just a part of who they are, what they do. They have over three hundred million scent receptors compared to our measly five million. Think of it this way. You can get a whiff of a teaspoon of sugar in your coffee. A dog can detect a teaspoon of sugar in an Olympic-sized swimming pool. It's not just that they have sensitive noses. The part of the dog's brain that's dedicated to analyzing odors is forty times greater than ours. When you think of it that way, we're not training them so much as we're harnessing those abilities and finding a way to communicate what we want them to find."

"Hey, Jason! What are you doing here?"

Both Creed and Jason turned to see the man waving at them from one of the hallways. His feather-white hair stood straight up like he had just crawled out of bed. But Creed thought the rest of the old man — his trousers, buttoned shirt, and cardigan — all looked neat and pressed as if he had just stepped out of a business meeting. Until Creed noticed the pink bunny slippers.

Creed heard Jason stifle a groan before he said, "That's my granddad."

The man clapped Jason on the shoulder as his rheumy blue eyes took in Creed and the dogs.

"You must be working," he said, then offered his hand to Creed. "I'm Gus Seaver."

"Ryder Creed. It's a pleasure to meet you, sir."

Before another word was spoken, Creed and Jason noticed the dogs. Both Grace and Molly were sniffing the air, rapid breaths. Then suddenly the two of them lay down right at the feet of Gus Seaver.

8

CHICAGO

Despite the hood's plastic shield, O'Dell immediately could smell something slightly rotten when she crossed the threshold into the room. Beyond the narrow alcove she saw that everything looked curiously neat. Bedcovers were pulled up and tucked in at the end, though on closer inspection she saw the imprint in the top pillow where someone had laid his head.

Still, there was no clutter occupying the nightstands. The desk's surface had a hotel phone and notepad that hadn't been disturbed. A room service cart in the corner had plates with stainless steel lids still in place. That was where the smell was coming from. O'Dell walked over and gently lifted a lid to find overripened strawberries. They were carefully stacked in an untouched pyramid.

Platt watched her from the alcove, arms crossed, eyes intense. She was getting the first look before he began taking samples. If Jacks was correct, the victim was the last one inside this room.

Then she turned and saw the flat-screen TV. Something had been sprayed across the surface, thick droplets that had dried. She noticed that the wall behind had been splattered, too, with rust-brown flecks that O'Dell suspected might be blood.

She glanced at Platt, inviting his input.

"I'm thinking bloody sputum."

She looked back at the screen and the wall and said, "Seems like a lot."

"The autopsy report has photos of his lungs. I'll forward everything to you."

She went back to examining the room. She'd do an overall view first, then come back and work a grid.

Nothing was missing from the minibar. One glass from the tray held what looked like water. Half full. The other glasses were still upside down on their rims, the coasters on top. The ice bucket was dry. There was nothing out of the ordinary.

"There doesn't appear to be any kind of ritual," she said while her eyes continued the search.

"Ritual?"

"Sometimes when a person commits suicide there'll be small, sort of ritualistic things they'll do. They might take off their glasses, empty the change out of their pockets." She gestured toward the bed. "Make the bed."

"I'm told he had his wallet in his back pocket."

"How about a cell phone?"

Platt shrugged. "That I don't know. There's a duffel bag on the floor of the closet."

She thought about checking out the bag but decided she wanted to see the balcony first. She stopped in front of the sliding glass door. It was unlocked.

"Was this closed when you arrived?" she asked.

"Yes."

She was careful how she touched the handle, using the top and pushing with two fingers instead of grabbing it so she wouldn't destroy any prints. It took some effort to open and when it did slide, it made a grating sound of resistance.

The cement patio was small and the cast-iron railing looked antique. It came as high as her waist. She could hear the traffic below. Through the plastic faceplate the snowflakes glittered. One glance down and she needed to take a step back until the palms of her hands could feel the glass door.

The cold wind swirled around her and she swore she could feel the patio sway underneath her feet.

"It doesn't make sense," Platt said, startling her. She hadn't noticed that he had come to the door. "If you're going to jump, why bother to close the door?"

"Sometimes they're beyond the point of making sense," she told him as she edged her way back inside. Then she carefully closed the door using the same two-finger method. "The small stuff is still instinctive. You close the door without giving it a thought, especially if you have no plans of going back inside."

"How does a criminal profiler know so much about suicide?"

She recognized a hint of admiration in his voice. Their mutual respect and admiration were two things that had brought them together as friends.

"I've investigated a number of murder-suicides." Those were some of the hardest cases, too, trying to climb inside the mind of someone who takes out his entire family or a department store full of strangers before putting the gun to his own head.

"Suicide with an agenda," she told Platt. "Or a mission. The suicide is simply the last step."

She started across the room, heading to check out the bathroom, when she noticed a small wastebasket tucked underneath the desk. She pulled it out to see inside. Carefully using only fingertips again, she plucked through the contents without pulling them out: a torn ticket stub from the Museum of Science and Industry, a folded map of downtown Chicago, several brochures for other tourist attractions, a flyer from the Art Institute, and a napkin from a local pizza place.

She looked up at Platt. "When did he check in?"

"I think Detective Jacks said he'd been here for two days before he jumped."

"You said his lungs looked like the virus was in an advanced stage."

"Definitely."

"How long does it take for that to happen?"

"I'm not sure. Humans rarely get the bird flu, so we don't know a lot of statistics. The information we do have is on victims mostly from Asia. Some of those cases haven't been reported in as much detail as we're used to getting. The theory is that bird flu is mutating so quickly that eventually it'll jump to humans. We know Shaw was working on a strain that would be highly contagious."

"And just how would she accomplish that?"

"By making it airborne. Right now, for humans to get infected they'd need to handle a sick bird or be in direct contact with the bird's blood or droppings. But if Shaw was able to make the virus airborne, all that changes. It could easily spread from birds to humans, then from human to human. We could have a mess on our hands."

O'Dell let that sink in, then asked, "If you had to guess, how long would you say it would take for the lungs to be in an advanced stage?"

"A week. Ten days at the most. Why? What are you thinking?"

She gestured him over to take a look. "Seems like a lot of sightseeing for a guy who's already coughing up blood."

O'Dell watched Platt's face through the face mask as his eyes examined the contents of the wastebasket.

"You don't look surprised."

"It's what we suspected," he finally said. "Actually, it's what we feared."

"Would have been helpful if you had shared those suspicions."

"They were just that — suspicions."

Probably classified suspicions, but she didn't say that. This was a touchy subject, one that had caused a major rift in their friendship. Last fall when they worked together during the North Carolina mudslides, Platt had withheld information. There were details he'd argued were classified and he could only share on a need-to-know basis. Not knowing some of that "classified" information had almost gotten her killed. She had hoped things would be different now.

"We have to be careful with this," he told her when he recognized her irritation. "Unwarranted suspicions trigger alarms. We can't have the media and the public in a panic."

"I'm not the media, Ben, and I'm not the public. You and Roger Bix are going to have to trust me."

"Of course we trust you."

"I'm the one who's supposed to be tracking Shaw. So let me get this straight. You suspect that Dr. Shaw might not have just infected this man, but she sent him out to infect others? Like a suicide bomber, only with a virus instead of shrapnel?"

Platt met her eyes, waited a beat, and said, "Yes."

9

NEW YORK CITY

Christina Lomax stood in the hotel atrium looking out at the street. The watchers had slipped a handwritten note under her hotel room door. It must have been during the two hours she'd finally slept. She hadn't heard a thing.

They'd told her there would always be someone watching over her to help her complete the experiment. But she never saw them. They were like ghosts. Once yesterday she thought she had seen a reflection behind her in a storefront window, but when she turned no one was there. It was getting more and more difficult to tell what was real and what was fever-induced.

They'd warned her about feeling a bit feverish off and on. And there was a reminder in today's message. But they made it sound like it was no big deal. By now she had done enough of these experiments that she knew the discomfort was temporary.

Others had made her light-headed and one even made her nauseated for two days, but every time those minor symptoms didn't last long. Still, she was glad they'd prepared her that it might be several days of feeling bad.

She remembered thinking at the time, how bad could it be? She'd done enough drugs early in life that she didn't think there was much her mind and body hadn't experienced. And although she never considered herself a fighter, she knew she was a survivor. No matter how low she had sunk in the past, she always found a way to make do . . . to survive.

Last summer after her second divorce Christina had lived in her car for two months. When she ran out of gas money she parked at a busy shopping plaza, moving the vehicle from one corner of the lot to another. A Goodwill drop-off box was close by, as were several fast-food restaurants. She had clean clothes and half-eaten sandwiches. When you were hungry enough, Dumpster diving — or trash can diving — was far from gross, especially if you timed it right. Sometimes the discarded fries were still warm.

The more difficult challenge was finding a way to cool off during the hot humid days.

She walked through one of the huge retail stores, pretending to browse and using the bathroom. The women's restrooms at the Home Depot were rarely used during the morning hours, allowing her time to wash her hair and brush her teeth. She'd gotten good at slipping small necessities like deodorant, toothpaste, and shampoo from the department store shelves into her purse. She knew where all the cameras were hidden. She even knew what shifts were lightly manned.

Yes, she had gotten quite good at surviving.

It had almost become a game for her. Until the night she got caught rummaging through a load of donations at the Goodwill drop-off box. She'd expected to hear police sirens. At the very least, a righteous lecture. She never in her wildest dreams expected a job offer. As it turned out, someone recognized that her skills would come in handy.

Ever since then, the money she made from being a part of a few experiments once or twice a month was enough for her to move out of her car and into a studio apartment. But this time — this experiment was huge. Yes, she'd be sick for three to five days, but she'd make more money for those several days than she'd ever made in a year's time.

Now, as Christina stood in the atrium of the Grand Hyatt, she wished she could stay between the cool sheets of her king-sized bed. The fever made her head swim.

She didn't know New York very well, but they had told her that would make her even more convincing in her role as a tourist. They insisted what she saw as a weakness would end up being her biggest asset. And besides, the notes offered ideas of places for her to go. Yesterday the watchers had even slipped a folded map under the hotel door.

They had, however, warned her to stay clear of law enforcement officials. That she could be arrested for loitering if she stayed in one place too long. It was best to keep moving. Not a problem. Christina didn't trust cops, though she realized it was a leftover reaction from her rebellious drug-using days.

As soon as she stepped outside she immediately noticed several men in military fatigues in front of Grand Central Terminal. She walked by two police cruisers. Two officers were across the street, pacing, looking, watching.

Christina made her way to the corner and drew close enough to one of the men in fatigues to make unwanted eye contact. His face was young. She guessed he was about her son's age. His eyes were intense. There was an energy and discipline about the way he moved.

She raised her hand to hail a cab. The soldier was still looking her way.

For a second or two her stomach flipped.

He knows. How can he not?

A taxi swerved up to the curb in front of her. She froze. She waited, expecting the young soldier to yell at her. To stop her.

Finally she stepped forward. Out of the corner of her eye she watched him. Was he quickening his pace?

She grabbed the taxi's door handle and pulled the door open. Just when she thought he would start running at her, he turned on his heel and headed in the opposite direction.

Christina slid into the backseat. A wave of relief washed over her. Only when the cabdriver stared at her did she realize she was drenched in sweat on a cool spring day.

She gave him her destination and sat back.

They were right. She was as good as invisible. She could relax. She was just a forty-something-year-old woman. A tourist.

10

CHICAGO

Platt started pulling out each brochure, each ticket stub and flyer.

"We'll need to track where he's been."

O'Dell couldn't imagine the enormity of that task. Thankfully it was up to Platt and the CDC. Her job was to find whatever she could to track down and stop Shaw.

She moved on to check the man's duffel bag on the floor of the closet when Platt stopped her.

"I'll be damned," he said.

She turned to find him lifting a black-cased cell phone out of the wastebasket.

O'Dell pulled an evidence bag from a pocket in her Tyvek coveralls, but Platt waved a hand at her.

"Sorry, nothing leaves the room until we're sure it's not contaminated."

"Can I at least turn it on and take a look?"

He thought about it for a few seconds, then handed her the phone.

She tried to power it on. The battery was dead. *Of course it was.*

After gently rifling through the duffel bag, she found a power cord and plugged the phone into a nearby outlet. Then she went back to the duffel and kneeled beside it. She kept the bag on the floor of the closet, attempting to move things around as little as possible.

"I need to call Bix," Platt said. "Are you okay to be in here alone?"

"I'll be fine."

"Decon is down the hall to your left if you need to leave before I get back. Two techs are waiting to assist us."

She nodded and listened to him leave as she pulled out the bag's contents item by item. Extra underwear and socks, a couple of T-shirts, a pair of jeans. Nothing out of the ordinary. Same with the zippered pockets, until she got to the last one. Tucked inside was a four-by-six photograph. The corners were frayed from being handled. She gently tugged it out, carefully pinching one of the sturdier corners.

The photograph was of four young men in army fatigues with dusty boots and helmets. Their weapons were slung over their shoulders, their arms wrapped around one another's backs as they posed, smiling and laughing. Behind them was a craggy rock wall.

She flipped the photo around. Written in black marker:

Afghanistan. Me, Jason, Colfax & Benny

She turned the photo around again and studied the faces under the dirt and grime and the rims of the helmets. She thought she recognized one of the men, but she couldn't place him.

O'Dell packed all the items back into the bag, but she kept the photograph out. She took it with her as she went to check on the cell phone. This time when she pressed the On button, the faceplate came to life. A tiny yellow envelope in the corner indicated there were unread text messages. Another icon showed that several voice messages were waiting as well.

She tapped the text messages first. As soon as she saw the name attached to the most recent one, she knew who the familiar young man in the photograph was. She hadn't recognized Jason Seaver at first, because this photo was taken when he still had both of his arms.

11

FLORIDA PANHANDLE

Creed and Jason had just gotten back from Pensacola. He wasn't sure he had convinced the kid that his grandfather would be okay. It was a good thing that they had caught the *C. diff* now.

Creed noticed the dogs' reactions before he looked up and caught a flash of black metal moving through the tree line. Several of the dogs jumped at the fence, restless and alarmed with ears pitched forward. Noses sniffed the air. Heads turned. All of them pointed toward the driveway, a quarter-mile stretch that wound through the forest.

His view was limited. All Creed could see were slivers of the black vehicles and glints of light reflected off the windshields. But it looked like a long caravan, reminding Creed of a funeral procession. His stomach tightened. His jaw clenched.

This wasn't good.

He weighed his options.

How long would it take to run up into his loft and get the revolver he hid underneath his mattress? The shotgun was clear across the property, locked up in the training facility. Before he had time to choose, the first SUV made the turn onto the property.

They knew enough to drive past the two-story house and the sign that directed visitors to the K9 CrimeScents office on the first floor. But the house was also the residence for Hannah and her two young boys, and Creed felt a slight relief. It was short-lived as he watched the huge black Suburban drive up over the grass and head directly toward him and the dog kennels.

A second followed. Then another. In minutes Creed's front yard was filled with five identical black SUVs. Tinted windows. Shiny and new with only the dust from Creed's driveway.

"What the hell is this?" Jason asked.

Creed hadn't even heard Jason come up beside him. From the corner of his eye he saw Dr. Avelyn coming out of the clinic. He glanced at the house and hoped Hannah would stay inside.

"Settle," Creed told the dogs, keeping his voice calm.

The dogs stayed quiet but the tension was

easily visible. Tails stayed down. Hair at the back of the neck stood on end. Eyes were locked. Ears were still pitched forward.

Creed dug a remote from his pocket. He clicked a button preventing any of the other dogs from coming out into the yard, keeping them safe inside the kennel.

With the engines still idling, car doors opened and men in dark suits and sunglasses sprang out with a sense of urgency. A couple of them had Kevlar vests over their suits. Three men who exited the last Suburban carried automatic rifles. The sight of them made Creed's hands ball into fists. The panic in his gut was quickly replaced with an instinct to fight and protect.

"Son of a bitch," Jason muttered under his breath. "Who the hell are these guys?"

One of the Kevlar-vest guys started walking toward them, and Creed finally recognized the man.

"I must have missed your phone call," Creed called out to the man. "What's going on, Agent Tabor?"

"It's best if everyone stays calm, Mr. Creed. We just need your cooperation."

"It's hard to stay calm when you come onto my property without warning or an invitation."

"This is official government business."

"Did I forget to pay some sort of tax?" Creed tried to keep his voice casual for the dogs. When Tabor didn't answer, Creed asked, "What's this about?"

"Those birds you bagged. I understand they may be carriers of a deadly virus."

Tabor hadn't seen Creed bag up the dead robins. Sheriff Wylie must have told him. By now, Dr. Avelyn had joined Creed and Jason.

"I have them sealed and isolated," she said. "I can get them for you."

But Tabor didn't seem interested in what she was saying. He waved at someone and more car doors opened. The four men who exited this vehicle wore white jumpsuits with surgical masks dangling at their necks. They crossed to the back of their SUV, opened the tailgate, and started pulling out equipment.

"It's highly contagious. I've been told it's a new strain of the bird flu," Tabor said, while he gave more hand signals to a couple other men who joined him. They ventured closer to the kennel yard where Creed, Jason, and Dr. Avelyn stood in front of the fence.

"Just give us a minute and we'll get the dead birds for you," Creed told him.

"I wish it were that simple."

"I sent off samples two days ago," Dr. Avelyn told him. "They may already have the
results."

"I'm afraid that's not good enough," Tabor
said. "We'll need to quarantine everyone."

"None of us touched them," Creed said.

"But one of your dogs did. Sheriff Wylie
told me it had the robin in its mouth. If it's
the strain of the bird flu that we think it is,
by now your entire kennel has been contaminated," Tabor said. "And all of you might
be, too."

And suddenly Creed realized what this
was. He glanced at Dr. Avelyn and quietly
asked, "They can't do this, can they?"

She looked up at him but didn't attempt a
response. He caught a glimpse of fear in her
eyes.

"We'll make it as quick as possible," Tabor
said, his demeanor distracted as he waited
for the men in the protective gear.

"No one touches my dogs except my staff.
If you need samples, my vet will get them
for you."

Now Tabor shook his head at Creed.

The realization hit Creed like a punch to
the stomach. Tabor didn't intend to take
samples and quarantine the dogs. He was
here to euthanize them.

"I'm told it spreads very quickly," Tabor

said. "All of your staff will need to be put under quarantine. But the dogs . . . I'm sorry. From what I understand, even if they test negative they could still be carriers. I'm just following orders."

He glanced back at the men in white who carried cases and tranquilizer guns slung over their shoulders.

"Whose orders?" Creed wanted to know.

Instead of answering, Tabor said, "We'll try to make this as quick and painless as possible."

"They can't frickin' do this, can they?" Jason asked, fidgeting beside Creed.

Creed moved toward the gate. Inside his head a wind tunnel had begun to swirl. Ice water rushed through his veins as his hands clenched the gate rail tightly. They'd have to shoot him first.

When the first gunshot fired, Creed thought it was his heartbeat exploding inside his chest. Only when he saw Tabor duck for cover did he realize it was real.

12

The second gunshot sent the men scrambling back, diving behind their vehicles. Only then did Creed realize the gunfire wasn't coming from Tabor's gang.

Tabor and the men closest to the fence crouched behind the trees. Even the men with automatic rifles stayed low behind car doors, their heads pivoting, eyes darting, trying to see where the shots had come from.

Creed stood perfectly still. Dr. Avelyn was beside him. Jason had disappeared. The dogs were pacing. Creed grabbed a whistle and the remote from his pocket. He put the whistle to his lips at the same time that he opened the kennel doors. The dogs ran inside on command. After every single dog was safely inside and the kennel doors shut, he turned his attention back to Tabor and his men.

"We're here on official business," Tabor

yelled. "Put the gun down now before someone gets hurt."

Creed saw Hannah come out on the lawn in front of the house. She looked like a trained marksman with the shotgun level in front of her ready to shoot again, and this time not in the air.

"I don't care what your official business is," she yelled back. "I need to see a warrant."

"We don't need a warrant for this," Tabor called out as he ventured from behind the tree. "I advise you to put that gun down before you get yourself hurt."

A shot fired above his head, sending him back to take cover. But this shot didn't come from Hannah. It came from the tree line behind Jason's trailer.

"What the hell?" Tabor was down on one knee now that he realized he had two shooters.

Creed exchanged a nervous glance with Dr. Avelyn. Jason had lost half his arm in Afghanistan, but his army training as a sniper hadn't been affected.

"I think it's best you go back and get a warrant," Hannah yelled.

"I don't need —"

"Oh, I work with the federal government enough to know you folks love your paperwork. I'm filling out twelve pages' worth every time you need to use one of our dogs."

"That's entirely different," Tabor insisted. "I have the authority —"

"Now see here," she interrupted. "I have my own authority right here." And she racked another shell into the shotgun's barrel like it was second nature to her.

This time Tabor looked over at Creed and said, "She's only making this more difficult for you and your employees. Especially if you all get sick. You have no idea what you're dealing with or who you're dealing with."

"You have no idea who *you're* dealing with, Tabor. I suggest you and your men get off my property."

Tabor stared him down.

"You're making a very big mistake."

He cautiously stood up, waited to be sure there would be no additional gunfire, and then walked back to the first SUV. Glancing over his shoulder at Hannah, Tabor gestured to his men to follow suit.

Car doors slammed. Engines rumbled to life. Tires spun and spit up grass. The long black line formed, and piece by black shiny metal piece it disappeared between the trees. Leaving behind exhaust fumes and silence.

13

Stephen Bishop dragged the roller bag through the busy terminal. There were long lines to the security check-in. A place against the wall opened up and Bishop grabbed the chance to stop and observe. This was the third trip to this airport, in this terminal, in less than a week. Bishop pulled out a cell phone and pretended to read messages, while watching over the top of heavy-framed glasses.

They were short one body scanner today. The machine was corded off, and the TSA official gestured for passengers to use another lane. The PreCheck line was longer than usual but moving quickly. Bishop wasn't in a hurry. There was no flight to catch. This trip, like the others, was strictly for observation and ultimately preparation.

By now Bishop recognized several of the TSA officials. The tall black man with the shaved head and muscular arms was named

Oscar. He usually worked the PreCheck lane. His narrow-set eyes scrutinized everything, so even though passengers didn't have to take off their shoes or remove liquids from their carry-ons, they still had to get past his approval.

LeKeesha sat at one of the X-ray machines. Last time Bishop had heard one of her colleagues call out her name. The others treated her like she was more senior than them. She was big and brassy. Even her purple-streaked hair demanded attention. When she stopped the line and asked that a case be pulled for a search, it got done immediately.

Of all the terminals, this was the one Bishop had chosen. Despite having a guaranteed PreCheck boarding pass, it would still be important to feel confident and look confident so that someone like Oscar or LeKeesha had absolutely no reason to stop and say those dreaded words "Please step aside."

That old saying "Never let them see you sweat" became a vital mantra. And not an easy one today.

Bishop's suit was snug. The extra weight was difficult to get used to. It was exhausting, especially while plodding through the airport. But the extra weight had one benefit. It created — actually forced — a new walk that came instinctively with little risk of slipping into old habits.

Bishop's discomfort, however, didn't stop there. The beard itched. The short, square-trimmed fingernails and the heavy-framed glasses were annoying. Bishop had given up everything fashionable and chic in exchange for ordinary and invisible. It was a small price to pay for future notoriety, possibly even making the annals of science history.

Bishop's grandfather, who had been a renowned scientist during the Cold War, loved to say, "You can change the world or sit on the sidelines and let the world change you. It's your choice."

The cell phone started vibrating, and Bishop plucked it from the suitcase pocket with a quick glance at the incoming call's phone number.

"What is it?" Bishop said, using the new commanding voice that came with the new image.

"Is this Bishop?"

"Who the hell is this?"

"The colonel needs to know —"

"If the colonel needs to know anything, he needs to call me himself. I'm not talking to a lackey of his."

"Excuse me, but I'm the director of the

division for —"

"Good for you. Congratulations and never call this number again."

Bishop ended the call before the caller had a chance to respond. The phone stayed in Bishop's hand. It would take only a few minutes for the lackey to report his failure to his boss.

Colonel Abraham Hess was a necessary evil. They had formed an unholy alliance that suited both their needs. Bishop had agreed to spare the colonel's precious reputation, while Hess provided Bishop with protection. The old man still held an undisputable amount of power and influence, but sometimes that same power triggered what Bishop called an arrogant ignorance. The colonel believed he was infallible. Stupid mistakes like trusting some low-level assistant with classified contact numbers would eventually bring the old man down, but he wouldn't be taking Bishop with him.

The phone started vibrating again. The same incoming number. Bishop swiped the faceplate to answer but said nothing.

"Bishop? What the hell's going on?"

"Don't ever share my phone numbers with anyone. Do you understand?"

"He's a high-level —"

Bishop hung up and waited. The colonel

would be furious. No one dared treat him with such disrespect.

The phone began vibrating and Bishop let it continue, answering just before it went to voice mail.

"What is it that you need to know?" Bishop asked in place of a greeting.

"I need to know what the hell's going on. I don't expect to be updated through rumor and eventually cable news. There's a young girl who was found dead in a river. What the hell —"

"Stop. Say no more," Bishop said calmly. "I'll call you but not on this phone. I'll need to get you a new phone number."

"Oh, for Christ's sake. Isn't that the reason we're using these silly disposable phones? There was not a breach just because —"

Bishop ended the call again. The vibration started after only three seconds.

"Okay. Give me the new phone number," Hess said in a conciliatory tone that sounded like he was biting his tongue at the same time.

"Someone will deliver the new number this afternoon."

"Another handwritten note? This is ridiculous. You're a scientist. What's with this archaic ritual you insist upon?"

"When was the last time someone was convicted because of an incriminating handwritten, courier-delivered note? You know as well as I do that any and every electronic footprint can be and is watched, listened to, recorded, sorted, and filed. You'd be surprised how many of your D.C. friends use this exact method."

"There's such a thing as handwriting analysis, too."

"Wouldn't matter. It's not my handwriting. You have your ways of protecting yourself and your interests, allow me mine. Which reminds me. I need a guaranteed PreCheck. You'll need to handle that."

"You'll need to be fingerprinted."

"Not happening."

"There's no way —"

"Figure it out."

Bishop ended the call, finished with the old man for now.

There was no SIM card to pop out and destroy, so the entire phone went into an empty coffee cup with the lid tightly replaced. Finished for the day, Bishop tossed the cup and phone into a nearby trash can and headed for the exit, dragging the empty roller bag.

14

"Is it possible?" Creed asked Dr. Avelyn.

They had settled the dogs down and were now all seated in Hannah's kitchen. She made them coffee and pulled out a plate of homemade oatmeal cookies like this was an ordinary day and a typical staff meeting. With two exceptions — the guns set carefully in the corner by the back door and the bottle of Baileys she passed around like it was creamer for their coffee.

He was surprised at Hannah. She hated guns. Never allowed them inside her house. Even to get the shotgun she had to have sneaked over to the training facility. She was the diplomat of the two of them. In fact, the first time Creed met her, she ended up giving him a sermon about how violence never resolved anything. This was after he started a fight in Walter's Canteen, where Hannah was bartending. Years later her husband, Marcus, was killed in Iraq. She helped start

Segway House, a safe house for returning veterans, domestic abuse victims hiding from their abusers, and drug addicts wanting to go straight. She dealt with the brutal results of war every single week as she made sure there was shelter and jobs for amputees, like Jason, returning home.

Every once in a while the cases they took on for K9 CrimeScents came with violent and dangerous consequences. Their dogs sniffed out cadavers, drugs, and explosives, and sometimes the killers, drug dealers, and terrorists decided they were fair game. Truth was, he and Hannah had seen their share of violence. Both of them. But he'd never seen her take up a firearm and shoot at someone.

He watched her pacing around her own kitchen, waiting on them. When she passed by, he gently grabbed her hand.

"Sit down, Hannah." He stood and pulled out a chair for her. "Please, just sit down."

When she finally did, Creed focused his attention back on Dr. Avelyn.

"Is it possible what Tabor was saying? That those robins were infected with something?"

"It's possible. But I didn't see anything unusual."

"Would you know? How could you know?"

"I sent tissue samples in the day you

found them. But also I spent a month in Iowa last year. Remember? We gassed millions of laying hens infected with the bird flu that swept through several commercial poultry farms. It's tough because the birds don't always show any signs of being sick."

"But it's just birds that can be infected. Dogs can't get it, right? Is it possible Grace could be infected?"

She didn't answer, and Creed felt a kick of panic again. "You gotta know, because I possibly just exposed a bunch of old people to a deadly virus." He rubbed a hand across his jaw when he realized what this could mean. "Grace. Please tell me dogs can't get this. Tabor made it sound like he believed they can."

"The virus has been known to mutate. And yes, it has jumped species. Not just to humans, but I believe there have been cases of pigs and, in lab settings, ferrets."

Silence. All Creed could think about was Grace bringing him that robin, so proud to show it to him.

"Look," Dr. Avelyn said, "there's no way I can tell you anything until I know more. We shouldn't panic, but we should be careful."

Creed watched the veterinarian wrap her hands around her mug and stare into the coffee. He hadn't seen her take so much as a sip.

"What are you thinking?" Hannah asked her.

"Until we know more, I think we need to quarantine Grace."

"She's already been around most of the other dogs," Jason reminded her.

Dr. Avelyn's eyes darted around the table, then came to rest on Creed.

"We need to quarantine all of them. It doesn't mean cages. We can do it in the kennel. They just can't leave to work. We should consider using gloves and surgical masks when we're around them. Perhaps even limit how many of us have contact with them."

"Lord have mercy," Hannah said under her breath. "You think we can get it, too?"

Creed knew she was thinking about her two boys.

"We can't rule it out."

"What about the senior care facility?"

"Let's wait until I get the results back on the tissue samples. I'll call. See if I can get them to expedite the results." Then she looked at Creed and asked, "Did you handle either of the robins?"

He had to think about it. All he remembered — now so vividly implanted in his memory — was Grace with the bird clamped in her teeth. He had put the birds in plastic bags, opening the bag and carefully keeping the plastic between his palm and the dead bird. But when he asked Grace to drop it? Had she dropped it on the ground? It was instinctive for him to have his dogs drop the errant object into his hand so he could examine what it was. Bad habit. Perhaps a deadly habit.

Creed finally answered, "I had her drop it in the palm of my hand."

"Did you have your working gloves on?"

He shook his head and avoided looking at Hannah. He didn't need to. He could already feel her anxiety. It was as thick as the coffee she had served them.

"I'll run blood and saliva samples on all of us and the dogs." Dr. Avelyn's voice remained calm, trying to be reassuring. It was that steady, unflappable attitude that Creed had admired enough to trust her with his dogs' lives. And now he'd be trusting her with the lives of all of them.

"If it's bird flu," she continued, "the risk to humans is considered low. The virus has never been airborne. Those who have been infected worked closely with live poultry, or helped slaughter them. Actually the virus is easily spread by bird droppings, so just unsanitary conditions can be enough. It doesn't have to be blood.

"Most of the fatalities have been in China, where they don't take a lot of precautions in handling live birds. Sometimes they don't wear protective gear even when they're slaughtering them. In fact, there's always concern during their Chinese New Year because so many travel to be with family, and it's customary to bring along live chickens or ducks as gifts.

"In 2014 for the first time we saw the Eurasian H5N8 virus in the United States. It was bound to happen. Migratory waterfowl were the original culprits, bringing it with them into the Pacific Flyway. By the time the virus made its way to the Midwest it had already changed and mutated in order to survive. H5N1 is genetically different than the Asian or Eurasian strain."

"I never thought about it before," Hannah said. "How easy it would be for migratory birds to bring diseases from clear across the world."

"Most of the time it doesn't kill the waterfowl. They're convenient carriers. But once it infects the domestic bird population like it did with commercial turkeys and chickens in the Midwest, it's devastating. They're literally sitting ducks. There's no way to cure it. No vaccines. Slaughtering the flocks has been the only way to destroy the virus."

"And that's what Tabor wanted to do with our kennel," Creed said. "I have to think he was out of line. Maybe just misinformed? He said he was following someone else's orders."

He had been clenching his jaw so tight that it now ached. The coffee had set off an acid storm churning in his gut.

"Please tell me," he said, searching the veterinarian's eyes, "that euthanasia's not the solution if we find out Grace has contracted this virus."

"Let's wait for the results," she said.

It was not the answer Creed was hoping for.

"In the meantime," she continued, "we need to take precautions for ourselves, too. We'll need to follow our standard decontamination procedures — coveralls, masks, shoe covers, gloves, and goggles anytime we go into the kennel. And one last thing — none of us should leave the grounds."

15

CHICAGO

Now in her own hotel room several floors above the victim's room, Agent Maggie O'Dell finished jotting down all her notes. She had already made several phone calls and guzzled down a Diet Pepsi. The television was turned to a news channel, but only for background noise. She hadn't unpacked yet except for her notebooks, copies of documents, and her personal laptop, all of which were strewn across the desk and the foot of the bed.

There was something that troubled her about Tony Briggs's suicide. Never mind that he had left behind no signs of a ritual or a single good-bye note. His room had been too tidy. Other than the spray on the TV screen and the wall behind — what Platt suspected might be bloody sputum — there were no bloody tissues anywhere. She hadn't found a single bloody washcloth or towel. In fact, the bathroom actually looked as though someone had cleaned it, and yet the hotel remained adamant that house-cleaning had not entered Briggs's room. And if they had, the wastebasket would have been emptied.

So did Briggs clean his bathroom? Did he make his bed? Could that have been his ritual? To clean and tidy up his room before he stepped out onto the patio and jumped to his death?

Anything was possible. She'd seen stranger things in her career as an FBI agent and criminal profiler. *Much stranger things.*

And yet she couldn't help but wonder if someone else might have come into the room. If not housekeeping, then someone who knew exactly what Tony Briggs was doing.

O'Dell picked up a sheet from one of the piles. Attached to the corner was one of the few recent photographs they had of Dr. Clare Shaw. The scientist looked younger than her forty-two years. For this photo — one that had been taken and used for her ID badge at the research facility — Shaw had chosen to pull back her dark hair, leaving only bangs that dangled over her eye-glasses. She was attractive, with only subtle wrinkles at the corners of her mouth to hint at her real age.

She had earned several degrees from Johns Hopkins University in molecular biology, concentrating on genetics and biomedical engineering. Her advanced studies focused on neuroscience and human behavior. She had spent time at several different laboratories across the United States, but only a few years at each, moving often and rarely making lasting relationships. During O'Dell's investigation she'd had difficulties finding anyone who knew the scientist very well.

Shaw had never married and had no children. She was an only child; her parents had been killed in a car accident. Her only living relative was a grandfather with advanced-stage dementia. O'Dell had found him at a nursing care facility in Panama City, Florida, close to the community where he had lived, then retired to some ten years earlier. The staff told her that Dr. Shaw had visited at least once a month and in between those times, she sent small gifts. The visits and the gifts stopped after the North Carolina mudslide, and everyone there believed that she was killed in the disaster.

Shaw had been at the University of Wisconsin in 2012 when she attracted the attention of DARPA, the Defense Advanced Research Projects Agency, landing her the director position at the research facility in

North Carolina. There she had freedom to conduct experiments along with the resources to pay test subjects. One of those subjects, a man named Daniel Tate, had survived the mudslide. More importantly, he had survived the executions that had occurred moments before the slide. Someone had shot one scientist and two test subjects. The FBI believed the killer was Dr. Clare Shaw.

However, there was a catch. Shaw disappeared that night. Her cell phone had gone silent. Her apartment looked exactly as if she had gone to work and never come home. Nothing of value appeared to be missing. Her car was one of those destroyed in the mudslide. Even her credit card charges stopped the day before the slide.

The FBI had issued a BOLO (Be On the Look Out) nationwide and contacted other research laboratories across the country in search of Shaw. In five months there hadn't been a single sighting, not even a false one. O'Dell was beginning to wonder if the woman had perhaps been killed along with her colleague and her test subjects.

O'Dell's cell phone interrupted her thoughts. It was a number she didn't recognize. One with the Chicago area code.

"This is O'Dell."

"In the spirit of sharing, how about we share dinner?"

It was Platt. The bureaucratic tone was gone, replaced by a warm and inviting one, reminding her that he could be very charming.

16

FLORIDA PANHANDLE

Creed had just finished taking care of the dogs for the evening. He had stripped out of the coveralls and protective gear, stuffing everything into a decon bag. From the window in his loft apartment he could see that the light was still on in the building Dr. Avelyn used as their veterinary clinic. She had already told him that it would be a long night. Hannah had offered her guest room, and Creed knew she'd make sure the veterinarian got some sleep.

Several years ago Creed and Hannah had decided it would be better for their dogs if they didn't take them off-site for their vaccinations and medical needs. Instead they contracted with Dr. Avelyn Parker. She had her own practice with two other veterinarians in Milton, Florida, but had agreed to handle the needs of K9 CrimeScents. Since then Creed knew she had certainly gotten more than she bargained for, and yet she never complained. She treated these dogs like they were her own.

His hair was still wet from his shower when he heard the soft tap on the back door to his loft.

It was Jason, and the kid looked like he had seen a ghost.

"Come on in." He had to coax him.

Jason had barely stepped into the room when he said, "Tony's dead. His mom just called me."

His voice was deadpan. His eyes darted everywhere else to avoid meeting Creed's, but it didn't matter. Creed had already caught a glimpse of the emotion.

"What happened?"

Creed didn't know Tony Briggs well, but the few times he'd been around him, the young man had been volatile enough for Creed to now suspect that Tony's death had not come peacefully. And from Jason's hesitancy, he guessed he was right.

"They're saying he jumped from his hotel room. Nineteen stories."

Creed winced. He was glad Jason's eyes were now examining his bookshelves and missed it.

"Where?"

"Chicago."

"Why was he in Chicago?"

"How the hell should I know?"

There it was. Jason's trademark anger. It was his refuge. He used it to protect himself. Creed was actually relieved to see it. Wasn't right for the kid to pretend that he felt nothing. This was someone who meant a great deal to him. Anger seemed appropriate.

"He didn't tell you he was going to Chicago?"

"I'm not his goddamn keeper." He wiped at his face out of frustration and in an effort to catch any rogue tears.

"Why don't you just tell me what you do know instead of biting my head off?"

Jason's arm crossed his chest and his hand grasped the stub of his amputated arm. It was a nervous gesture Creed had noticed the young veteran made often. Jason rubbed at the stub like it still hurt, or maybe like he needed the reminder his lower arm was gone. Creed didn't push him. He let the silence settle until Jason was ready. The news was still fresh, the shock still raw like a rip in the skin.

"He didn't say anything about going to Chicago. At least not to me. His mom said it was some fancy hotel on Michigan Avenue. That doesn't sound right. Doesn't sound like Tony."

He stopped there. Noticed his hand and

let it drop.

"They know it's him for sure?" Creed asked when the silence lasted too long.

"Had his wallet still on him."

"That doesn't mean —"

"Fingerprints matched. It's him."

Another long silence.

Jason's hand went back to rubbing while he fidgeted, shifting his weight from one foot to the other. He looked miserable, all the while trying hard not to telegraph it.

Creed wished Hannah were here. She was much better at this. He wasn't good with comforting people. Dogs he understood. People, not so much.

"The son of a bitch. I can't believe he did this. The bastard."

"Why are you judging him for something you've thought about doing yourself?"

And that was when Jason's eyes met Creed's. The anger slipped for a second or two, replaced by a flicker of surprise. Maybe he'd forgotten that he had confessed to Creed, months ago, that he'd thought about suicide. That he'd seriously considered it when he first got back from Afghanistan. Hell, maybe he still thought about it.

Creed also knew that Jason had lost friends. Tony wasn't the first. But Tony would mean the most. They'd grown up together. Gone off to war together. Came back, both of them broken, although in different ways.

Finally Jason said, "I'm not judging him." His eyes were gone again, as if in search of answers in the horizon. The fidgeting became more pronounced.

Creed went to his refrigerator, pulled out two bottles of beer. He twisted the caps off and handed one to Jason. The kid took a sip.

Creed thought about calling Hannah. She was used to working with troubled veterans. She was a cofounder of Segway House and played an active role in helping residents find jobs in the community. That was where Jason had been staying. It was because of Hannah that he had come to work for them.

Creed rescued dogs. Hannah rescued lost souls. Jason was one of those.

"I didn't think he'd do it that way," Jason said, then took another sip of the beer. At least having the bottle in his hand kept him from rubbing the stump of his arm.

Creed waited.

"We talked about it sometimes," Jason told him. "Like when we'd be drinking. You know, talking big. We've had friends eat their guns. I told you, one guy I know even hanged himself."

"So what was your and Tony's preferred method?" Creed asked it as casually as if they were talking about sports.

Ironically it seemed to relax Jason. His eyes stopped darting for a few seconds.

"For one thing, we agreed we wouldn't do something that would make such a mess our moms couldn't look at our bodies." He glanced back toward the door as if expecting someone. "You're not gonna tell Hannah any of this, are you?"

So much for suggesting that was who Jason should talk to. Reluctantly Creed shook his head.

"I mean, I don't know what jumping nineteen stories does to a body, but I'm guessing it's not pretty."

"Maybe he was drinking. Not thinking straight. Could have been an accident."

"Tony's one of the few guys I know who thinks better drunk. Especially after his TBI."

Creed knew that although Tony looked normal, with none of the outward scars that Jason and his buddies came back with, his traumatic brain injury had had a tremendous impact on him.

"It's like alcohol settled him down," Jason continued. "He said it quieted the demons in his head."

"So what are you saying happened?"

Jason shrugged. "We both know Tony pissed off quite a few people. Some of them people you should never piss off."

Creed nodded.

People like drug cartels. Jason, Tony, and their friends had come to Creed's rescue last summer when members of Choque Azul, a Colombian drug cartel that used the Gulf of Mexico, had targeted Creed and his dogs. If it weren't for Tony, Creed would have never known when the cartel's attack was coming. He would have never been able to prepare for it, and even then, he wouldn't have survived if Jason, Tony, and their vet buddies hadn't come to his rescue.

"I had a text message from him," Jason said. "It might have been that same day." He patted the back pocket of his jeans, but the cell phone wasn't there. "I'll need to check."

"What did he say?"

"Something about getting himself into a mess."

"That could mean anything," Creed told him.

"Maybe. Maybe not."

A silence fell between them. Creed knew it was tough to convince yourself that a friend or loved one had actually committed suicide. When he found his father slumped on his own sofa with a bullet hole in his temple, Creed had searched the house for signs of an intruder. He remembered telling the 911 operator that someone had shot his father while he stared at the revolver still dangling from his father's fingers.

"What if Tony didn't jump?" Jason finally asked, this time meeting and holding Creed's eyes.

"You think someone pushed him."

17

CHICAGO

O'Dell and Platt bypassed the hotel's luxurious four-star restaurant and chose a booth at the bar and grill. They ordered burgers and beers. O'Dell asked for a side salad. Platt chose the house-cut chips instead of fries. They were comfortable in settings like this, though they hadn't spent any time together since the holidays. Both of them recognized that North Carolina had driven a wedge between them, one that would take more than time to dislodge.

However, Platt was the quintessential gentleman and tonight was no different. Sometimes O'Dell felt guilty when some of his good-mannered habits annoyed her. She had spent her entire career trying to get male colleagues to treat her no differently than they would one another. Platt knew that, but he operated by a rigid code of ethics, one that included being a gentleman in the presence of a woman.

An army colonel, medical doctor, and director of USAMRIID, he saw many things as black and white, right or wrong, where O'Dell would argue there might be a sliver of gray. Both of them worked for the same government. Platt trusted it. O'Dell did not. Platt was a follow-the-rules guy. O'Dell pushed the limits, crossed lines, and sometimes stretched the rules. But there was one thing they did have in common — they did the right thing, or what they believed was the right thing. And sometimes they did so at a high risk to their careers and their well-being.

So it was difficult for O'Dell to understand how Platt could justify some of the research his facility and others like Dr. Clare Shaw's were doing. Working to create vaccines, she understood. And yes, it was necessary to have samples of the deadliest viruses in the world in order to develop antidotes.

Places like DARPA and USAMRIID made good arguments that they needed to prepare and protect U.S. citizens from any and all possible bioterrorism threats, some of which might include these viruses. In digging through the classified files on Shaw's research facility in North Carolina — files that had only recently been made available to O'Dell — she found studies Shaw had conducted that in O'Dell's mind stretched common scientific ethics.

There were experiments in which paid volunteers were injected with hallucinogenic drugs. Others were subjected to sleep deprivation and asked to undergo a battery of tests every hour on the hour.

Shaw also seemed fascinated with mosquitoes as possible carriers for deadly viruses and might have released swarms infected with dengue fever in an attempt to test the efficiency of the insects as possible bioweapons.

After investigating other DARPA research facilities — what little access was available to her — O'Dell suspected that Shaw's experiments were not unusual by comparison. Other projects seemed more interested in a desired outcome of doing harm — granted, harm to an enemy, but nevertheless, harm. In fact, O'Dell wondered if these facilities had more stockpiles of bioweapons than they did vaccines.

"What have you heard from Roger?" she asked after their food arrived.

"He's certain it's a strain of bird flu. The assortment is different than H5N1 or even H7N1." He glanced up. "Sorry, I know those identifiers are confusing."

"Is it what Dr. Shaw was working on?"

"A bit different. Roger thinks she altered it, trying to make it airborne, just as we suspected."

"So was Tony Briggs a test run?"

"Briggs and possibly others."

"You said that before. If you and Roger have information that I don't have about —"

Platt held up his hands in surrender. "Hold on, Maggie. I told you, we don't know anything for sure. Just supposition. The FBI's been tasked with finding Shaw. You'll have to trust us. It's up to the CDC and USAMRIID to be prepared for what she might be doing with the viruses she stole."

"You're wrong, Ben. Motive is just as important in tracking a killer as knowing physical characteristics and last known whereabouts."

"We've only been speculating about her motive."

"Well, do me a favor and include me in those speculations from now on."

He nodded as his eyes glanced at the booth across from them, and only then did O'Dell realize how obvious her irritation was. Forget irritation, she was still angry with him. At one time they were beyond colleagues and friends, on the fringes of a real

106

relationship. Or at least the closest she'd gotten to one since her divorce.

"Tell me what else Bix knows," she said, poking a fork at her salad instead of meeting his eyes.

"His team is checking area hospitals and urgent care centers. Unfortunately most of the early symptoms that we know of are similar to the traditional flu."

"How serious could this be?"

"You were exposed to Ebola, so you know how deadly that virus is." His eyes met hers. "But Ebola spreads through contact with an infected person's bodily fluids. Unless someone with the virus gets on a plane, there's no way for it to travel. Now consider a virus just as deadly. The bird flu is spread by migratory birds."

Platt glanced around, planted his elbows on the table, and leaned toward her so she'd be able to hear his quiet voice despite the restaurant noise.

"If Shaw has succeeded in making it airborne, she'd need very few carriers like Tony Briggs. You said you wanted to be in on our speculations. Well, look at it this way — all she'd need to do is figure out how to infect flocks of birds. That would be one way to spread the virus across the country and do so very quickly. If she's successful"

— and Platt paused as his eyes scanned the surroundings — "if she's successful, then we could have a pandemic on our hands."

18

"In China," Platt explained, "people contracted the bird flu by actually handling
infected birds. I think the mortality rate was
around fifty-five percent. In 2013 there was
a new strain, H7N9. It's so genetically
unstable that since then, there have been
forty-eight subtypes found. It's a good
example of how the bird flu is able to swap
genes with other flus, not just to survive but
to get stronger. If it does that in nature, can
you imagine what we'd have with a hybrid
strain created specifically to infect humans?
And if there's a way to make it airborne and
transfer from birds to humans, then human
to human . . ."

"What about a vaccine?" O'Dell asked.
"Surely the CDC has been working on
something."

"They've stockpiled a vaccine for H5N1.
But it might be useless. The virus mutates
quickly. The best way to create an effective

vaccine is to reverse engineer the actual virus that you're trying to protect against. But we need to have that specific virus first."

"So if Bix can isolate several victims that have been infected, will he be able to do that? Create a specific vaccine for this one? Isn't that what the CDC does with the common flu?"

"Yes, but it could take months. Seasonal flu vaccines cause antibodies to develop within our bodies about two weeks after the shot is received. The antibodies provide protection against infection caused from viruses that are included in the vaccine."

"And how do they know what viruses to include? Surely seasonal flus are different from one year to the next."

"Yes, that's true. They use available research that indicates which ones will be most common for the upcoming season."

O'Dell raised an eyebrow.

"I know, it sounds like a crapshoot — but you did not hear that from me. So imagine trying to do that with a new virus that might even mutate by the time you've created the new vaccine. This is one of the trickiest. That's why it could be so dangerous. I can't even tell you how many millions of dollars and valuable hours have been spent on vaccines that are too little, too late."

Platt kept looking up at one of the big-screen TVs. She knew he was watching for breaking news despite all the precautions they'd taken to keep this under wraps.

"You can't keep this quiet for much longer," O'Dell said. "People need to know or else they'll think they just have the regular flu."

Platt's eyes darted around again. "That's Roger's call."

She sat back and let out a frustrated sigh.

"Listen," Platt continued, his eyes intense, and she saw his frustration. "Hurricane Katrina taught us the need to be faster and quicker in evacuating cities. But we still have no idea how to quarantine an entire city. I have to trust Roger Bix and the CDC on this one, because I'm the guy who's used to looking at these situations from behind a microscope back at USAMRIID's labs."

His eyes returned to the big-screen television as if he didn't want to witness any more of her skepticism. O'Dell knew he was also watching the news crawl.

She took the opportunity to study him. He hadn't changed. He was still handsome, with thoughtful intelligent eyes. He wore his hair military short. His clothes always fit him like a glove. Whether he was wearing a uniform or jeans and a sweatshirt, like tonight, he looked polished and professional. He moved with discipline and precision so that everything he did appeared to be a skilled process. Even the way he opened a bottle of ketchup — first giving it a side turn, then a slap on the bottom with the palm of his hand before he turned the lid with two long fingers, a surgeon's fingers.

He caught her watching.

"What?"

"Just waiting for the ketchup," she lied, then thanked him when he finished and handed it to her.

"Is there anything in your investigation of Shaw to lead you to believe she could still be in the Chicago area?" Platt asked. "Why did she choose Chicago? I understand Briggs is from Florida, right?"

"Pensacola." She had searched out all that information as soon as she knew the victim's name. "He had a layover of one hour and twenty minutes in Atlanta. Roger must have a team checking out the exposure there?"

Platt nodded and picked up his hamburger.

"I'm coming late to the game," Platt told her in between bites. "He called me late yesterday afternoon and asked me to be here when he realized this could be Shaw's bird flu. The fact that Briggs flew here makes the contamination a much larger scope. It's not just the people he came in contact with at the airport but every passenger and member of the crew on both those flights."

"When does an infected person become contagious?"

"Again, we know very little about the bird flu in humans. To be safe we have to assume that with this strain someone infected may be contagious immediately. Is it possible Briggs met Shaw in Pensacola?"

"It's more likely that she has someone recruiting for her, because we haven't found a trace of her since she disappeared. Pensacola could be the best clue so far. It could mean she's still in the Southeast. What would she need to be able to do this?"

"What do you mean?"

"She took one sample from the North Carolina facility. Even I know that can't possibly be enough to start an epidemic, right? What would she need to create more virus? I'm guessing it's not like meth where all you need is a trailer or a garage and no nosy neighbors."

"She would need a laboratory to grow more. It wouldn't need to be elaborate, but in order to protect herself from exposure, the lab or suite of labs would have to provide the isolation and adequate containment for a Level 4 pathogen."

"What about another research facility?" she asked. "The one in North Carolina worked off the grid with little oversight."

"A lot of them do, especially those associated with DARPA. But surely you've already checked that route?"

"We did, but there's no way to even locate all of them. There's no registry, and in some cases, no federal regulation. I've talked to scientists who've worked with Shaw at other labs, but that was a dead end. The FBI put out alerts. She's wanted for suspicion of murder. If anyone risks taking her in they'd be harboring a fugitive."

"Has DARPA been cooperating?" Platt asked.

The director was a mentor and friend of Platt's. Colonel Abraham Hess was such a legend that even a barrage of congressional hearings last fall couldn't put a dent in his reputation.

"Hess will only talk to AD Kunze," O'Dell told him. Kunze was her boss at the FBI, and he was a political animal who sometimes was too concerned about his own reputation with D.C. elites. "He's been very willing to provide any information I need, only it seems to take forever for his staff to get it to me."

Platt shook his head. She knew he didn't like having to defend the man and for the moment, he didn't bother to try.

They finished their dinner. Platt ordered a Scotch. O'Dell declined to join him. Told him she had some phone calls to make and excused herself for the evening.

She shared the elevator ride with three people. One was a dark-haired young man she recognized from the booth across from her and Platt. He didn't glance at her, keeping his eyes glued to the ascending numbers above the elevator doors, almost as if he were trying hard not to look at any of the other passengers.

She got off on her floor and the young man followed, but when she turned right to go down her hallway, he turned left. At her door she looked to see him still walking. But at the sound of her keycard's bleep, she noticed — out of the corner of her eye — that he glanced over his shoulder.

O'Dell went inside her room, held the door handle so it didn't click shut, and then waited and listened. She eased the door open without making a sound. She peeked out just in time to see the young man turn the corner, headed back to the elevators.

She listened for the ding of the elevator's

arrival, waited for the swish of the doors to open, then close. Then she hurried down the hallway.

Above each elevator, digital numbers showed the floors as the elevator descended or ascended. There was only one in motion at the moment. It was headed back down.

19

O'Dell pulled out her cell phone.

Perhaps it was a coincidence that the young man had gotten out on the wrong floor. After all, hotel floors all looked the same. The only problem was that she didn't believe in coincidences.

Platt answered on the second ring.

"Are you still at the restaurant?" she asked him.

"Just left."

"There was a young man in the booth across from us," she said as she watched the elevator continue down without stopping. "Dark hair. Wearing jeans and a blue shirt. He's going to be getting off the elevator in the lobby in the few seconds. Can you get a picture of him, then see where he goes?"

He didn't question her. Instead, all he said was "I'll call you back."

It was twenty minutes later — what felt like an hour — when Platt called.

"He was on his phone when he stepped out of the elevator," Platt told her. "Picked up a suitcase from the concierge. He's in a cab now. Looks like he's headed to O'Hare."

"How do you know he's going to the airport?"

"Because I'm in a cab right behind him. I remember him from the restaurant. I thought he looked too interested in our conversation. You think he's part of this?"

"I don't know. He followed me up to my floor. Pretended to go the other direction like he was going to his room, but as soon as I got inside mine he headed back to the elevators."

"He wanted to see what room you're staying in. Maybe you need to get a different room."

"I'm sure I'll be okay. I can certainly protect myself. It's not in anyone's best interest to start killing off investigators."

"Unless the investigator is getting too close."

"We can't get paranoid. What are they going to do? Push me off the balcony?" She was trying to make light of the situation. She didn't want Platt worrying.

"Do you think someone pushed Briggs?"

"It's possible. Ben, relax. You're following the only person we think might be a threat."

There was a knock at the door.

"Room service."

O'Dell started across the room to answer the door.

"He wasn't alone in that booth in the restaurant," Platt said.

She stopped suddenly.

"What's wrong?" Platt asked when she paused too long.

"I didn't order room service. I'll call you back." She ended the call before he could protest.

She grabbed her Glock from the closet. Through the peephole she examined the man dressed like the waiters in the restaurant. She tried to remember the other man from the booth. She was certain this one was older, stockier with thinning hair.

Yet she couldn't help but remember another room service tray delivered to her hotel door years ago in Kansas City. It was the kind of thing that set off alarms in her head. Something she'd never forget. A killer had left a victim's spleen splayed on a porcelain plate and tucked neatly under the stainless steel lid.

With her weapon down at her side O'Dell opened the door but only as wide as the chain would allow.

"I didn't order room service," she told him.

Flustered, the man flipped open the receipt wallet and his eyes darted to the room number.

"My apologies, ma'am. I do indeed have the wrong room. I'm so sorry to have disturbed you." Embarrassed, he turned and quickly pushed the cart down the hall.

She waited and listened for him to knock on another door, but instead, she heard the elevator open, the clank of the cart, and the swoosh of doors closing. Was it odd that he'd get not just the room number wrong but the floor wrong as well?

Her cell phone was ringing. It was Platt — impatient. Though when she answered he sounded only concerned.

"What's happening?"

"Wrong room." She left it at that even though the knot in her stomach refused to quit twisting.

"This guy's heading back to Atlanta."

"How can you know that?"

"I stood beside him at the self-serve kiosk while he printed out his boarding pass. I could see it on the screen. It could mean that he's a part of this."

"Did he look sick?" she asked.

"No, but —"

"Ben, there's no evidence he's a part of this."

Usually she could count on her gut instinct, but maybe she really was just being paranoid. Being in that hazmat gear had triggered not just memories but that helpless feeling of not fully being in control. Killers she could handle, but invisible viruses were a whole different threat.

"I could at least have him detained," Platt offered.

"On what grounds? Getting off the elevator on the wrong floor? I don't think that's wise. Were you able to get a photo of him?"

"I did. I'll text it to you before I head back."

"Great! I can run it by Agent Alonzo and see if anything comes up. Thanks."

"Maggie."

"Yes?"

"Just be careful, okay?"

She assured him that she would and that everything was fine. As soon as she hung up she called down to the front desk and asked for a different room.

20

FLORIDA PANHANDLE

Creed handed Jason another beer over the countertop that separated his kitchen from his living room.

"Maybe I just don't want to believe Tony would do something like this without me," Jason said.

His eyes darted to Creed's, looking for judgment, checking to see if Creed might think it odd that friends would share suicide. That Jason would be disappointed that his friend didn't include him.

Creed shrugged and asked, "How long you guys been friends?"

He was relieved when Jason started telling him how he and Tony had been best friends since grade school.

"We actually didn't have much in common. Even in sixth grade Tony had girls fawning all over him," Jason said. "I was a bookworm. He was the athlete. I helped him study and pass tests, and he helped me figure out how to get girls and not get clobbered in football."

Creed couldn't relate. He'd never had a friendship like that in grade school or high school. He was fourteen when his sister Brodie disappeared. He couldn't even remember what life was like before that. For many years it hurt too much to think about it. It seemed wrong to think of happier days when he had no idea what was happening to his sister.

He watched Jason as he talked. The kid was actually smiling.

"Tony was the one who wanted to sign up for the army. I didn't give it a second thought," Jason said. "Of course I was going, too. The recruiter made sure that we trained together and shipped out together."

Something crossed Jason's mind, and Creed saw the smile fall almost as if a shadow had passed by. His hand went to the stub of his arm and started rubbing.

"He told me he felt like it was his fault. Me losing my arm. Just because he talked me into signing up. And yet, he came back with his own problems. Yeah, sure, his body looks okay. Not like Colfax with his glass eye and Frankenstein scars, or Benny with both legs sliced off above the kneecaps. Hell, compared to those two, I even feel lucky. But Tony . . . he came back looking normal, but his mind hasn't been right since Afghanistan."

Creed noticed that Jason was talking about his friend going back and forth from present tense to past. Not unusual. The shock of Tony actually being dead would need to wear off. And yes, Creed understood that Tony didn't just have PTSD (post-traumatic stress disorder) but had been diagnosed with traumatic brain injury.

"Tony calls them his brain fevers," Jason continued. "I've seen them. Looks painful. He said it feels like his head is getting ready to explode — pressure, pain, sometimes even a pounding sound. Still able to joke about it. Every once in a while he'd ask us guys if we could hear it and cock his head with his ear toward us." Jason smiled.

Suddenly Jason sat up straight on the bar stool as another memory came back to him.

"I just remembered. Tony told me he actually called the VA's suicide hotline."

"When was that?"

"Last summer, during one of his episodes. It ended up being something we joked about. They put him on hold."

Creed just shook his head. He'd heard enough stories like this one that they no longer surprised him.

"He waited thirty-seven minutes. By then he was pissed off and more focused on telling them to screw off."

Creed opened the refrigerator to grab a couple more beers but stopped.

"Are you hungry?"

"You cooking?"

"Of course not, but I have some leftovers that Hannah brought over."

"Yeah, I could eat something." But the kid didn't need to answer. His eyes lit up at the mention of Hannah's cooking.

Creed pulled out the glass casserole dish and was about to peel off the foil when he decided to leave it and turn on his oven. Ordinarily he'd grab a fork and eat it cold right out of the dish. Bad habits of living alone. From the counter he unwrapped a loaf of homemade corn bread. Sliced a couple of pieces and slid a plate over to Jason.

"The chicken and black-eyed peas will take about fifteen minutes to heat up."

Jason was biting off chunks of bread before Creed brought out the butter. The kid's appetite always made Creed smile. Both men were in their twenties — Creed at the end and Jason at the beginning — yet most of the time Creed felt like decades separated them instead of years. Maybe part of it was because Creed had already gone through much of what Jason was going through now. Only for Creed it felt like a lifetime ago.

"Hannah promised to teach me how to make this," Jason said about the bread.

"You cook?"

"A little bit. And making bread is baking, not cooking."

When Creed raised an eyebrow, Jason said, "My little sister and me were latchkey kids. My dad worked the night shift and my mom didn't get home until five or six. I got tired of frozen pizzas and grilled cheese."

Creed had never heard Jason talk about his family. Maybe seeing his grandfather had reminded him of them.

"They live in the area?"

"Mobile."

Fifty miles away and yet Jason had lived at Segway House in Pensacola when he came back. The kid must have suspected what Creed was thinking.

"It was hard on them, you know," Jason explained. "When I came back. It was like they didn't know what to say to me. My mom wanted me to stay with them, but I couldn't." He shook his head, looking down at the plate of homemade bread. "I just couldn't take them staring at me, all sad and stuff. So frickin' polite and careful. I felt like I was being crushed under their pity."

Jason grabbed the neck of his beer bottle and took a long gulp.

"My dad didn't even come to the hospital," he continued. "Said it was too hard on him to see me like this." He raised his amputated arm to emphasize "this." "It was too frickin' hard on *him.*"

Creed understood. He'd never been able to rely on his own family. That was why he'd joined the Marines. Now his family was Hannah and the dogs. There was nothing he could say to Jason to make any of it better. No wise words. No sage piece of advice.

Instead he glanced at the time and said, "Why don't you stay here for the night?"

"What?"

"The sofa's pretty comfortable. Scout's downstairs in the kennel with the other dogs. You can check up on him during the night if you want."

"You're worried I'm gonna off myself if I'm alone. Because of Tony."

"No, it's not that." But it was exactly that. "Look, it's been a tough day. It was just a suggestion." He pretended like it was no big deal.

"Oh, I get it," Jason said with a smile.

Creed braced himself for the kid's indignation. Sometimes he wanted to ask Jason if his shoulder ever got tired with that huge chip on it.

But the kid surprised him when he said, "You're missing Grace and Rufus."

It wasn't a secret that the Jack Russell and the old Lab usually slept with Creed. Before he could respond, Jason added, "Okay, yeah. I wouldn't mind being closer to Scout."

21

NEW YORK CITY

Christina Lomax pushed her way through the crowd of people. She'd taken Broadway by mistake. She was trying to get back to Fifth Avenue when the evening shows finished, and suddenly Christina found herself swept up in a wave of people. She no longer knew which direction she was headed. And yet, this was exactly the kind of thing her handlers had wanted.

They had emphasized over and over for her to make contact with as many people as possible. Touch objects that many others would touch after her — taxicab door handles, elevator buttons, café menus.

Now all she wanted to do was find her way back to the hotel. She needed a cab. It was too far to walk, especially with the muscle fatigue. She swore it wasn't half this bad when she'd left the hotel. Her knees felt wobbly and so did her stomach. The only thing she had eaten for the day was a hot pretzel from a street vendor. The salt had soothed her sore throat and the warm doughy bread filled the void. But that was hours ago, and even though she didn't have much of an appetite she knew she needed to eat to keep her strength.

Through a slice of the crowd she could see a line of yellow taxis and black sedans. Christina tried to elbow her way to the curb. In front of her, theater patrons piled into the cars. She twisted through bodies, but every time she got close enough someone beat her to the cab door. She kept getting shoved back. It was like swimming against the current.

Finally she gave up.

She decided to walk to the nearest hotel. She'd go inside for a few minutes, then come back out and ask the doorman to hail a cab for her. It had worked earlier.

She was dressed well enough to be mistaken for a tourist who could afford to stay at a midtown luxury hotel. Though it didn't really matter. Christina had learned years ago that it wasn't so much about how you looked but how you carried yourself.

Confidence. That was what it took.

An air of confidence could work better than Cole Haan leather flats. She never had designer shoes or clothes all those times she used the bathroom at the Home Depot or replenished her necessities at Walmart, and no one had given her a second look. No one would have ever guessed that she was homeless and living out of her car.

She was on the fringes of the Broadway crowd when the man beside her leaned down and said, "I have something for you, Christina. But don't look at me."

Her entire body went rigid, but she managed to keep from looking over at him. They walked together, only it was more like they were being swept up in the same direction.

"Try not to look surprised or anxious," he told her as he faced forward.

Out of the corner of her eye she tried to see if she recognized him. He was only a few inches taller than her. He wore a dark sports jacket and matching trousers, shiny leather shoes. His hair and beard were trimmed short with streaks of gray, though Christina guessed he was close to her age, somewhere in his forties.

"I don't understand," she said, keeping her voice calm and her eyes from glancing at him. "Who are you?"

"My name's Howard, but that's not important. I've slipped something into your jacket pocket. Don't reach for it now. Wait until you're back at your hotel."

Her pocket? When? How was that possible? She hadn't felt a thing. But she refrained from questioning him.

"Keep it on you at all times. When you're done, it's important the authorities find it on your body."

What in the world was he talking about? No one had mentioned that she needed to carry something. But he was already gone.

On her body? It sounded like he meant when she was dead.

22

Stephen Bishop ate a late dinner alone in the corner office just two doors down from the suite of laboratories. Not an uncommon habit for scientists. At least for dedicated scientists. Dr. Howard Getz had cancelled their scheduled evening meeting. Something about a family emergency he needed to attend to in New York.

"My sincere apologies," he had said earlier over the phone.

Family could be a scientist's weakest link, especially during the launch of an experiment like this that had monumental ramifications. But the man sounded so pained that it was difficult to question him.

Bishop knew absolutely nothing about Dr. Getz's life and didn't care to, although it was hard to avoid the display in his office. His walls and bookcases were interspersed with dozens of photos of Getz and a smiling wife with or without several children in various stages of life.

Bishop didn't trust the man, but Getz was one of the two scientists Colonel Hess had recruited for this project. Getz and Dr. Sheila Robins didn't know all the details about the operation; however, both of them — at one time or another — had worked on creating various strains of the bird flu at different DARPA facilities.

Getz's goal was to ultimately make a universal vaccine. Of course he understood that in order to do that he needed to first make it contagious. Robins's work was more in line with Bishop's: to make a potent strain that easily transferred from bird to human, then human to human with very little contact. Birds would be the perfect carrier. Robins saw the same advantage as Hess did in creating a new biological weapon.

The research facility was huge, though you'd never know that unless you could first find it along the winding back roads. It was tucked into the woods at the base of the Smoky Mountains; few outsiders even knew it existed.

Bishop had no clue how many scientists and staff worked here. The number was enough that no one cared about or noticed three new faces. That was one of the nice things about scientists. Most were intensely private people, and in a DARPA research facility, many were secretive and protective about their own projects. They had no extra time or inclination to care about anyone else's.

Bishop knew there were dozens of facilities like this one across the country that operated off the grid with little regulation and much independence. When Hess was pressed to find a laboratory suite for Bishop to use to run this experiment, he had no problem making the arrangements.

Still, it had taken some convincing on Bishop's part. Perhaps Hess might even call it blackmail. Bishop simply appealed to Hess's own goals and ambitions. As head of DARPA, Colonel Abraham Hess had spent decades investing in research that would facilitate the protection of soldiers and the death of the enemy. The enemy had changed through the years. It was no longer the Russians and the Cold War. Now it was the medieval forces like the Taliban and radical Islamist terrorists.

Bioweapons were just a part of the dirty secrets that Hess and his minions didn't want the world to know about — and heaven forbid the bleeding-heart ruling class should be confronted with that reality, the ones who had no stomach for offending the enemy, let alone killing them.

Bishop and Hess disagreed on many things, but the one thing they did agree on was that for every twisted quasi-immoral weapon that DARPA could dream up, the enemy was already two steps ahead of them. And there was no easy method to combat this new enemy — terrorists who strapped bombs to their chests and were willing to blow up hundreds of civilians along with themselves.

Bishop's grandfather had been a scientist in the 1960s, when there was a race to build and stockpile bigger and better and more bombs than the Russians. He and Hess came up in their careers during a time when biological weapons like VX nerve gas and sarin gas were considered the latest tools in a growing arsenal of alternative weapons.

In fact, Bishop's grandfather was one of the first to test the use of mosquitoes as carriers for dengue fever. Back then they used the military's enlisted men as test subjects. Fifty years later when those facts came to light — after being hidden and buried in classified documents — the American people were appalled.

Last fall Colonel Hess had faced a congressional hearing — a political firestorm —

and somehow he had risen out of the ashes. And he'd managed to do it without releasing any information about DARPA's current research, nor did he sacrifice a single DARPA research facility or project. That was if you didn't count the unfortunate loss of the North Carolina facility, which really couldn't be counted. Its demise came from a massive mudslide and not the political firing squad.

The new cell phone started ringing.

Speak of the devil.

"This is Bishop."

"You were going to call me." The old man's voice sounded like gravel on sandpaper.

"I see you received the new phone number."

"Tell me again why it's so important these carriers be eliminated," Hess said.

"We cannot risk them telling how they became infected." Bishop had already explained this to the old man. "If we wait until they get too sick, they may end up saying things."

"One of your watchers killed a young woman and left her body in a river."

"They're supposed to make it look like suicide."

"I'm told he panicked. The woman had

called the county sheriff."

Bishop sat up and gripped the phone. This was new information.

"What did she tell him?"

"Some fantastical story about being a part of a government experiment that was making her ill."

This was exactly what Bishop worried about. "Did he believe her?"

"It doesn't matter. I sent one of my men to clean up the mess. From now on we use only recruits that I choose."

"I really can't be bothered by those minor details," Bishop said, hiding the wave of relief. "We'll use yours for the next phase."

"And your watchers," he said, "they need to report to my man."

Hess had sensed vulnerability like a shark in bloody water and was using it to seize even more control. It wasn't out of concern for the project's success as much as his own self-preservation.

Bishop swallowed years of preparation along with pride and pretended this was no big deal, then simply said, "Fine."

23

CHICAGO

Almost midnight and O'Dell couldn't sleep. Hotel management had overcompensated giving her a new room, this one with a view. She kept the television on, leaving it at one of the cable news stations though there was no news that interested her.

She had left a message for Agent Anthony Alonzo back at Quantico. She'd sent him the photo Platt took of the young man who had followed her. Alonzo could download it into their face-recognition program. If they were lucky maybe they'd get a hit.

She also e-mailed a list of information requests. Alonzo was a data wizard. These days almost everyone left an electronic footprint of some sort. If there was even a crumb, Alonzo would usually find it. Except for Dr. Clare Shaw. Nothing. They had come up empty, time after time.

She told the agent what Platt had said would be necessary for Shaw to grow the virus and asked that he try one more time to find a research lab in the Southeast. Was it possible they had missed a facility in their earlier hunt? Perhaps somewhere near Pensacola.

Alonzo also agreed to see if there was anything else he could find about Tony Briggs. Tracking his last days might lead them closer to Shaw. Past experience had taught O'Dell that sometimes you could learn vital information about a killer by examining his victims. That was when she realized there was someone who could tell her more about Briggs than Agent Alonzo.

She was thinking about Jason Seaver when her phone rang. She recognized the area code. The call was from the Florida Panhandle. But it wouldn't be Jason calling. She thought immediately of Ryder Creed, and she hated the annoying flutter of anticipation.

"This is Maggie O'Dell," she answered.

"Maggie, it's Hannah. Hannah Washington."

Of course. Ryder wasn't the only person she knew within that area code. But that his partner had called, and that her voice sounded anxious, turned O'Dell's anticipation to worry.

"Hannah, what's wrong? Are you okay? Is

Ryder okay?"

"Mercy, I'm sorry to be bothering you at this hour. No one's hurt. Not yet anyway. I've been racking my mind trying to think of someone who might be able to help us. I know Rye won't ask. But I'm not too proud. I have my boys to think about."

"What is it, Hannah? Of course I'll help. Tell me what's going on."

"We had quite a scare today."

Hannah went on to tell O'Dell about the men in black SUVs who had come to their training facility. Armed men.

"Several of them wore hazmat suits. They were here to . . . dear God, I can't even say it. They were going to put down our dogs. Every last one of them."

"I don't understand. Who were they?"

"The man in charge is an FBI agent named Lawrence Tabor."

Hannah explained about the missing girl, Izzy Donner. How Ryder and Grace had helped find her body. And about the dead robins. Before today none of what Hannah was telling O'Dell would have warranted much concern.

"We got them to leave," Hannah said. "But I know he'll be back. Is there any way you might be able to talk to him? Dr. Avelyn has the dogs quarantined. She sent samples of the dead birds in for testing, and she's waiting to hear from someone at the CDC. But I'm just afraid he'll be back sooner than all that."

O'Dell jotted down as much information as Hannah had about Agent Tabor.

"Can they do that?" Hannah's voice was calmer now, but O'Dell could still hear a trace of fear.

"I'm not sure. I know someone at the CDC. I'll do everything I can to stop them."

"Oh, thank you."

"Hannah, tell me about the young woman they found in the river."

"Actually I don't know much about her. Rye said she looked peaceful."

"Peaceful?"

"Said it looked like she loaded her jacket pockets with rocks, walked into the river, and just lay down."

Suicide?

Instead of saying it out loud, she asked, "Why was Agent Tabor there? What was his interest in the case?"

"You know, I don't rightly know."

"Is there any way you or Ryder could find out what happened to her?"

"Rye knows the medical examiner. I suppose he could give him or Sheriff Wylie a call. You think this has something to do with her? It's not just about some dead robins with the bird flu virus?"

"Wait a minute, Agent Tabor actually told you the robins might have the bird flu virus?"

"I believe that's what he said."

O'Dell sat on the edge of the bed. She'd been pacing dressed only in her nightshirt, and now she was chilled. How would this Agent Tabor know? Or was he just guessing?

"Hannah, I'm in Chicago, but I'll be coming down to Pensacola perhaps tomorrow or early Wednesday." She couldn't tell Hannah about Tony Briggs. She didn't know if his family had even been told yet.

"That would be a blessing to have you here."

"If Tabor shows up again, call me or have him call me directly."

"Thank you, Maggie."

She ended the call and immediately pulled on a pair of jeans and a sweatshirt to ward off the chill.

Pensacola, Florida. Tony Briggs's hometown. Dead robins and a dead girl in a river that sounded like another suicide. She needed to add another name to Agent Alonzo's list. She grabbed her laptop to send the e-mail. Then she'd search for flights.

But the television screen caught her eye.

O'Dell reached for the remote and turned up the volume. A woman was talking to a reporter. The boxed graphic at the bottom of the screen identified her as Amee Rief, a biologist with the U.S. Fish and Wildlife Service. What caught O'Dell's interest was behind the biologist.

Right at that moment the camera panned the area, giving her a better view. The lake looked huge, and every inch of its surface was covered in white snow geese. Rief was explaining that these were migratory birds that usually stopped here every spring on their way to breeding grounds on the Arctic tundra.

Only these geese were dead. All of them.

■ ■ ■ ■

TUESDAY

■ ■ ■ ■

24

"You look like hell," Dr. Avelyn told Creed when he walked into Hannah's kitchen.

"Did you get any sleep?" Hannah asked. She was scrambling eggs in one skillet while bacon fried in another.

He shook his head and rubbed at his unshaved jaw. The bristles were longer than he usually kept them, but he figured that wasn't what the two women were noticing. He knew his eyes were bloodshot. He'd finished the morning chores and it was still dark outside. It had been a mistake letting Jason spend the night in his loft. The kid snored. Sounded like a chain saw.

He poured himself a cup of coffee. There were dark circles under Hannah's eyes. Dr. Avelyn looked rested and she smelled good, something citrus with a hint of coconut. He tried not to notice how good she could smell or look. He knew she was single, somewhere around his age, and she was attractive. But years ago he'd made a promise to himself and to Hannah that he wouldn't get involved — code word for "sleep with" — any women he worked with. Hannah insisted it would diminish their professional reputation. Bottom line, Creed would never do anything he thought might hurt Hannah.

"I may have some good news," Dr. Avelyn told him as he sat down across from her at the kitchen table.

He glanced up at Hannah. She already knew.

"You heard back from the CDC?"

"No, not yet. But I did hear from the state health department. Remember I sent them tissue samples of the robins the same day you found them? Yesterday after Tabor and his goons left, I called a friend who works there and told him about the situation. He tracked down the lab results. There's absolutely no indication of disease or the bird flu virus."

"Any idea what killed them?"

"I only sent the tissue samples. They'd need the whole bird to check for trauma. Would you like me to do that?"

"There's no need, right?"

"No, the lab results eliminated the possible risks to the dogs and to us."

Creed breathed a sigh of relief, so deeply

148

Hannah looked over and laughed at him.

"That was almost my reaction."

"With a string of hallelujahs," Dr. Avelyn added.

"Grace is okay?" he asked.

"Yes. No worries of contamination. No quarantine. I did send tissue samples to the CDC, but I'll send them these results."

"So we shouldn't have to worry about Tabor?" Hannah asked.

"I wouldn't think so. If he returns, I can share these results with him," Dr. Avelyn said.

Creed's cell phone started to ring. He checked the time as he looked at the caller ID. It was awfully early for a call from the Santa Rosa County medical examiner.

"Dr. Emmet."

"Ryder, it's not my place to be calling you, but I can't get ahold of Sheriff Wylie. They told me he went fishing. Left for his cabin the other day. He's not even returning messages."

Creed knew the medical examiner. They had worked on many cases over the years, and even though Creed wasn't a part of law enforcement, Dr. Emmet always extended him the courtesies as if he were one of them. He had even given Creed samples for training purposes — unclaimed teeth and bone, sometimes bloody clothing that the victim's family had declined.

"Is this about Izzy Donner? I haven't talked to Wylie since we found her body."

"You didn't touch her, did you?"

"Excuse me?"

"How about your dog?"

"Neither of us touched the body." Creed saw Dr. Avelyn and Hannah stop. Both women were staring at him.

"She didn't drown."

"I figured as much."

"No water in her lungs, but there was a lot of hemorrhaging. I didn't think too much about it when I did the autopsy. There was petechial hemorrhage. You know what that is, right?"

Before Creed could answer, Emmet continued, "It usually occurs when blood leaks from the tiny capillaries in the eyes. They rupture when there's increased pressure on the veins in the head when a person's airways are being obstructed. Lack of oxygen sometimes can cause hemorrhaging in the lungs too, but this girl's lungs looked messed up. She was sick — very sick — before she ended up in the river."

"Let me guess," Creed said. "She may have had a deadly virus."

"I don't know. I didn't get a chance to

find out, but Agent Tabor said she may have had a new strain of the bird flu."

"Tabor called you?"

"He was here. They took the girl's body late yesterday, stormed the place with what looked like a SWAT team. Assholes scared the crap out my staff. He had us locked up here. Had his own medical team poking us, taking blood and saliva samples. They finally cleared us about three this morning. I'm concerned about Wylie. Do you know how to contact him? I understand he helped fish her out of the water."

"But how did she end up in the river? Could she have walked that far if she was so sick?"

"Oh, I'm sure someone put her there. Probably the same person who killed her."

"Killed her? You mean she didn't die from the virus?"

"Sorry, I wasn't more clear. The petechial hemorrhage in her eyes wasn't from drowning. Based on bruising around the neck, I'm almost certain she was strangled to death."

25

Christina had spent the night tossing and turning. By the time she got back to her hotel room she had been exhausted, weak, burning up with fever, and shivering uncontrollably.

She had done exactly what the man had asked and had not even put her hand in her pocket to feel what he had left there. It wasn't until she was safely inside her hotel room that she rushed to turn on all the lights. And then she had sat very quietly, rubbing her shoulders, waiting for the courage.

His words raced in her mind. Was he friend or foe? Certainly he wasn't one of the watchers if he didn't want anyone to see them talking together. And yet he seemed to know everything.

Most troubling was when he told her to make sure this item was on her at all times. *When you're done, it's important the authori-*

ties find it on your body.

The authorities. Not her handlers. Not the watchers.

Maybe she had misunderstood him. But her mind was still sharp enough to remember his words exactly even though she didn't want to accept what they meant. He spoke of her death as if it were imminent. But her handlers had told Christina that the watchers were there to help her carry out her mission. They had injected her with a virus. She knew that. She allowed that. She knew she was supposed to spread the germs to as many people as she could.

She was told that it was a test, an experiment just like the other tests and experiments that she had volunteered for at the research facility in North Carolina. Each time she had been rewarded and paid well. Sure, some of the tests left her feeling disoriented, even nauseated, for several days after, but she had always been okay. Twice they had even provided a serum to help make her feel better afterward. So why was this man talking as if he expected her death?

And the object he had slipped into her pocket only added to the confusion.

The whole incident along with the fever had brought her strange dreams; some of them felt like hallucinations. At times she couldn't tell whether she was asleep or awake. She kept a lamp on, hoping it would help. It did not. It only added to her mind's confusion.

Her bedsheets were drenched with sweat. Finally, she had gotten up and wrapped herself in the luxurious soft robe that the hotel provided and tried to sleep in the chair instead of the bed. She was awake when she heard the rustle at the door. When the piece of paper slid underneath, she startled to her feet. On tiptoe she raced to the door, smashing her eye against the peephole. All she saw was a blurred thin figure hurrying away.

Christina carefully picked up the folded piece of paper and carried it to the chair. Right now she had no interest in looking at what instructions the watchers had for her day.

Without unfolding it she placed it next to the item the man had slipped into her pocket. The small flash drive was useless to her. Without a computer she couldn't even look to see what was so important that it needed to be found on her dead body.

26
OMAHA, NEBRASKA

Instead of Pensacola, O'Dell booked a flight to Omaha. Before she left she spent the morning tracking down the biologist she had seen on the newscast the night before. She called Platt about her plans only when she was getting ready to board, leaving him little time to talk her out of it or try to convince her this was a wild-goose chase. Besides, he had his hands full, and she asked him to fill her in on the CDC's progress.

Roger Bix's staff had spent the last thirty-six hours with Chicago hospital personnel and checking with urgent care facilities. Platt told her that Bix was reporting a total of seventy-three people in the Chicago area who might have come in contact with Tony Briggs and were now sick. They were in the process of testing them for the virus. But Platt admitted it was early and most people might not seek medical help until the more severe symptoms hit. They were expecting that number to rise in the next several days, especially after they tracked down the passengers who were on both flights Briggs had taken, one from Pensacola and the other from Atlanta.

O'Dell's flight from Chicago to Omaha was short but bumpy. She was relieved that the biologist from the U.S. Fish and Wildlife Service was able to meet her and even offered to pick her up from the airport.

Amee Rief wore blue jeans, a bright yellow ski jacket, and stylish hiking boots. O'Dell was surprised. On television Rief had been dressed in a pea-green jacket with a patch on the sleeve that identified her department.

Rief seemed to notice and smiled as she said, "Off camera I like to go rogue."

O'Dell had decided she liked the woman before she met her, recognizing even on the phone that she was sincere and genuine in wanting to do the right thing. Though she was the department's spokesperson and investigator on this case — and O'Dell knew she was doing her best to keep the media and locals from panicking — Rief had not tried to hide any of the details from her. Coming from a federal employee, O'Dell found it refreshing.

It took almost two hours to drive from the airport to the lake. By the time they arrived they had only a few hours before dusk. During the drive Rief pointed out a huge flock of snow geese in the distance. O'Dell couldn't help thinking the sky looked like a snowstorm of birds. Their white wings glittered in the sunlight.

"So not all of them have been affected."

"So far I've only found dead geese on this one lake. I've taken water samples to check for any chemical leaks or pesticides. But the other flocks appear to be okay. Millions of snow geese stop here to feed before they head up to their breeding grounds," Rief explained. "They're not the only migratory bird to choose the Platte River Valley. Lots of them come through here along the Platte and the Missouri. In a few more weeks we'll start to see sandhill cranes."

"They're gorgeous," O'Dell said, mesmerized by the sight of them, a thick wave rising and lowering, their movement as smooth as water in the sky.

"Pairs mate for life," Rief continued. "They'll have two to six chicks. Families stay together through the young one's first winter. About a hundred years ago they were almost extinct, but populations are thriving again. So much so, they're back on the hunting list. Sometimes overpopulation of a particular waterfowl can be a problem. But we haven't seen much disease. Until now."

"Is that what you're thinking, or do you already know?"

"We don't have any results back yet, but I've never seen anything like this. Migratory waterfowl have always been suspected carriers of bird flu, but they don't usually get sick themselves."

O'Dell had told the biologist that they suspected a new strain. She needed Rief's expertise. She hoped she hadn't misjudged the woman by confiding in her. Besides, how could she in good conscience not share what she knew when Rief and her colleagues would be processing and disposing of thousands of dead snow geese in the weeks to come? They needed to know that they might be at risk.

"You know, we've all anticipated for some time now that the bird flu would hit the United States," Rief said. "It was just a matter of time. I don't know if you're aware of this, but when it did show up — that first case in Washington State in the fall of 2013 — it didn't resemble the Asian strain or the one that they were seeing in Europe."

"I've been told it mutates easily."

"Oh, it wasn't just that it might have mutated," Rief told her. "We wondered if it didn't resemble the others because it was leaked from one of our own research labs."

27

The rain had finally stopped by the time Creed found the dirt path. His tires skidded on the red clay. He slowed down and let the four-wheel drive do its job.

A glance in the rearview mirror assured him that Grace was unfazed by the continued rumble of thunder. It seemed to grow louder as they advanced up the hill. The seats in the back of his Jeep were laid flat to accommodate her kennel and their gear. She stood in the middle so she could see in between the front seats, as though she were helping him navigate.

The Jack Russell knew they had brought her working gear, so she was ready to work. But Creed hoped they'd find Sheriff Wylie fishing in between cloudbursts. Maybe he would have some answers about Izzy Donner.

Creed remembered how desperate the old sheriff had been to find the young woman, despite sticking to the story that she had simply wandered off. It wasn't like Wylie to leave without even checking with Dr. Emmet to see what had happened to Donner. Creed remembered during the search for the young woman how Wylie and Tabor seemed to know more than they were telling. And now Creed suspected that Wylie might know exactly what the hell was going on.

It could even be the reason the sheriff had taken off. If not to hide, then to get away for a while.

The small cabin was nestled deep in a forest of longleaf pines. The thick trunks with patches of green shot well above the roof, and the wood of the cabin blended in. On this dark, dreary day, it'd be easy to miss the cabin entirely and continue up the dirt path that fishermen used as a road.

It had been years since Creed had been up here. Not much had changed. Wylie usually invited a handful of colleagues for an annual fishing excursion that ended with a fish fry and all the beer you could drink. Creed had missed a few. Grace had never been here, but he noticed her nose already working the air.

He pulled up alongside Wylie's pickup. Several different tire tracks crisscrossed in the mud. Creed realized the sheriff might not be alone.

"Would help if you returned phone calls," Creed muttered.

Grace cocked her head at him.

"Nothing to worry about," he said to the dog.

There were no lights on inside the cabin. But even on a dark and dreary day the place probably had enough natural light for a miser like Wylie.

As Creed got out of the Jeep, he looked for the river between the trees. There was a footpath behind the cabin. From here he could see the water and the old wood dock. But no fisherman. No surprise. The clouds looked like they could burst open again at any minute. What did concern Creed was that Wylie's boat wasn't at the dock.

Creed raised the Jeep's tailgate and Grace met him. He expected her to be squirming and excited. Instead she stood stock-still, her head back and nose twitching. Her ears were pitched forward. That was when Creed realized how quiet it was. There was only the rumble in the clouds. No birds. Nothing flapping in the breeze. No humming of a generator.

It was too quiet.

Creed clipped a leash to Grace's collar

and lifted her out and onto the ground. He hadn't given her any instructions or commands, but she was straining at the lead, pulling him toward the back of the cabin.

"We're not staying for dinner," he told her when he got a whiff of a recent wood fire.

Grace's nose would be able to smell not only the ashes, but what had been cooked on that fire, even if it had been the previous night.

There were several pairs of footprints in the mud. Different soles. Different sizes. Wylie had probably invited some of his fishing buddies. And now Creed was starting to regret crashing a party he hadn't been invited to.

Still, something didn't feel right.

He followed Grace's lead. He was a bit surprised when she passed the fire pit without giving it an extra sniff. She was headed for the water. By the time they got to the boat dock she was breathing fast. Her tail was straight up. She didn't change her pace even as she jumped up onto the rickety boards and marched to the edge, where she came to a dead stop.

Then she looked back at Creed, staring straight into his eyes.

He wasted a few seconds checking the riverbank. Another precious minute or two

163

went by as he dropped to his knees and looked down around and under the dock.

In the meantime, Grace was getting impatient with him. Her paws danced and her head bobbed almost as if she were trying to point her nose in the right direction.

His eyes started darting across the surface of the water. There was a gentle swish. He listened to the breeze skimming through the tops of the pine trees. Again, the clouds above rumbled.

This part of the river was only about a hundred feet from bank to bank, but around the bend Creed knew it opened up wider. Tree branches leaned down in places. Some had toppled into the water, making a natural habitat for beavers, insects, and water moccasins. But Creed saw nothing.

He looked back at Grace.

She stared at him again, then poked at the air with her nose.

"I'm trying," he told her.

This time he focused on the bend where the river curved, about three hundred feet away. Close to the opposite bank he saw something, an object in the water. A red object that caught his eye. It bobbed on the surface but didn't appear to be moving with the current. He couldn't think of anything that grew or bloomed red in these parts at this time of year.

Creed pointed in its direction and looked down at Grace.

She pranced on the edge of the dock, and Creed's pulse quickened. Grace was never wrong.

28

Creed peeled off his hiking boots, then his vest and shirt, shedding everything that might bog him down.

"You have to stay, Grace."

She twirled.

"I'm serious."

She twirled a second time.

"Stay, Grace."

The water was cold. Creed was glad he had left on his jeans. In places the river ran waist-high, but through the middle Creed knew it was as deep as twenty feet. It ran shallow on the other side of the bend, where it spilled into a much wider area. It wasn't a problem. Creed was an excellent swimmer. His facility housed an Olympic-sized pool for him and his dogs to train in. But almost as soon as he started swimming, the sky darkened. What had been a soft rumble overhead now crackled with electricity. The Florida Panhandle witnessed more lightning strikes than anywhere else in the country, and spring was the most unpredictable season.

Creed needed to be quick about this. He raised his head. Still couldn't make out what the red object was.

A flash of lightning.

He kept his head down and increased his pace. At one point he glanced back at Grace. She was waiting at the end of the dock, right where he had left her. Right where he had told her to stay. And he knew she'd stay even when the downpour started, even when the crackles became crashes. Loyal to a fault. That was his Grace.

He hated leaving her out in the open for some wild-goose chase. Then he reminded himself that Grace had alerted at the water's edge. He hadn't asked her to search out anything, and yet she had alerted to something.

Closer to the bank now, Creed dug his feet into the sand and raised himself up. The water lapped against his thighs. The current had gotten stronger. The breeze had kicked up a notch.

The red object had disappeared from sight. Or the current had taken it.

His eyes darted over the water's surface. Then he searched the overhanging branches that dipped into the river. It looked like a pile of debris-tangled brush, broken branches all twisted together. He was about to give up and head back when the flash of red bobbed up just three feet in front of him.

It was a red baseball cap with the letter *A*, what Creed recognized as the University of Alabama's logo. Wylie was a huge Bama fan.

His heart started pounding. Was the sheriff somewhere in the water? Had he knocked himself out and off his boat?

The water was shallow enough here for Creed to swipe his hands underneath the surface. He hadn't gone far when he saw the boat on the other side of the debris pile. And now he knew Wylie had to be here somewhere.

He dived his head beneath the water's surface, but it was too dark to see anything other than roots and branches.

"Wylie!" he called out.

If the man was injured maybe he could hear him.

He looked back at Grace. She pranced around, agitated.

Creed shoved his way around the debris pile, his eyes focused on the small boat. It was wedged between the pile and the bank. Maybe Wylie had gotten caught underneath.

He made his way to the boat and was about to dive underwater again when something above caught his eye. Something in the trees up on the riverbank. Something swaying with the breeze, hanging from one of the branches.

It was Wylie.

29

Christina set out to the streets just as her watchers expected her to do. Her first stop was a little shop on the corner. They had made sure that she had plenty of cash. She usually left most of it in her hotel room, dividing it in three wads and stuffing the wads inside socks, then stuffing the socks into the toes of her shoes. Today she'd stuffed some of it inside her clothing.

She tried to take as much of it with her as she could fit. Some of it was flat against her shins inside her knee-high socks. A couple layers filled her bra, making her so buxom she wore a baggy sweatshirt she had bought from a street vendor on her first day. Last, she ripped a seam in the lining of a baseball cap and tucked in as many bills as she could. Then she put her hair in a ponytail and weaved it through the open back of the cap to make it more secure on her head.

She did all this in case she decided not to

come back to her hotel room. She'd need money for another hotel room, food, and maybe a ticket to get back home.

It wasn't until the man in the crowd — the man who had slipped the flash drive into her pocket — had talked about her death as though it were a foregone conclusion that Christina realized that perhaps the watchers were not necessarily her allies. And now she realized she wouldn't be able to go back home.

She wasn't stupid. She knew that all the information and all the help the watchers had given her so far was simply for her to be able to go out and spread whatever version of the cold or flu they had infected her with. But the more she thought about it, the more she realized that no one had talked about them helping her get better after this experiment.

Sometime during the night, while she tossed and turned in her sweat-drenched sheets, it occurred to Christina that maybe she was really stupid. What if this time instead of providing her with an antidote, they meant for her to simply die?

Was that possible? Or was the fever starting to make her paranoid?

Safe inside the small shop, tucked in the back aisles, she reached through the neckline of her sweatshirt and the T-shirt underneath. She fingered the bump on her upper left arm. The tiny microchip was barely visible. It was put there months ago. Another experiment. For something different.

But what if it wasn't? What if it was being used to track her?

She bought a carton of orange juice, a small bottle of Tylenol, and three protein bars. While she walked down the street she forced down two of the bars. She stopped long enough to pop three Tylenol and washed them down with the orange juice.

Yesterday she had accidentally gotten off on the wrong floor of the hotel. She remembered seeing computers and printers in a room — a business center. But there had been several men and women inside. And the watchers were always slipping notes under her room's door. They were obviously here at the hotel. There was no way she'd be able to use one of the computers.

But other hotels must have similar business centers. She'd go out and pretend to walk the streets just as she did yesterday. Somehow she'd find a computer.

She slipped her hand deep down into the pocket of her jeans and made sure the flash drive was still there. She wanted to see what was so important.

30

THE PLATTE RIVER VALLEY
SOUTH-CENTRAL NEBRASKA

Nebraska didn't have the snow that Chicago had gotten. Brown grass, tinted with the beginning sprigs of green, surrounded the lake. The sky was a brilliant blue turning to deep purple at the horizon as the sun began its descent behind the trees. As the SUV pulled closer, O'Dell couldn't help but think that the surface of the lake looked like it was covered in snow.

The birds were crammed so tight and so close that not a sliver of water could be seen. Some of them even lay on top of one another.

There was no one else around. No traffic. No buildings or homes for miles. Not even any other birds in the trees. The only sound was the breeze whispering through the tall grasses.

"I thought it was best that we wait for the results before we start handling the birds," Rief told her. She pointed out the few tire tracks. "We even made the news media walk from the main road and limited how close they could get. Not that difficult since, as you can see, there's not easy access."

"Still, I'm impressed you were able to limit them."

"National news agencies picked up the local feed. So far they've been satisfied with running with that."

They parked on a field road and walked the rest of the way. With the sun low on the horizon the breeze started to turn cold. O'Dell was glad she had put on her coat. Mud sucked at the soles of her boots. In the distance she could hear a train whistle. There was a hint of musk in the air, but not at all what she expected. The cool weather had kept the birds from decomposing quickly.

"I'm not sure what I hoped to see or find," she told the biologist.

"Maybe you just needed to see it."

On closer inspection the birds looked as if they had lain down to rest in the water and simply died. There didn't appear to be any trauma. No deformities. No molted feathers. No injuries or blood. They looked quite peaceful.

They were headed back to the vehicle when Rief put her arm out in front of

O'Dell to stop her.

"Just stand still."

O'Dell didn't understand until she saw the coyote coming out of the trees. He was approaching the lake, slowly. He seemed to be focused on the dead birds and paid little attention to the women.

O'Dell glanced at the biologist only to find her looking in the opposite direction. From the other stand of trees three more coyotes were making their way to the lake. When she looked back she saw that two more were following the first one she had seen.

"What do we do?"

She kept her voice low and soft. In her own head she could barely hear it over the drumming of her heartbeat. She knew from working with Ryder Creed that dogs could actually smell human fear. Something about hormones and chemistry. None of it mattered right now because she imagined that a coyote's sense was probably even more heightened. Her fingers automatically slipped inside her jacket only to find that she hadn't put on her shoulder harness and weapon after the flight.

"Just keep still," Rief instructed with a steady and calm voice.

O'Dell was feeling anything but steady and calm. And "keeping still"? That was easier said than done. O'Dell couldn't help noticing that they were caught between the lake and the coyotes. And their vehicle was about a hundred feet away. About the same distance as the nearest coyote. It would be a sprint that she imagined might end badly.

The biggest one turned to look at them. The others didn't seem to care. All of them were more interested in the dead birds. O'Dell realized that made sense. It was less work for them to snatch and grab food that was already dead than to challenge the humans. Still, she tried to access her memory bank for any information about coyotes attacking people.

"Were they here last night, too?"

"No. They don't like fresh meat," Rief said. "They'll leave dead stuff until it starts to decompose a bit. Easier to digest."

"They have a lakeful. So we're okay?"

Just as O'Dell asked, another coyote looked over at them.

"Depends," Rief said.

She waited for the biologist to continue.

"Usually a lone coyote won't attack, but a pack can be more aggressive."

It was not what O'Dell wanted to hear.

Soon the sun would be sinking behind the tree line along with O'Dell's stomach. She hoped coyotes couldn't smell fear, because

she was certain she was starting to reek of
it.

31

FLORIDA PANHANDLE

Creed sat on the boat dock with a blanket wrapped around him. He didn't remember which crew member had given it to him. Grace sat next to him. It had taken almost two hours for anyone to arrive. Too much time for Creed to sit and wait and think.

His initial reaction was to get Wylie down.

He had started to climb the riverbank. He'd climb the tree if he had to just to get the sheriff to stop hanging by his neck. But he stopped himself, knees buried in the mud. Halfway up the bank he realized he might destroy crime scene evidence. And he wanted to believe that a crime had been committed. He did not want to believe that Wylie had done this to himself.

So Creed had stayed there, staring up at the body. His eyes couldn't look away.

"You didn't do this to yourself, did you, Wylie?"

The rope had been thrown up over the

branch. One end looped around the sheriff's neck. The other was attached to the boat. Creed could see the skid mark in the clay bank. The boat had been on the bank. All it would have taken was a shove to make it slide down into the water and make the rope act like a pulley. The weight of the trolling motor and the downward slide looked like it was enough to yank Wylie's body up and keep him there. If his neck wasn't broken by the impact, he might have struggled. Creed didn't want to think about how long it could have taken.

At the same time he reminded himself that sometimes things weren't what they seemed. There were so many easier ways to kill yourself. Like Tony Briggs's way of jumping nineteen stories. Or putting a .22 to your temple like Creed's father had done.

Creed didn't want to think about that right now either. He'd spent the last eleven years of his life trying to forget. Sometimes it was too much work to stop it. Too painful to juggle the memories, to decide which ones to release and which to lock away. Brodie's disappearance. His dad's suicide. They leaked into each other.

In his head he could still hear the play-by-play of a football game. It was on the car radio. It was the reason his dad hadn't gone with Brodie to the bathroom at the rest stop. Because his dad couldn't miss a goddamn second of the game. And it was the reason Creed couldn't go with her either, because he was supposed to keep the dog quiet so his dad could listen to the game.

Creed always wondered if it was some sort of odd poetic justice that when he found his dad a football game was playing on the television. His dad was slumped over on the sofa as though he'd fallen asleep watching.

Grace nuzzled him and only now did he realize he was breathing hard, taking gulps of air. He needed to slow down, steady himself before he started to hyperventilate.

He wrapped his arm around the dog and pulled her close to his side, tucking her under the blanket with him. The rain had stopped, but both of them were soaking wet.

The rescue unit finally had a boat in the water. They had to wait on the CSU team. It was getting dark and two of the men were hooking up spotlights. One of the technicians stopped beside him and handed him a thermal cup.

"Hot coffee," he told Creed.

"Thanks."

Then the man put down a stainless steel bowl with water for Grace. She looked to Creed first.

"Go ahead," he told her, and she lapped at it.

"I appreciate that," he told the tech.

"Deputy Mason said to tell you, you're free to go. Oh, and your ride's here," he said, pointing a thumb over his shoulder.

"My ride?"

"You look like hell," someone said from behind him.

Creed turned to find Jason and his friend Colfax. Colfax served in Afghanistan with Jason. He'd lost an eye, and that side of his face was scarred so badly it looked like half his face was melting.

"I have my Jeep. You didn't have to come all this way."

"Hey, I only do what Hannah tells me to do."

Jason kneeled beside Grace and she greeted him with tail wags and face licks. He took a plastic bag from his jacket pocket and held out a handful of kibble. He looked out over the water while the dog took bites and crunched.

"You think he did it?" Jason asked.

"I didn't know him well enough to say."

"Yeah, well, I thought I knew Tony pretty well and I still didn't see it coming."

He pointed to Colfax and told Creed, "One of us will drive your Jeep back. You and Grace can sit back, relax. Enjoy the ride. Have something to eat. We brought food for you, too."

When Creed didn't answer, Jason added, "Please don't make me have to call Hannah."

Creed smiled at that, and suddenly he was too exhausted to argue.

32

The largest coyote was the first to approach the lake.

O'Dell swore her legs were starting to ache from trying to stand so still. But now she was captivated with watching the coyotes.

Two stayed back as if acting as guards, occasionally looking over at Rief and O'Dell. The others drew closer to the lake, but even they didn't go to the edge. They appeared content to let their leader check it out first.

He had to crouch on his front legs to reach over the shallow ledge. Slowly he stretched until his teeth could grab a bird, and even then, he took it gently by the wing, tugging and pulling it, separating it from the others. He did this as he backed up, dragging the bird up onto the shore.

The others watched patiently. They waited while their leader sniffed the bird's dead body. He left it. Went back to the lake and began again the same process, bringing another one to the shore. This time he nudged it several times with his snout. He left this one, too, and walked to another spot on the lake. He brought up two more birds. By now the others had come over and started to inspect the ones he had rejected. None of them attempted to take a bite.

Then suddenly their leader turned and headed back into the woods. One by one the others followed. All of them left without dinner.

"They could smell that the birds were sick," Rief said. She didn't seem surprised.

On the drive back O'Dell was thinking about Ryder Creed's dogs. The coyotes reminded her that the last time they had spoken, Creed was training his scent dogs to detect different health issues in humans. His team had already trained several dogs especially for private owners with epilepsy and diabetes to help detect seizures before they happened and insulin levels before they dipped. She also remembered that she owed Hannah a phone call.

"If you need a place to stay tonight, my guest room's available." Rief offered. "I do have to warn you, I have a black Lab and a cat."

O'Dell would have been surprised by the

offer except that she had worked several cases in Nebraska and the surrounding states. Oftentimes she'd been met by generosity beyond what she'd ever expect. In western Nebraska an Indian woman, a retired coroner named Lucy Coy, had opened her home to O'Dell during an investigation. The two women had remained friends, consulting each other on various cases. But ordinarily O'Dell wasn't comfortable staying in someone else's home. She liked — no, she needed — her own space to recharge or to stay up all night if she wanted.

"I really appreciate the offer, but I have a room reserved at the Embassy Suites in the Old Market." She shrugged. "It's close to the airport and I have an early flight out. But thank you."

"Sure, no problem."

"What are their names?"

"Excuse me?"

"Your Lab and cat? I have a white Lab named Harvey and a black German shepherd named Jake."

"Tommy is my big baby. Harry is my cat."

"I would like to buy you dinner if you have time."

"That sounds nice." Then, gesturing to O'Dell's cell phone, she added, "We'll run into a dead space pretty soon. Not enough towers out here. Which to me is great. I can't tell you how many thousands of warblers we lose every year when more towers or wind turbines are added."

"They run into them?"

"Most birds have very poor night vision. You probably have a few miles before we get into one-bar country."

O'Dell took the advice and started checking her messages. She had a missed call from Agent Alonzo and one from Platt. It looked like Ben had sent her an e-mail with attachments. She had forgotten that she had asked for the autopsy report and photos of Tony Briggs.

She was about to go to her text messages when the first thump on the windshield startled her. She looked up in time to see something slide off the hood of the SUV.

"What was that?"

"I'm not sure," Rief said as she let up on the accelerator.

Another thud and a smear of black and red.

This time the biologist slammed on the brakes just as the windshield, hood, and roof were being pummeled. Everywhere around them — on the two-lane highway, in the ditches and in the fields surrounding them — birds were falling from the sky.

It was raining birds.

Rief pulled the SUV to the shoulder. The biologist pulled out her own cell phone and immediately was talking to someone about highway barricades while O'Dell turned her cell phone on to video.

The sky had gone dark, but not from the impending sunset. Streams of black birds with red-tipped wings flew overhead, thick flocks blocking out the sunlight. And hundreds of them were falling from the sky.

Smears of blood and feathers streaked the windshield. O'Dell kept the phone steady as she panned across the highway to the ditches and to the fields. Everywhere there were dead birds. She zoomed in to record those on the ground. There appeared to be no movement — no injuries. Just dead birds, and they seemed to be dead as soon as they hit the surface, if not before.

"State Patrol is on the way," Rief told her.

A pickup flew by on the highway. It was the first vehicle they'd seen since they'd left the lake. O'Dell noticed Rief wince as she started tapping in another phone number. To O'Dell she said, "We need to get this stretch of highway barricaded. If these birds are infected, we don't want pieces of them being transported to other places on the tires of vehicles."

As the biologist explained the situation on the phone, O'Dell kept her video going but looked out over the long stretch of road. Dead birds littered the highway for as far as she could see.

She glanced at the timer on the video: five minutes and forty seconds. And birds were still falling.

Ten minutes later what was left of the flock overhead was gone. The last of the birds had fallen, but O'Dell and Rief stayed inside the vehicle.

The sun disappeared behind the tree line, leaving layers of pink and purple as it set. It was a pretty spring evening, except of course for the hundreds of dead black birds dotting the fields and highway.

"Do you know what they are?" O'Dell asked. Several of the birds were laying on the hood in front of them.

"Redwing blackbirds."

"Migratory?"

"Yes." The biologist looked distracted, watching for the State Patrol and keeping an eye on her cell phone and occasionally replying by tapping in a text message. "Birds falling out of the sky en masse isn't an unusual occurrence. There have been incidents when flocks have been startled and flushed out of their roost by loud noises. It sets them off and they fly too low, crashing into buildings or, as I said before, into cell towers or wind turbines. Sometimes electrical lines. Wind, fog, lightning — all of those factors have been known to cause incidents like this."

O'Dell stared out the window and refrained from saying out loud what they were both thinking. None of those factors applied here. Not only was the weather beautiful, though the temperatures a bit crisp, but there were no buildings, no wind turbines, no cell towers or water towers anywhere in the distance. It was still light out, so even the birds' poor night vision didn't explain this.

"It looked as though they were dropping rather than flying down into our vehicle," O'Dell said.

"Yes, I noticed that, too." Rief was reading something on her cell phone. "A colleague is telling me that last year in Idaho he witnessed a flock of geese falling out of the sky." She paused as she scrolled through the message. "About two thousand. They later determined it was avian cholera. Not sure where the birds picked up the bacteria. But it spreads so quickly that infected birds can have no signs of illnesses and suddenly die in flight."

O'Dell didn't bother to keep quiet her immediate reaction. "I wonder if there were any research labs in Idaho conducting studies on avian cholera."

Before Rief could respond they both noticed the flashing blue and red lights in the distance. O'Dell started to breathe a sigh of relief until she noticed that coming from the opposite direction was another vehicle. And even from this far away she could make out the satellite dish on top of the news van.

33

NEW YORK CITY

Christina reluctantly trudged back to her hotel room at the Grand Hyatt. Although she had been taking a steady regimen of Tylenol, protein, water, and vitamin C, her body was struggling to fight off the muscle fatigue. She had developed a cough and her chest already ached. On her way back she had stopped at the little shop and picked up cough medicine and more orange juice. But she was too exhausted to think. And after getting a look at what was on the illicit flash drive, she was now afraid.

She had forgotten to put the DO NOT DISTURB sign on her door as the watchers had instructed, and now she was grateful for her mistake. Housekeeping had changed her sweat-drenched sheets for clean ones and had even replaced the fluffy robe with a fresh one wrapped in a plastic bag.

She guzzled down the complimentary bottle of water as she put away her stash of supplies. Carefully she took off all her clothes, putting them on a nightstand and keeping the layers of cash in between. She'd put them all back on again tomorrow and try to come up with a plan.

She turned on the television, not wanting to be surrounded by silence. All day she'd had the noise of traffic and voices, whistles and honks, music and shouting. In the silence she could hear her heart pounding and tonight a new wheezing sound in her chest. She needed to drown out the sounds of her sick body.

She was still trying to decipher what she had seen on the flash drive. Earlier she had gone into a luxury hotel off Broadway. It was one she had been in before when she wanted the doorman to hail a cab for her. So when she walked in this time, she confidently marched to the elevators like she was a guest.

No one rode with her. No one saw what floor she exited, but just in case, she got off two floors above the business center and took the stairs back down. No one else was in the room.

When she viewed the flash drive, Christina had realized there were way too many documents for her to sort through. She knew she couldn't sit there all afternoon.

Eventually other people would be coming in and out of the room. One of them could be a watcher and she wouldn't have any idea. And if her watcher saw her go into this hotel he'd be waiting for her to leave. How much time before he came looking for her?

With quivering fingers, she had jotted down things that drew her attention. The Tylenol had helped relieve her fever, but she still felt the muddled effects. She had tried to concentrate and even commit some of the information to memory.

There were flight manifests, statistical data, and summaries of experiments. And then there was a file called TEST SUBJECTS. Curious, she had clicked on it, and when she saw her name on one of the lists a chill washed over her body as if someone had opened the door behind her and let in a cold draft.

Now back in her hotel room at the Grand Hyatt, she busied herself with trying to take care of her body. She took her evening dosages of the medicines she had bought. She ran a hot bath and let the steam soothe her aching muscles. She tried not to focus on the words she had read in the file with her name. Phrases like "expire on their own" or "assisted suicide if necessary."

She was pulling out a map of the city from the desk drawer when something on television caught her eye. Christina hadn't seen anything like it before. She reached for the remote and turned up the volume. A woman was explaining while the camera showed a highway and a field covered with hundreds of dead birds. Christina grabbed for the notepad from the desk and frantically jotted down the woman's name and all the information she could gather.

Then she sat down with fingers still shivering. One of the documents she had looked at on the flash drive described future experiments that would infect flocks of birds. She never imagined that it was already happening.

34

Jason had seen it before. How a man he looked up to and admired like Ryder Creed could be rendered speechless by death. Not just any death, but suicide. Somehow it made them feel vulnerable, helpless, like they could have caught it and stopped it if only they had been there earlier. If only they had seen it coming. He figured that might be how Ryder was feeling.

Jason saw it a bit differently. He considered suicide a relief, an escape, a promise that you didn't have to put up with feeling vulnerable and helpless and half a man.

He had brought Creed home and taken Colfax back to Segway House. Now he was back in his double-wide trailer, staring at the box from Tony. Earlier he and Colfax had picked it up from Tony's mom. She said it had Jason's name on it and explained that Tony had dropped it off with the instructions that if anything should ever happen to him, this box was to go to Jason. She said he was adamant about it even though he joked that of course nothing was going to happen to him. In tears she told Jason and Colfax that she should have seen it as a sign.

Everybody thought they should have seen it coming.

Jason had pulled up the tape and peeked inside. He recognized the assortment of Tony's belongings. He closed the lid and set the box in the corner.

Did this mean Tony knew he wouldn't be returning?

Colfax seemed convinced it was proof that Tony had killed himself. But why travel all the way to Chicago to do it? Was it just as possible that Tony feared he wouldn't be coming home because of whom he'd gotten involved with?

Jason shared his suspicions with Colfax. He told him about the text message that Tony had sent, and what he'd said about getting himself into "a fine mess."

"What if someone pushed Tony?" Jason had asked Colfax.

His friend shook his head at the idea and said, "Seems like a lot of trouble to go through. Any of the guys who wanted Tony dead wouldn't have cared about making it look like suicide."

And maybe Colfax was right. Maybe Jason just didn't want to believe that his longtime friend — his best friend — wouldn't have confided in him one last time. Wouldn't have given him a chance to talk him out of it.

Jason looked around his trailer. This was the first place that felt like home since he came back from Afghanistan. Hannah and Creed had provided it for him along with a job and a dog and most importantly, a purpose. Yet tonight he couldn't stop thinking about Tony. Everyone seemed willing to believe that he had killed himself.

Maybe it was that simple. After all, Jason knew exactly how Tony must have felt. He knew how tempting, how comforting the lure of suicide was.

It was usually after dark — mostly late at night — when the black thoughts came to him. Sometimes they came in a whisper. Sometimes in a roar. He sensed the pressure building now and knew it could grow so intense that it threatened to explode inside his head.

Closing his eyes didn't help. It brought images of body parts and splattered blood. Pools gathered on the top of crusted rock, otherwise so dry and dusty that the blood reminded him of liquid mercury sliding around.

Jason hadn't felt the IED that had taken his lower arm. He had no idea his arm was missing the whole time he lay with his cheek against the hard dusty rock. He watched his sergeant flailing before him, limbs twisting and jerking. Half the man's face was gone. His mouth was an open scream, though Jason couldn't hear it. The blast had replaced all sound with a hurricane wind tunnel.

In Afghanistan, Jason and his fellow soldiers — including Tony — had talked obsessively about home. How much they missed it. They longed for the simplest of thing, like ice-cold beer and the smell of fresh-cut grass . . . or just grass, period.

So much of their conversation began with "When I get back home . . ." It was all they talked about. Dreaming about home helped them sleep despite the sounds of IEDs being tripped in the distance — beyond the wire. Getting back home kept them going. It was the secret treasure they held deep inside them that they would not allow the Taliban to take away. It was a rallying cry, a promise, and their one true inspiration to get up every morning.

The only problem was that none of them realized when they returned home they would be different men. They'd be taking back with them nightmares filled with images they couldn't share with their families. Some would bring back with them brain fevers, paranoia, tremors, and an aversion to loud noises. Nor did they ever anticipate what they might be going home without — limbs, fingers, an eye, half a soul.

They weren't prepared for the struggles that met them stateside. Many of them hadn't learned a trade. Tanks, assault weapons, how to detect roadside bombs — these were skills no longer needed. But they had become ingrained into the fiber of their being.

How do you shut off your survival instinct? How do you not flinch and dive for cover at the metallic crash behind you, even if it's shopping carts being racked against each other in a supermarket parking lot? And forget about the Fourth of July. Jason's first was spent curled into a ball deep inside his closet's corner at the Segway House, waiting, praying for the explosions to please stop.

Maybe it simply was impossible to go home again after you'd been to hell.

Jason hadn't experienced his black thoughts and gone through the ritual for a while. It'd been long enough ago that he couldn't remember the last time. You'd think that'd be a sign of improvement, some measure that perhaps he wasn't quite so screwed up.

But tonight he was thinking about Tony, and he couldn't believe his best friend had left him behind.

35

Jason kept the pill containers in his shaving kit. He used to keep the case hidden, but it wasn't necessary now that he had a place of his own.

All the tablets and capsules could fit into two or three containers, but he left them separated, each in its original bottle. It had become part of the ritual to spill them out, one container at a time. Each had its own separate pile, too. The assortment was his personal collection amassed over the months of hospitalization and rehab.

The doctors had kept prescribing — in fact, they still kept prescribing. First was one painkiller, then another. When Jason mentioned trouble sleeping, they threw in a variety of sleeping pills.

One doctor had asked him about depression. Jason had only shrugged at the time instead of saying, *You think? Son of a bitch, I lost half my arm. Am I depressed? Hell yes.*

"Depression" didn't seem like a strong enough term to even scratch the surface of what he was feeling. So another prescription was written.

Post-traumatic stress was diagnosed next, along with an additional med.

He and his buddies laughed about Jason's "collection." Because unlike his buddies, he refused to take any of the drugs. More times than not, they made him feel fuzzy-headed and nauseated. He couldn't imagine all these pills being a remedy. But he could see them being a helpful alternative if and when he decided he was tired of living.

So Jason stockpiled the pills.

In the beginning their presence comforted him. When that wasn't enough he started the ritual of bringing them out, spilling them into their individual piles as if he were assessing his arsenal.

He had devised a cocktail of which ones to take and in what order to guarantee the most success. He figured out how many sleeping pills to take first before he took the most potent ones to ensure that he'd be too sleepy to change his mind and throw them up. Once when he was still living at Segway House, he was interrupted by someone knocking on his room's door. He had just taken the sleeping pills and had to stash the rest away. By the time the person left, Jason was too sleepy to continue. He ended up sleeping for eighteen hours straight.

He wouldn't make that mistake again.

Jason glanced at the box with Tony's belongings. Scout, his eight-month-old Lab, was stretched out on the floor beside it. Tony had taught the puppy to play fetch. Scout was destined to become an awesome scent detection dog, and the fact that he was treating the cardboard box like it was something he needed to guard and watch over made this harder.

Jason felt like a fist was pressed against his chest, the pressure so real it was almost difficult to breathe. The puppy could smell his fetching partner. Jason had caught him glancing toward the sounds outside their trailer's door as if he expected Tony to come knocking at any minute now.

All of it only seemed to justify Jason's ritual even more.

"I can't believe you left me behind, buddy." Jason said it out loud, and Scout cocked his head. Sometimes he called the dog "buddy." Jason was only adding to his confusion.

Jason began opening the containers and spilling the pills onto this makeshift coffee table. One pile, then two. He had lined up the containers in order, following his self-devised cocktail recipe. This time he'd get it right.

There was rhythm to Jason's ritual. Blue pills, then yellow. He focused on their texture and shape and color. The rest of the world went away so that the only sound in his head was the constant counting. No more explosions. No more waking in the middle of the night and discovering that the nightmare of his arm being blown off was no dream but his new reality.

He was so tuned in to what he was doing that he didn't notice Scout had gotten up. The dog had come over to watch, mesmerized by this new game.

Jason spilled another container onto the tabletop, and this time the round tablets rolled to the edge. Scout went to catch them.

"No, stop it!"

Jason shoved the dog away, surprised by his presence. Then he realized Scout might have gotten some of the pills and his stomach clenched.

"Son of a bitch! Did you get one?"

He grabbed the dog and pulled at his mouth.

"Spit it out, goddammit."

He was frantic. Panic sent his fingers digging into Scout's cheeks, desperately trying to hold the dog down with only half an arm.

Jason's breath chugged. His heart pounded in his ears. Then he heard the low whine, the soft cry of a frightened animal.

He stopped. Saw the dog's wide eyes. He pulled his fingers out of the dog's mouth, and gently he pulled the frightened dog against his chest.

"I'm so sorry, buddy. Dear God, I'm sorry, Scout. What the hell was I thinking?"

He held him tight, petted him, and apologized over and over again as his eyes darted back across the table. Had the dog swallowed any of them?

He counted the scattered tablets. He knew by heart how many he had of every pill. Two had fallen to the floor, and he added those to the total. Then he counted them again, all the while his mind reeling over how few could kill a puppy this size.

What the hell was he doing? What the hell was he thinking?

He scratched Scout's ear and continued to hold him, telling him what a good boy he was.

Jason counted the pills a third time. He had to be certain. There was no second-guessing.

They were all there. Scout would be okay.

36

It was late by the time O'Dell got to her hotel. Both she and Rief were exhausted but agreed to keep each other up-to-date. The biologist had bagged and taken several of the dead birds but only after donning gloves and a surgical mask. She promised to have results as soon as possible, telling O'Dell that she would oversee them herself if necessary.

O'Dell had been impressed with the woman. Even as the television news van swooped in, Rief remained composed. When the news reporter inquired about O'Dell, Rief simply made it appear as though she were a colleague, then took charge. The locals were already used to Rief being their source. None of them questioned it further. Though O'Dell was captured in some of the video, she remained unnamed. She told Rief that she owed her one. And even more so since they ended up getting their dinner by picking up fast food and eating in the SUV as Rief drove them back to Omaha.

Again, as was O'Dell's routine, she didn't unpack. Instead she turned on the television as she popped open a can of Diet Pepsi. It was too late to call Agent Alonzo. Hannah's voice message from earlier in the day was a mix of good and bad news. The robins had not been infected, nor did they show any signs of disease. However, the young woman's body may have been. The medical examiner said there was hemorrhaging in the lungs and also in the petechiae. He suspected she had been strangled and left in the river. There was no way of telling for certain because Agent Tabor had confiscated the body.

Who the hell was this Agent Tabor?

O'Dell didn't like this. It sounded like someone was covering his tracks. If the girl was infected, why bother to kill her? And was Tabor part of the cover-up or was he helping contain the contamination?

She made a quick note to call Agent Alonzo first thing. In his message he said he had some interesting information to tell her. She hoped that included who Tabor was and what authority he was working under.

When Hannah had first told her about the robins and the young woman found in the river, O'Dell wondered if it was possible that there was a connection with what was happening in the Midwest. It seemed a bit far-fetched. Except that Tony Briggs was from Pensacola. She was having Agent Alonzo check to see if Tony and Izzy Donner knew each other or had crossed paths. If Alonzo had tracked down Tabor, O'Dell would ask him herself.

She downloaded the e-mail attachments that Benjamin Platt had sent her, and though she was exhausted she pressed herself to take a look. The autopsy of Briggs reported pretty much what she already knew. She pulled up the photos, enlarging and examining them one by one. Nothing out of the ordinary. Front torso, back torso, close-ups of hands, feet, face . . . *wait a minute.*

She clicked on the back torso. Across his lower back, right over his buttock, there was bruising — a straight line from his right to his left side.

O'Dell scanned the autopsy report again. There was no mention that the body had hit anything on its way down. And he was found facedown.

She zoomed in on the area. It was a line of bruising about two inches high and stretched clear across the back. Maybe he had done something earlier that day or prior to his trip to Chicago.

Except that the color of the bruise looked recent. The ME noted that the bruise was premortem, but he made no attempt to explain it.

Then she remembered the cast-iron railing on the balcony. It came to about her waist. She checked how tall Briggs was and guessed that the railing would come to about the small of his back. It made sense that it could be the culprit. But leaning backward would be an awkward way to throw yourself over a balcony.

She pulled up Platt's e-mail. He was finished with the room and handing it over to Detective Jacks. But if they accepted that Briggs had committed suicide, there wouldn't be any investigation.

O'Dell thought about the room again and how odd that it was so neat and tidy. Why would a man who was getting ready to jump to his death care about cleaning up beforehand? And if he did care, why leave the bloody sputum on the television screen and the wall?

She looked at the photo again of Briggs's lower back and decided she needed to call Jacks. They needed to get a CSU team to process the room. If her suspicions were correct, Tony Briggs might have been shoved over that balcony.

37

O'Dell was still going over the autopsy report when a text message from Benjamin Platt came through.

CALL ME WHEN YOU HAVE A CHANCE.

He answered on the second ring, "Maggie, where the hell are you?"

"That wasn't exactly the greeting I was expecting."

"Sorry. It's been a long day."

She told him about the dead snow geese on the lake and then the redwing blackbirds falling out of the sky.

"If Dr. Shaw is responsible, how and where could she have infected them? To my knowledge there's not a DARPA research facility in that area," he said.

"It wouldn't matter. The biologist I spent the day with says that Nebraska is just a stop before they move on to breeding grounds in Canada, Alaska, and the Arctic tundra. Snow geese winter in a number of southern states from Texas and Louisiana to Georgia and North Carolina."

"So it's possible she infected them somehow before they started their spring migration."

"There's more, Ben. A lot more."

O'Dell told him about her phone conversation with Hannah. About the robins that Agent Tabor believed were infected. She explained what the medical examiner had said about Izzy Donner. That she might have been infected with something. He couldn't confirm his finding because Tabor and his team had confiscated Donner's body.

"Are you thinking this Donner girl may have been one of Shaw's recruits?"

"Possibly. I'm not sure. I'm trying to find if there's a connection between her and Tony Briggs. Donner's body was found in the Conecuh National Forest. That's close to the Pensacola area. The medical examiner believes she may have been strangled."

"Why kill her? That doesn't make sense," Platt said. "If Shaw wants to infect as many people as possible — which looks like what Briggs was trying to do — then why kill her before she's able to do that?"

"I don't know. I'm beginning to think Briggs didn't kill himself."

She explained about the bruise and her suspicion about the railing causing it.

"We thought the young man you followed to O'Hare may have been with Briggs. What if he was there to make sure Briggs didn't leave? What if Shaw has others to watch and make certain the virus carriers don't survive?"

"Or make sure they don't end up in a hospital telling their story."

"So maybe it's not so far-fetched? There must be others," she said. "Have Roger and the CDC figured out how to find them?"

"He's convinced DHS there's a large-scale threat. Charlie Wurth is putting together a multiorganizational task force with him in charge."

O'Dell had worked with Charlie before. He was deputy director at the Department of Homeland Security. She liked and respected him. Several years ago the two of them had been sent to investigate after two suicide bombers blew up themselves and parts of the Mall of America on Black Friday. Since then Charlie had been trying to lure her away from the FBI to come work for him.

"I'm afraid we have a bigger problem on

our hands than finding Dr. Clare Shaw," Platt told her. "We need to find and stop her virus carriers before they infect more people."

"How can we do that if we don't even know what cities they're being deployed to? Or how many there might be? Ben, she can't be doing this all on her own. She'd need someone helping her, recruiting the carriers and those who might be watching over them. For an operation this size, she needs someone with leverage."

In the silence that followed she sensed his frustration. And more importantly, he knew what she was implying.

When the two of them were working to find the remains of the North Carolina research facility that had been buried in the mudslide, Platt had kept classified information from her. But it hadn't just been O'Dell who had been kept in the dark. The director of DARPA, Colonel Abraham Hess, a friend and mentor to Platt, had kept even more classified information from Platt.

Colonel Hess had gone a step further. He had sent a crew to secure the remnants of the facility, but a member of that crew had gone rogue, according to Hess, going way beyond his original instructions. Before it was all over, the man had attempted to kill

O'Dell and Ryder Creed.

In O'Dell's search for Dr. Clare Shaw over the past five months, she continually wondered how it was possible for the scientist to simply disappear. Unless she'd had help.

"Do you know an Agent Lawrence Tabor?"

"No, and Maggie, I honestly don't know anything. And if I knew anything that would help I'd certainly tell you. Listen, Wurth believes we need to concentrate on airports. And I agree with him."

"Airports?"

"Tony Briggs didn't get infected in Chicago."

She understood. And neither would the other carriers. She grabbed the notepad and started jotting down reminders.

To Platt, she said, "Just like the snow geese and the blackbirds. They would have been infected somewhere else before they arrived in Nebraska."

"Yes. So where the hell is Shaw?"

"There are a couple of military bases in Pensacola."

"No," he interrupted her. "I can't believe she could be working undetected at a military base. It's not possible."

She stopped from telling him that military bases didn't seem any less likely than government-funded research facilities or state universities.

"Wurth thinks we can narrow it down to several airports," Platt went on to say.

"It's still an overwhelming task," she told him.

"He asked Roger Bix and me to figure out a way to help his TSA agents so they could start screening for infected passengers, but most of the symptoms are the same as the common flu. Bix said the CDC might be able to come up with a swab test."

"A swab test? You mean like inside the mouth?"

"Exactly. Then you dip the Q-tip into a solution. Sort of like a home pregnancy test. It turns a certain color if the sample is positive."

"They actually have something like that?"

"They've been working on it, but they'd need to devise it for this particular virus strain."

"And how long will that take?" she asked.

"Ten to fourteen days. But it could be longer to get approval to use it." It sounded like it pained him to admit it. "They've never tested it before."

"So it might not even work."

"It's all we have."

"Maybe not," she told him. "I might have a better idea."

216

Creed was in bed but far from sleep. He couldn't shake off the image of Sheriff Wylie's body hanging from the tree. Somehow his mind managed to loop it together so that when he closed his eyes he saw not only Wylie's face but also his father's.

He left his window open, hoping the fresh air would clear his senses. The breeze had gotten chilly enough that Grace curled into his side. He could hear the soft snores of Rufus down on the floor alongside the bed. When the phone rang Creed grabbed it off his nightstand. Instead of being startled, he welcomed the distraction despite the late hour.

Then he saw the caller ID.

"Maggie? Are you okay?"

"I'm fine. Sorry, I know it's late."

"It's okay. I couldn't sleep."

Chronic insomnia was something the two of them shared. They had talked only a handful of times since they last worked together in North Carolina. Creed had avoided contact on purpose. There was chemistry between them that he hoped would dissolve with time, but just hearing her voice canceled that idea. It also reminded him that there was something deeper between them. They had saved each other's life. Shared things. They trusted each other all the while knowing that trust was a precious commodity to both of them.

"I talked to Hannah yesterday," she said.

"About Tabor's visit?"

"Yes."

"Do you know who he is?"

"Not yet. I have Agent Alonzo working on it. Hannah left me a message today that the birds weren't even infected."

"No. He would have euthanized my entire kennel for nothing."

Creed tried not to think about it. He knew that if Hannah hadn't stopped Tabor, he and his men would have had to kill Creed before getting to his dogs.

"I think Izzy Donner and Agent Tabor might be a part of a larger scheme," she told him. "Something that involves Dr. Clare Shaw."

"The director of that DARPA research facility in North Carolina?" Creed asked.

He hadn't thought about it before. "Let me guess — the bird flu was one of the viruses she took with her."

"Yes. It turns out she was working on creating a strain that would transfer easily to humans. And possibly one strong enough to transfer from person to person by casual contact."

"You think Izzy Donner was infected by Shaw?"

"I'm not sure how any of it works. I've been hunting Shaw since last fall and still have no idea where she is. She literally disappeared that night of the mudslide. There were no calls on her cell phone after that day. No charges on her credit cards. No bank account withdrawals. We've put out APBs and contacted other research facilities. It's as if Dr. Clare Shaw ceased to exist that night, and yet we still suspect she killed her colleagues and stole three samples of deadly viruses."

"Maybe she had an assistant? Someone from the outside to help her?"

"That's what I'm thinking. The virus that we're seeing is definitely the strain she was working on. I don't believe there's any way she could be doing this without help."

"Wait a minute, you've already seen the virus?"

"In Chicago. The CDC is trying to down-play it. I can't imagine that that'll work for too much longer. Now that his parents have been contacted I can tell you that one of the victims was Jason's friend, Tony Briggs."

"What do you mean? We heard Tony jumped from the nineteenth floor of a hotel. You're saying he had this virus?"

Creed was on his feet now, at the window. The breeze was cold against his chest.

"There's a lot we still don't know for sure. I'm heading down to Pensacola to retrace Tony's footsteps for the last several weeks. But that's not the only reason I'm calling. I remember Hannah telling me about the DHS contracts you have with them to train dogs for TSA."

"That's right. We also have a contract to provide patrols for a certain number of hours each month. The demand for detection dogs has increased ten times faster than the trainers can keep up. The government's using private contractors more and more."

"I know you've used your dogs to track diabetes and are working on cancer. Do you think they might be able to detect this virus?"

He was still thinking about Tony. "If you can get enough samples for us to work with, I'm sure they'd be able to detect it."

"Would you mind talking to Ben and the deputy director of DHS?"

"Ben's involved with this?"

There was silence, and Creed wanted to kick himself. Did he really just sound like a jealous teenage boy? He tried to backtrack and redirect his focus.

"Tabor made it sound like dogs could get the virus," he said. "Do you know if that's true?"

"Ben knows more about that than I do. We only talked briefly about this. He doesn't believe there's enough evidence that they would be at risk."

Creed shook his head. It sounded like a bureaucratic response, probably the exact words Platt had told her.

"Look, Maggie, I know he means something to you, so you trust what he tells you. But there's no reason in the world that I trust him. And you're asking me to trust my dogs' lives based on a theory that they might not get infected."

"Could you just talk to them? No obligation. If we can stop this virus at the airports before it spreads across the country, we could be saving hundreds, even thousands of lives."

"I'll talk to them. But no promises."

"Of course. That's all I ask. And Creed, if you do agree, maybe don't use Grace."

■ ■ ■ ■

WEDNESDAY

■ ■ ■ ■

39

NEW YORK CITY

Christina ordered hotel room service, then made herself eat as much as her stomach would allow. The Tylenol was keeping her fever manageable. At least she had been able to sleep on and off. But she still woke to sweat-drenched sheets. Her muscles ached so badly it was difficult to get out of bed. Even with the medicine her cough was getting worse. Her chest hurt when she tried to take deep breaths. It scared her but she tried to use the fear to keep herself going.

All the more reason to hurry.

She might not be able to get out of bed at all tomorrow. She had to do what she needed to do today or it would be too late for her. Of that, she was certain.

She prepared again for the day. Yesterday she had bought a zippered tote bag in which she could carry all her cash, meds, bottled water, and other necessities. When she put the strap up over her head she almost cried out in pain. It hurt just to lift her arms that much. How in the world would she be able to walk the streets of New York?

Yesterday she had tried to take a cab, and all the idling, the stop-and-go, and the exhaust fumes had made her so nauseated she almost threw up. She knew today it would be worse. Vomiting was not something she wanted to add to her list of ailments. It was already difficult enough to keep fluids down and stay hydrated.

For some reason Christina had expected the watchers to look more like her. Now she was beginning to believe they looked like soldiers — muscular and strong, walking with ramrod-straight backs, heads pivoting, eyes darting around and missing nothing.

She walked past Grand Central Terminal and continued for several blocks before she realized that the same soldier who had been on post at the entrance two days before was now watching her again. Only this time he wasn't wearing military fatigues. At first she thought she must be mistaken until his eyes met hers. She'd recognize those intense black eyes anywhere.

Christina tried to pretend that he was of no interest to her. That she didn't notice that he appeared to be following her. She stopped in front of a small shop to admire the decorated pastries in the window. She could see his reflection. He was definitely watching her.

The drumming of her heartbeat made her chest ache even more. Were they getting cocky or sloppy? Or perhaps they expected her to be so sick by now that she wouldn't notice? Either way it unnerved her. She'd never get away with what she had hoped to do. She tried to shake him out of her head.

Forget about him. You can do this, she told herself. How many times had she fooled store clerks who were standing in the same aisle as she swiped goods off their shelves in order to survive? The key was confidence. That was when her first coughing fit attacked her.

She leaned against the brick wall of the shop and dug a bottle of water out of her tote bag. Somehow she managed to contain it. Out of the corner of her eye she noticed that the soldier was now across the street buying a cup of coffee and not even watching. The cough must have convinced him he didn't need to watch so closely.

It was a small relief, and Christina felt the tension in her shoulders ease a bit. Then she started to wad up the tissue she had been coughing into and the panic returned. She had just coughed up blood.

40

PENSACOLA, FLORIDA

Creed didn't want any more government men on his property, so he agreed to meet them in Pensacola. He watched the black SUV enter the parking lot of the Coffee Cup. On the edge of downtown, the mainstay breakfast place had a varied clientele. Businesspeople in suits filled tables alongside construction workers in boots and hospital staff in scrubs. It was the one place Creed thought two Washington, D.C., outsiders might not draw attention.

Now he wasn't so certain about that as he watched the two men get out of the vehicle — one in a leather bomber jacket and jeans, the other in turned-up shirtsleeves, trousers, and leather shoes so polished Creed could see the glint off their shine even from his corner booth. Although he had to admit neither man looked like the stereotypical government official. They didn't even look alike. Creed would have been able to identify Colonel Benjamin Platt as a military man even if he hadn't already known the man's background. In his casual attire Platt walked like an officer: ramrod-straight back, chin held high, head pivoting as he checked out his surroundings from behind the dark-lensed sunglasses.

Beside him the tall lanky black man surveyed everything from behind his designer shades, too. But this guy had an easy gait, shoulders rolling, arms swinging, his whole body in motion like he was moving to music, a silent beat that only he could hear.

Creed waited. Sipped his coffee. He kept his hands on the table and his eyes on the men but didn't gesture or wave, letting them search and find him. After all, they were the ones who wanted something from him. Suddenly he smiled to himself, realizing the reversal of roles. The last time Creed had seen Platt in North Carolina, Platt had something Creed wanted. Now the tables had turned.

Creed had never met the other man. Charlie Wurth came in first, and it was obvious this wasn't the DHS (Department of Homeland Security) deputy director's first visit to the Coffee Cup. He flicked off his sunglasses and offered a veteran waitress a wide smile.

Then he asked her something and she actually smiled back. She turned and pointed at Creed from across the room.

At the table Platt started to make the introductions, but apparently he made them too formal or too slowly for Wurth.

"Call me Charlie," he told Creed as he stretched his hand from across the table to shake Creed's. He slid into the booth while gesturing to their waitress, who was bringing two mugs of coffee.

He waved off the menu she handed him.

"I'm gonna have some of those fantastic grits of yours," he told her with a familiarity as if he ate here every morning.

"Eggs?" she asked.

"Scrambled."

"Bacon or sausage?"

"Sausage."

"Toast?"

"Wheat."

Wurth looked to Creed. "You having breakfast?"

"Already did about two hours ago."

Wurth let out a whistle. "Early riser, huh?" Then to Platt he said, "Best breakfast you're gonna have."

Platt looked distracted. Maybe a little uncomfortable. No, actually Creed thought he looked irritated, like he didn't have time for something as frivolous as breakfast. As if to please Wurth, he told the waitress he'd have the same.

"Ryder, more coffee?" she asked before she left the table.

"I'm good. Thanks, Rita."

An awkward silence followed. Creed was in no hurry to fill it. Again, these men had asked to meet him.

"Last time I was here there was a hurricane barreling up the Gulf," Wurth said. "Had Pensacola smack-dab in its crosshairs."

"Which one?" Creed asked, only slightly curious.

"Isaac. Agent O'Dell was here with me."

"I remember that," Platt said. "I was here, too. Over at the naval base."

Creed remembered it, as well. He and his dogs had spent days afterward looking for people in the rubble. Just then, he realized Maggie was the one thing the three of them had in common. And he figured that was about all.

He glanced at Platt's hands wrapped around his coffee mug. They looked well taken care of. An officer's hands. A surgeon's hands. Creed's, in contrast, were callused. He had a cut on the back of one, and although his fingernails were neat and trimmed, the left thumbnail had been ripped down below the quick, snagged on broken concrete he had unloaded for the dogs' obstacle course. Wurth's hands were well kept, too. Not an untrimmed cuticle in sight.

"Maggie told me about the mudslide in North Carolina," Wurth said.

Creed noticed that the deputy director switched from "Agent O'Dell" to "Maggie" almost in a calculated way, as if he wanted Creed to know that she was a friend of his.

"She said your dogs are pretty amazing," Wurth continued. "You already know it was her idea that you might be able to help us."

Creed thought Wurth might be trying to appeal to their shared camaraderie, so he was taken off guard when the man said, "So tell me, what makes you think your dogs are good enough for something like this?"

41

Creed thought it was an odd way for the man to ask for his help — by issuing a challenge. He saw that Platt recognized the mistake and shook his head as he sipped his coffee.

"What?" Wurth said, noticing. "I shouldn't voice my skepticism?"

"If you're skeptical, why are you wasting my time?"

"Look, I've been with Homeland Security for quite a few years now," Wurth said. "I'm well aware that we have canines that can sniff out bombs and drugs and find dead people. I've seen them do it."

"Then you know DHS is already using my dogs and my services."

"Sure, but again, for explosives and drugs. I get that. But seriously, how possible is it for them to sniff out sick people with this virus?" He stopped himself and glanced around at the tables behind them. "We need to track down these virus carriers that have been sent out with this thing. If we don't, we could have a major epidemic on our hands. So yes, I want to believe that your dogs can help or I wouldn't be here."

"We've already been training for *C. diff,* diabetes, and a couple different types of cancer," Creed told him.

"With proven success?"

"The tests for cancer have only been in our facility, but we've had a ninety-eight percent success rate. We've just started doing *C. diff* detecting in the field. Those results are trending around ninety-nine percent, but our testing field has been limited to a few skilled care facilities in the area."

Wurth sat back and let out a low whistle. "That's impressive. But I don't understand how the canines can tell the difference. I mean, I understand that they can smell and identify a sick person. But how are they able to differentiate between diseases and infections?"

Creed glanced at Platt. The man was an infectious-disease specialist. He'd certainly be able to explain it better.

"I'm not a biologist," Creed said, "but basically different antibodies are released by our immune systems to fight certain diseases. There are hormone and chemistry changes. Each disease, each infection has its own makeup, if you will."

"And canines can detect the differences by smelling the person?"

"With *C. diff* the dogs just need to be in the vicinity of the person. About a ten- to twenty-foot radius. Last year we trained a dog for a little boy with diabetes. He's able to play football with his dog on the sidelines and from there, the dog's been able to detect when his insulin level dips too low."

Wurth raised an eyebrow as if Creed were trying to pull one over on him.

Creed ignored him and continued. "Cancer's a bit trickier because the different types sometimes trigger different reactions in the body. For some cancers we use breath samples."

"Breath samples? So what do you think would work for this virus? I can't have you running your dogs up to people's faces while they wait in line at the airport."

They went silent and pushed back as Rita brought their breakfasts. Both men thanked her. Creed noticed that Wurth shoveled a bite of grits into his mouth before Rita left the table. However, Wurth's eyes were still on Creed. For the first time he felt like the man was sizing him up.

"We use breath samples to train the dogs. That doesn't mean they need to be in a person's face in order to detect it." Creed was getting impatient. Did Wurth not get the point he'd just made with the little boy and diabetes? Or did the man just not want to believe him?

"What exactly would you need then to train your canines?"

"Samples of the virus. Live samples. Lots of them from as many different people as you can get. At least a dozen or two."

"If the virus smells the same, why does it matter that the samples come from different people?" This time it was Platt who wanted to know.

"When we train the dogs we want to make sure they're picking out the virus. Not what that person ate last night or their brand of toothpaste or any other ailment that person might have. We want the virus to be the only common denominator that the dog is detecting."

Platt nodded, satisfied.

"I have a question for the two of you," Creed said. "How can you assure me that my dogs won't be infected by the virus?"

"The bird flu hasn't been known to infect canines," Platt answered too quickly.

"But this is a different strain. Tabor made

it sound like dogs could get infected. He came to euthanize my entire kennel."

Wurth waved a hand at Creed. "Look, that was an unfortunate incident by someone not affiliated with us."

"He presented himself as a federal officer."

Creed watched the two men exchange a look, and then Wurth shrugged as he slathered butter on his toast.

"You guys don't have a clue who he is."

Again, neither man attempted to answer.

"He took the body of a young woman who was strangled. He may have killed a county sheriff. And you guys don't care to even know who he is?"

"That's someone else's jurisdiction," Wurth said. "My job is to protect and secure the American people. We have others doing the investigating of who these assholes are. Now, what else would you need, Mr. Creed?"

"Reassurance that my dogs won't get infected."

Wurth shook his head and finally said, "I probably can't give you that. But listen, you can train any canines, right? I mean, that's what I hear. That you don't have to have a special breed like other trainers who insist on using shepherds or Labradors. Is that true?"

"What does that have to do with anything? My dogs are just as valuable even if they don't have pedigrees."

"Well, I'm sure they are and I understand you're attached to your own. What if we were to get you some disposable ones?"

"Excuse me?"

"You know, from a shelter or something."

"Disposable dogs?" Creed looked to Platt and finally saw a hint of distaste. Wurth hadn't done his homework or he would have known that Creed and Hannah rescue abandoned dogs, sometimes from shelters.

"Charlie doesn't like dogs," Platt said, as if trying to make light of the situation and regain common ground.

"It's not that I don't like canines. This is serious business. I'm trying to save human lives, not canine lives." He stabbed a piece of sausage but stopped before he put it into his mouth and added, "And yes, I don't particularly like dogs, but that's not the point."

He wagged the fork at Creed. "How is it any different than what the police or the military do? They train them and send them into the line of fire. I understand you were part of a Marine K9 unit. Don't tell me your canine didn't go first every single time you went into an area filled with IEDs."

Perhaps Wurth had done his homework, or more likely, Maggie had simply filled him in.

"That's different," Creed told him. "When we work with military dogs to detect explosives we don't train them with live explosives. In this case, my dogs will be exposed to the live virus while training to detect it. Is there a vaccine available to protect them?"

"First of all, we don't believe dogs are at risk," Platt said.

"CDC says they're working on one," Wurth said. "For humans, but it could be weeks, maybe months. If we get something we'll make sure your people are first on the list."

Creed hadn't even thought of his handlers and the risk to them. But they could wear masks and gloves. The dogs didn't have those precautions.

"How many dogs would you need?" Creed asked.

"For the short term we'd need enough to secure one major airport, twenty-four-seven."

"How soon can you get me samples?"

"We can have at least a dozen by late tomorrow," Platt told him.

"It takes about ten to fourteen days of training."

"In ten to fourteen days hundreds of people will already be dead and thousands of others infected. I can give you seventy-two hours," Wurth said.

Creed wasn't even sure that was possible, but instead of saying so, he asked, "What's in it for my dogs and me?"

"You save the world and become a hero," Wurth said sarcastically. When he realized neither Creed nor Platt thought it was funny, he added, "Tell me what you want. What you need to make it worth your while. I do understand this is a major undertaking."

Creed set his empty coffee mug to the side and stood up from the table. "Let me think about it. I'll get back to you."

And he left.

Christina stopped by the same shop where she'd bought her supplies yesterday. She figured her watchers might see it simply as a routine. Her note from them this morning told her that she was doing a good job. They suggested a couple of tourist attractions that she might want to visit. That was it.

Now that she had thought about all of the notes, she realized they were ambiguous enough that even if they were found, they would draw little attention. She imagined the watchers might come in and clean out her room before housekeeping. If she didn't return tonight they would probably already be letting themselves inside.

Still, she had left the DO NOT DISTURB sign on the door. Her suitcase was on the bed. She left a half-eaten protein bar and a cup of coffee on the desk. The television was on along with a light on the nightstand. If they came in, perhaps they might think they had simply lost track of her and certainly she was somewhere in the hotel. After all, she'd never leave behind her personal belongings.

As Christina walked through the small shop's tight aisles she kept looking up over the display cases and out the window. She could see the soldier on the other side of the street, sipping his coffee and reading what looked like a folded-up map. There was no way he could see the items she would be purchasing. Even the cash register at the front of the shop was tucked into a windowless corner.

And it would be impossible to see what she was choosing from the shelves. She picked out more cough syrup, tissues, and throat lozenges. She added a box of large Band-Aids, iodine, a small bottle of rubbing alcohol, and a quaint artist tool kit that included Krazy Glue, a straight-edged ruler, scissors, and an X-Acto knife.

At the register in the glass display case under the counter she pointed at the final item she needed. The store clerk had already rung up everything else. She didn't want this item to be sitting on the counter any longer than necessary. She wanted it to go directly into her tote bag as soon as he scanned it.

There were only two models to choose from. In the past she would have bought the burner phone with the most prepaid minutes. It was the better deal even if you didn't think you needed that much time. But today she pointed at the phone with fewer minutes and told the clerk she'd like "two, please."

She tried to steady her breathing before she walked back out the shop door and onto the street. She needed to carry on as if she'd just picked up a few supplies for a day of sightseeing and that there was nothing illicit in her bag. She had memorized the phone number she wanted to call and had practiced exactly what she wanted to say. She needed to find a place where she could do that without being seen or heard. But there was something else she needed to do first.

43

PENSACOLA, FLORIDA

Creed left the Coffee Cup and took the Bay Bridge. Pelicans skimmed the water surface below. One flew alongside his Jeep. The sky was a gorgeous blue, the water so calm it was slick as glass. He let the three miles steady him, breathing in the salt air that seeped in through his open sunroof.

He drove through Gulf Breeze, taking his time, letting his mind formulate a plan. By the time he got to Pensacola Beach he knew what he had to do. He parked near the water tower and took off toward the beach, taking only his cell phone.

First he called Hannah and ran his idea by her as he walked along the beach with his jeans rolled up and his shoes off, his toes enjoying the warm sand. The swish of the waves calmed him. He walked some more and ended up on the beach side of Walter's Canteen. He found an outdoor table with some privacy and ordered lunch.

Then he called Penelope Clemence.

He had relied on her countless times in the past to help him choose rescue dogs. She had an eye for those that were trainable and he'd learned to appreciate her expertise. More importantly, she saved him the gut-wrenching trips he'd otherwise need to make to the shelters where he knew he'd never be able to leave without bringing home dozens.

Though they had been working together for several years, Creed knew little about the woman. Hannah insisted that Clemence was a philanthropist who had chosen to spend her valuable time and wealth helping dogs at kill shelters find homes. Whenever Creed got together with the woman she looked nothing like a wealthy matron. She drove a beat-up Jeep Wrangler with thick off-road tires and a broken front grille that she didn't bother replacing. Usually she wore jeans — not any jeans, but threadbare, often with the knees ripped. Her hiking boots always looked like they had seen better days. But her fingernails were always manicured and her short hair cut and styled in what Hannah called "chic." Not like Creed would know.

Bottom line, he liked the woman. And more importantly, he trusted her. She had great instincts about a dog's personality and temperament, and sometimes she could talk him into taking a dog he might otherwise have reservations about. He knew her intentions were always to save one more dog, and he couldn't argue with that. But she also knew that detection dogs needed to be sociable as well as physically resilient.

"I need a dozen trainable dogs by tomorrow," he told her.

"Oh, sweetie, you just made my day," she said in a southern drawl that seemed to emphasize her excitement. "Any preferences? Any particular traits I need to look for?"

"Kill list gets top priority."

"You are a man after my heart."

"Penelope, what would it take to make Alpaloose Animal Shelter a no-kill shelter? How much?"

"It'd take millions to sustain it. Believe me, Ryder, if I had the money . . ."

"I'm not talking about you. Just humor me."

"To put in place education programs for people to —"

"I'm talking about adopting out dogs to other parts of the country. There're organizations that already do that sort of thing, right?"

"Of course, but it's expensive. You have to find transportation. It's a massive process that involves lots of volunteers and enough donors to keep it going."

"Could you put together some figures for me? Just an estimate of what it would cost to turn Alpaloose into one of those?"

"Oh, Ryder, sweetie. Don't you think I've already tried to do that? There's just not a large enough donor base in this area."

"Get me a cost analysis. Just a ballpark."

"I have some figures I put together a couple of years ago. I'll look over it and send you an estimate."

"Can you get it to me later today?"

"Actually, I can get it to you as soon as I have a chance to pull up my old file." Then she paused. "What are you up to?"

"I'll let you know if it works."

About twenty minutes later Creed had the e-mail with more details than he needed and an estimated cost. He called Wurth and was surprised that the deputy director answered on the third ring.

"The risk versus the reward isn't worth training these dogs for a onetime assignment," he told Wurth. "Nor is it worth training them just for this virus. If these dogs survive, we'll want to train them to be multitask dogs."

"I'm listening."

"I know DHS currently has a budget this year of $150 million to train one thousand dogs, and you're already going to come up short about two hundred and fifty dogs."

"What does that have to do with this?"

"Hannah and I already have a contract with your department. I'd like to expand it and talk long-term."

"Okay. That makes sense."

"In addition to what we're already doing, I'll provide you with five dogs and handlers for this initial test run. Within a year we'll add ten more. I'll procure and train twenty each year after. I want a ten-year contract to start, with a percentage of the money front-loaded."

"And how much is this going to cost me?"

Creed gave him the figure. Wurth whistled his response.

"Don't forget I already know how much you're paying for dogs, and some of those you're having to bring in from Europe."

"Yes, but this is a lot of money for a bunch of mutts."

"With my dogs you're paying a premium for my training. We'll also do a program to train your designated handlers. I know the government wastes more than this amount

248

on vaccines that don't work. You can spend three times that amount for more TSA personnel at your airports and you still won't be able to identify and stop infected people.

"Think about it, Wurth. DHS is already paying more than this for bomb detection dogs. Now you'll have a team that will be able to detect dangerous viruses — we can add others to the bird flu. There's already talk about adding dogs for detection not only at airports, but in stadiums and shopping malls, at campaign rallies, open-air concerts. And the best part — they'll never hound you for a raise or extra benefits."

"And if a canine has a false alert, I'll have a major lawsuit on my hands."

"Seriously? That's what you're concerned about? How many of your TSA agents have erroneously taken someone aside? How many times have they missed someone coming in with a deadly virus? We know they already missed Tony Briggs twice."

That silenced Wurth.

"You know, I'm told there's an app that can detect cancer. Hell, maybe I just need to invest in that technology."

"Go ahead. I guarantee it's not ever going to be as effective as a dog."

"How can you be so sure?"

"My dogs' batteries last longer and they can track without depending on a cell tower or a satellite signal. One thing's for sure — no app is going to help you in seventy-two hours."

"Why do I get the idea you just want to save a shelter full of mutts that are waiting to be put down?"

"Damn straight, and what's wrong with that? There's one other thing I want as a bonus immediately if we're successful in meeting this first deadline."

He told Wurth what it was and why he wanted it. To Creed's surprise the DHS deputy director didn't argue.

"That's the deal, Wurth. Let me know what you decide." And Creed ended the call.

Less than fifteen minutes later Charlie Wurth called and said he'd e-mail over a contract by the end of the day.

Creed should have felt a sense of victory. Instead he couldn't stop thinking that he might have condemned these dogs to a miserable death if they ended up infected with this virus.

44

Everywhere Christina went she saw the soldier. Twice he disappeared from sight and she thought he might be gone. Or that someone else was taking over for him and she'd need to find the new watcher. But he was never gone for more than a few minutes.

Usually he didn't follow her into any of the buildings. Instead he stayed on the sidewalk, across the street. Just when she convinced herself that she was out of his view and safe as long as she stayed inside, he proved her wrong. When she stayed too long in a café, where she sat with a cup of tea and a half-eaten sandwich, he came in. He looked impatient as he made his way to the restrooms. His movements were almost robotic as his head pivoted from side to side. When he came back out he took a different path, bringing him close enough to her table for him to check on her.

She could feel his eyes sweeping over her

and the entire booth despite the sunglasses that he kept on. She avoided looking at him, but her hand trembled as she raised the cup to her lips.

The place was busy and noisy but the booth made her feel like she was in her own little world. At least until he came back. Surely that wouldn't be within the next few minutes.

She dug out one of the burner phones. She had to do this now while she still had the nerve. While her mind was functioning. The fever was worse today. She had doubled up on the Tylenol and the vitamin C and yet she still felt a bit muddled.

She tapped the phone number in from memory and smashed the phone against the side of her face, hoping she could hear and praying that she wouldn't need to speak too loud. She expected to get a voice telling her to leave a message. She had prepared what she was going to say. Even now, it went around in her head like a recording on a loop.

"This is Amee Rief," a voice said.

Christina waited for instructions to leave a message, but they didn't come.

"Hello? Is anyone there?"

"I'm sorry, did you say you were Amee Rief?"

"Yes, that's right."

"The U.S. Fish and Wildlife biologist?"

"Yes. Is there something I can help you with?"

She waited too long. She was afraid Rief would hang up on her and then not take her call.

"Excuse me, ma'am, is there something you needed?"

What she needed was to find her voice. She needed to remember the message she had wanted to get to Rief. She had her on the phone. She was speaking to her directly. This was even better. If only she could speak.

"Look, unless you tell me what this is about, I'm hanging up now."

"No, please, don't do that." Panic pushed aside her confidence.

Oh God! She didn't mean to sound desperate, and yet that was exactly how she was sounding.

"I need your help. Only you. No one else. Please just listen. I'm sick. They infected me." She swallowed hard and felt a coughing fit coming on.

No, please not now.

She ripped the wrapper off a lozenge and popped it into her mouth.

"What's your name?"

"My name? That's . . . that's not important."

"Yes, it is. If you expect me to listen to you, to trust you, I need your name."

She hesitated. Was it a trap? No, she had chosen to trust this woman. She couldn't stop now.

"It's Christina. Christina Lomax."

"Why do you believe someone infected you, Christina?"

"Because they told me they did." Suddenly she realized she hadn't checked outside. Had it been seconds or a minute? Her eyes darted over the top of the booth. She couldn't see the soldier. In a whisper, she said, "They're paying me to walk around New York and give it to others."

"Who exactly do you think infected you?" Rief asked, and Christina couldn't help thinking that the biologist sounded skeptical.

"Whoever infected those birds in Nebraska."

There was silence on the other end.

Christina's eyes darted from the street to the door and back again.

"Please just listen. I'm not crazy. I don't have much time."

Then she tried to explain about the flash drive. About the man giving it to her and telling her to make sure it would be found on her body. She was interrupted by another coughing fit and once by a waiter. No one else seemed interested in her conversation, but she continued in bouts of whispers and a low voice.

Finally she told the biologist that she would give the flash drive to her, but only her.

Then she told her that it had to be today. It had to be this evening, because tomorrow at this time she might already be dead.

45

Creed had sent Charlie Wurth and Benjamin Platt a list of what he needed along with instructions on how to collect samples. He based it on the same process he had used for collecting cancer and *C. diff* samples.

Now with Hannah and Dr. Avelyn, he paced Hannah's kitchen while the three of them figured out if what he had just promised the DHS deputy director was even possible.

"I told them what plastic tubes to use," Creed said.

"With the polypropylene wool inside," Hannah reminded him.

"Yes."

Looking to Dr. Avelyn, Creed asked, "Do we know for sure that the bird flu smells any different than ordinary flu virus?"

"I believe so. I've been doing some research. No matter what strain of bird flu, it causes an intense response from the body's immune system. The dogs will be able to detect those changes. There's a release of proteins to fight the virus, but at the same time those proteins trigger inflammation. I also read that the virus tends to stick around the nose and throat, unlike the regular flu, which invades the gastrointestinal tract. If we get enough strong samples of the infection, we shouldn't have a problem training the dogs. But will we? Get enough samples? Are they going to be able to provide the quantity we need?"

"They claim they will. They're getting them from victims in the Chicago area who are already pretty sick, so they'll be strong samples."

"But how many different people?" Hannah asked. "We had over twenty-five samples from twenty-five different people when we started training for *C. diff.*"

"I told them that. They said it shouldn't be a problem. There're already over two hundred known victims just in Chicago."

"Oh Lord have mercy." Hannah shook her head.

The more difficult task would be training the dogs in such a short time span. Training of any sort was a series of repetitions. Over-stimulation and fatigue could muck up the process. Plus, this was still new territory for Creed. And he was learning alongside the dogs.

With explosives and narcotics detection, it was easy to isolate the single target odor for the dogs. Same was true for cadaver search. A dead body gave off certain gases during decomposition. Those smells were the same no matter how old the victim was and no matter what other ailments they had before death. But with disease and illnesses it was the opposite.

One inhaled breath condensation sample included thousands of organic compounds, gases, and scents. Dogs could smell all of them, including those that related specifically to that person, just as Creed had told Platt and Wurth. A dog could smell what toothpaste was used, or the contents of the last meal that was eaten.

Other variables contributed to different breath smells, like a person's age and even ethnicity. So the scent that cancer or diabetes or *C. diff* or even the flu gave off was only a part of the whole mixture that created that individual person's scent.

The best way to train was to have a large library of samples of that particular virus. He'd need to train the dogs on so many different people with the virus until the only common denominator was the virus scent itself.

"We'll also need as many healthy samples as we can get to use as controls," Creed told Dr. Avelyn.

"I'll start with all the staff."

"I can get some volunteers at Segway House," Hannah offered.

"Penelope will be bringing some dogs later today. Maybe she can drum up some volunteers, too."

Creed felt a dog pawing at his feet and looked down to find Jason's black Lab puppy. He picked him up and scratched behind his ears.

"What's Scout doing here?"

"Jason asked me to watch him," Hannah said.

"For how long?"

"I don't know. I guess until he gets back."

"Where did he go?"

"He didn't say."

"Did he tell you how long he'd be?"

"No, he did not. What's with you, Rye?"

Creed was feeling a panic knotting up in his gut. He was worried about Jason ever since he found out about Tony, and after Wylie . . . There was something wrong about this. He knew the kid would never hurt himself if he knew Scout would be left alone, but leaving the dog with Hannah instead of just putting him out in the kennel with the other dogs —

"Do we have a key to his trailer?"

"Yes."

"You need to get it for me."

"What in the world? Rye, we can't go into his trailer. It's his home."

"Hannah, please. Just get me the key."

Christina was exhausted. More than anything in the world she just wanted to go back to her hotel room and crawl back into bed. She had swallowed half a bottle of cough syrup and was popping more Tylenol than she knew was safe. The ache in her chest was now a knotted fist pressing against her lungs. She didn't look anymore when she spit mucus into a tissue. She didn't need to. She knew it was bloody.

She had given Amee Rief the phone number to her other burner phone. When she left the café she dropped the one she had used into a trash can, wadded up in a bunch of used tissues. If Rief didn't keep her word and somehow tried to track her by using that phone, she'd be in for a surprise and a dead end.

But before Christina could even hope to connect with Rief, there was something else she needed to do. She needed to shake this soldier.

Again, he had disappeared for almost an hour, and Christina was hoping the watchers had thought it a waste of their time to keep such close tabs on her. She had meandered through shop after shop, trying to think of somewhere she would be safe. She anticipated that she'd need twenty to thirty uninterrupted minutes. But every restroom she canvassed was too small and too busy.

She even thought about taking a cab to the Metropolitan Museum of Art, where certainly she would have plenty of space. She doubted the soldier would even come in. But she knew there would be security . . . and cameras. So she discounted the idea.

She was walking up Third Avenue, trying to convince herself to not turn around and go back to the hotel. Then she spotted the familiar orange-and-white sign. The Home Depot wasn't anything like the one she was used to back in her hometown. There was no huge parking lot. It was squeezed between a bank and another business. If nothing else, maybe there wouldn't be anyone in the women's restroom.

The store actually had quite a few customers. Christina busied herself pretending to be interested in a display by the window. The soldier kept walking up the street. He was probably wondering why she hadn't chosen Bloomingdale's instead.

She waited a few minutes, then casually made her way to the back of the store. The restrooms were in the far corner, women's on one side and men's on the other. And at the back of the hallway she saw another door marked FAMILY RESTROOM.

She couldn't believe her good luck. It was large. Wheelchair accessible with a diaper-changing table attached to the wall. And a lock on the door.

Quickly she started pulling out everything she would need. She took the Krazy Glue and the X-Acto knife from the artist kit, making sure that the blade was razor-sharp. She uncapped the iodine and rubbing alcohol. She brought out a stack of tissues and several of the large Band-Aids.

Yesterday one of her purchases was a cheap watch, and now she noted the exact time. She couldn't take more than twenty minutes or the soldier might come in looking for her. And lately the fever blurred her mind so much that everything seemed to take long minutes, but in reality it actually might be only seconds.

When she had all the items lined up on the sink, she took off the sweatshirt and T-shirt.

She stopped to take a long look at herself. Her cheeks were gaunt. There were dark circles under her eyes. Sweaty strings of hair had escaped the ball cap. But still she was relieved that she didn't look like the zombie she felt had taken over her body.

The microchip implant was just under the skin on her upper arm. Despite her current memory lapses she had remembered where they put it early last fall. She had no idea what it even looked like. They had used a syringelike instrument with a needle that poked under the skin. She was told that it was about the size of a piece of long-grain rice. It would act as a personal database, storing valuable information, not only her identification but also her medical history, medications, allergies, and contact information.

She remembered that the scientist who had done the actual injection had told her that it was the wave of the future. Never did she once consider that it might be used to track her and make sure that she didn't survive one of their experiments.

Her hand trembled as she picked up the X-Acto knife. She met her eyes in the mirror.

"You can do this. You *have* to do this."

She dabbed iodine on the bump where

she knew the implant was located. She poured alcohol over the blade of the X-Acto. Then she started cutting her own skin.

Creed tried to slow himself down, not just because Hannah and Dr. Avelyn were trailing behind him. He knew he needed to get control over his emotions.

"What in the world are you doing, Rye?"

"Listening to my gut," he told her.

He knocked on the trailer door but gave very little time for a response before he shoved the key in the lock. He realized he was holding his breath when he opened the door, bracing himself for what he might find.

Jason had said a couple of times that he never saw Tony's suicide coming. Had Creed been blind to Jason's depression? On the drive home last night Creed had been thinking about Wylie. He'd been fighting memories of his father's suicide.

"Jason!" he yelled.

Nothing in the main living area. No metallic scent of blood. But what had Jason said about suicide? Something about not leaving a bloody mess for his mother to see.

"Rye, please stop and tell me what's going on," Hannah said from the doorway.

Creed headed to the bedrooms, taking a breath before opening each door. In the bigger bedroom he noticed the bed neatly made, but a sleeping bag and pillow were on the floor. He marched on to the bathroom. The trailer had only one. The place was clean. There was nothing until Creed opened the cabinet under the sink and found the trash can.

He pulled it out and spilled the contents in the sink. Alongside a couple of used disposable razors, there was a pile of pill containers, each with a prescription label. He started opening them before he realized all of them were empty.

"Are you thinking he took those?" Dr. Avelyn asked.

"I'm sure he takes medication, Rye," Hannah said, standing at his elbow.

"All of these?" He started handing them to Dr. Avelyn, one at a time.

"Are you worried about an addiction?" The veterinarian was still confused. She had no reason to think Jason might hurt himself.

"Hey, what's going on?"

It was Jason.

267

Hannah and Dr. Avelyn backed out of the small bathroom.

"Can you give us a minute?" Creed asked them, and both seemed more than anxious to leave the trailer.

Then Creed waited.

"What the hell are you doing?" Jason asked when he saw the containers in the sink.

"Why do you have all of these and what happened to them?"

"That's none of your damned business."

"Do you have them stashed somewhere? Did you take a bunch of them?"

"Is that the way this is? I have no privacy? You can ram your way in here anytime you want?"

"No, of course not." Creed scooped up the containers and razors and threw them back into the trash can. "I was worried when I saw that you left Scout with Hannah."

"What?"

"I had a bad feeling," he tried to explain. "A gut instinct. After Tony . . . after Wylie. Thinking about my dad." He looked up at Jason. "I'm sorry. I made a mistake."

He followed Jason into the living room. Out the window he saw that Hannah and Dr. Avelyn had headed back to the house.

Jason noticed, too.

Creed was about to follow them when Jason said, "Your gut was right."

Jason's eyes met his and held him as he added, "I've collected and hoarded that stash since I was in the hospital. Doctors kept prescribing stuff, but none of it helped. I figured together they'd make a pretty effective cocktail. You know, if I decided to do something. I guess it was kind of comforting knowing that I had all of them."

"But you didn't take them?"

Jason shook his head. "I was going to the other night. Scout almost got a couple and it scared me. I flushed all of them — every single one — down the toilet."

Creed rubbed at his eyes, then his jaw, relief sweeping over him. Then he stopped.

"Promise me that if you ever think about it again, you'll come talk to me first."

Jason looked surprised and opened his mouth to protest but then changed his mind. "Only if you do the same."

It hit Creed hard that the kid was smart enough, intuitive enough to know that Creed had thought about it, too. But it was a long time ago. Before he had Hannah and the dogs. Instead of telling Jason that, he simply nodded.

48

The first flight O'Dell could get from Omaha to Pensacola had a two-hour layover in Atlanta. She found a quiet area — not an easy task — and decided to use her time wisely.

She and Agent Alonzo had been missing each other's calls. This time they finally connected.

"There's no Lawrence Tabor with the FBI," he told her.

"Maybe he's retired?"

"No, I would have found him. There is a Lawrence Tabor who's a federal employee but he works for one of the other alphabets."

"Which agency?"

"DARPA."

O'Dell's stomach slipped to her knees. She told herself that it might not be the same guy, and yet she still let the words slip — "Son of a bitch."

"Excuse me?"

"Sorry."

"Not your favorite alphabet?"

"Currently, no," she admitted. "It's not. But maybe this isn't the same guy."

"Oh, I beg to differ," Agent Alonzo said. "Now, I can't tell you exactly what methodology I used to find this information, but the Mr. Lawrence Tabor who's employed by DARPA spent five days in Pensacola."

"How can you be sure of that?"

"I know which hotel he stayed at."

O'Dell smiled. Alonzo was good. From past experience she knew there wasn't anyone or any agency that could keep their travel expense records secret from him.

"He worked for DARPA's Biological Technologies Office," Alonzo continued. "That was up until last summer, when he transferred to the Defense Sciences Office. He's still with DARPA, but now he's listed as being on special assignment. And that's where my magic ends. No one was authorized to tell me what that special assignment was or where he might be today."

"He's no longer in Pensacola?"

"Checked out of his hotel yesterday. He hasn't checked into another. If and when he does, I'll be able to tell you."

"Were you able to find anything on Izzy Donner?"

"The easily available stuff that you might already know. She was nineteen years old. Enrolled at University of West Florida."

"That's in Pensacola, isn't it?"

"Yes. But her last home address is Crestview, Florida, where her parents reside. Now, according to her checking account she recently purchased an airline ticket for Atlanta. Didn't find any credit cards, just the checking account. There were no other major expenditures. Nothing out of the ordinary. No major deposits. However, if you go back to last summer on August twenty-fifth there was a deposit by electronic transfer of three thousand dollars. I'm still working on where that deposit came from."

"Summer employment?"

"Unlikely they would pay one lump sum."

"How about Tony Briggs?"

"A three-thousand-dollar deposit on September fourth. Electronic transfer."

"He was back from Afghanistan. Any chance that deposit was military related?"

"No. I can see those deposits and they're different."

Her phone was vibrating.

"I have another call coming in," she told Agent Alonzo. "If you find out anything more, let me know."

"Sure thing."

She ended the call and clicked the incoming one.

"This is Agent O'Dell."

"Maggie, it's Amee Rief. I left you a couple of messages. I figured you were still in the air."

"Just landed in Atlanta. What's up?"

"I just talked to a woman who said she may have the bird flu."

"What? Wait a minute, why would she call you?"

"She said she saw me on TV last night. That's where she got my name and phone number. She told me she has information that says that flock of snow geese had the bird flu."

"But we don't even know for sure —"

"Actually we do. I just got the results back."

"Couldn't it be a lucky guess on her part?" O'Dell asked.

"She told me the exact strain. And she believes they infected her with it, too."

O'Dell ran her fingers through her hair, trying to keep steady. So it was true. There were more test subjects. Ben was right.

There was an announcement over the intercom. A flight was boarding at one of the gates nearby. She stood up and dragged her roller bag to find a quieter area.

"She actually said that? That someone infected her?"

"She claims they gave it to her as a part of an experiment."

"Did she say who?"

"No, said she wouldn't do that over the phone. But she claims she has proof. She wants to give it to me, but only me."

"Are you okay with that?" O'Dell reminded herself that even though she dealt with stuff like this every day, Rief was more used to birds falling from the skies than mad scientists releasing deadly viruses.

"I guess so. I'm not sure what to do."

"You don't have to do this."

"But she knows what I look like. She's expecting me. She said they have people watching her. She kept calling them soldiers."

O'Dell thought immediately of Lawrence Tabor and the dangerous bullying tactic he had tried to use with Hannah and Creed. His crew had stormed the medical examiner's office and taken Izzy Donner's body. His travel expenses were being paid by DARPA. No way he'd gone rogue. She could feel the familiar panic . . . and anger. And suddenly she was feeling duped again.

Technically Rief was a federal employee, but still, O'Dell wasn't comfortable putting her at risk.

"I can't ask you to do this," she told Rief.

"You don't need to ask. I'd never forgive myself if something happens to this woman after she reached out specifically to me."

"I can meet you. I'll be right alongside you. If she saw the newscast she won't be surprised to see me. She'll think we're colleagues. There's a Detective Jacks already working on the case in Chicago. She can provide us with backup."

"This woman's not in Chicago," Rief said.

"She's not?"

"No, she said she's in New York City. There's one other thing. She said I need to meet her today. She's afraid she'll be dead by tomorrow."

Creed didn't like that Colonel Benjamin Platt had insisted on accompanying the first samples. Then he saw the relief on Dr. Avelyn's face. He didn't realize that having the director of an infectious-disease-control facility — namely one of the top ones in the country, maybe the world — could be a tremendous advantage. As long as the colonel didn't think he could order everyone else around.

Yes, perhaps Creed had a chip on his shoulder like Jason when it came to military officers. Top brass always seemed to come in expecting to make life-and-death decisions after never being in the field or on the ground. Creed wouldn't allow Platt to do that with his staff and his dogs.

But that wasn't the sole cause of the rift between Creed and Colonel Platt. Of course it gnawed on Creed that this guy seemed to hold a piece of Maggie O'Dell's heart, enough so that she didn't feel free to move on. Creed didn't know exactly what the relationship was between Platt and Maggie, but he knew he had to back off. And that was exactly what he'd done since North Carolina. A part of him hated that Platt had the upper hand with Maggie. He certainly wouldn't give him the upper hand here at his own facility.

"Roger Bix with the CDC is continuing to get more samples," Platt told Creed and Dr. Avelyn.

"Does every sample have the patient information we need?" Creed asked.

Platt pulled out a sheaf of papers with grid lines, what Creed suspected was an impressive spreadsheet, hopefully with all the information he had asked for.

"We have the basics on everyone as far as age, gender, and ethnicity. Some were too sick to divulge past medical history. Those who shared about smoking and alcohol use are noted, as well as any current medical conditions. I believe one has diabetes. Another is a breast cancer survivor."

"How recent?" Creed wanted to know.

Platt stared at him for a second or two, and Creed thought it looked like the colonel was trying to decide if Creed was simply busting his chops or if having that additional knowledge was necessary. Then he started flipping through the other papers before finding something.

"She did share that," he said, reading the form. "She's been cancer-free for five years." Then he looked up at Creed to see if that was good news or bad.

"We'll make a note on her sample. If we use a couple of my dogs that are already trained in detecting cancer, we'll need to make sure they're alerting to only the virus."

"But she's been cancer-free for five years," Platt said.

"I'd feel better if it was seven."

"You're saying that your dogs might be able to detect if her cancer has returned when her oncologist obviously is saying she's cancer-free?"

Creed heard the challenge in Platt's voice, and with a glance at Dr. Avelyn to see her sudden discomfort, he realized he wasn't just imagining it.

"Yes. Dogs have been known to detect certain cancers — breast, prostate, lung, ovarian — at an earlier stage than any current lab test is able to detect it."

"Special breeds?"

Creed didn't have time for this. It didn't matter to him whether Platt believed him.

"No special breeds. And medical alert

dogs don't usually have the stamina or endurance requirements that a search-and-rescue dog needs to have for working a disaster site. A lot of the successful tests have been done with a variety of mutts and purebreds from beagles and cocker spaniels to Yorkshire terriers. The most important factors are a good sniffer, high energy, and the urge to please."

Platt stared at him again. Creed was about to thank him and send him on his way when Dr. Avelyn stepped between them.

"Why don't I show you around, Colonel Platt? We could use your help trying to figure out how to keep our staff and dogs from catching this virus while we work with it."

They had set up a room in their training facility as a sterile environment in order to receive, store, and prepare the samples. The breath samples that Platt had brought were taken or released onto fiber cloths that were then placed in sealed plastic tubes.

Dr. Avelyn explained the setup process to Platt.

"We don't use glass tubes. Too many opportunities to break," she told him.

The tubes, instead, were made of PVC with caps that could be screwed on and off at both ends. The sample was placed inside.

When they were ready to present them to the dogs, they would replace one cap with a cheesecloth that allowed the dogs to sniff the scent inside. The PVC tubes would then be placed in a stainless steel workstation.

Dr. Avelyn showed Platt the metal box and explained that most of their boxes had nine circular holes deep enough for the tube to sit inside without being disturbed by the dogs. Only one of the nine tubes would hold the target odor. The other eight would contain control samples.

"That's one of the reasons we wanted as much information about the patients before we use their samples," Dr. Avelyn said. "Whenever possible we try to match at least gender and age. We're successfully training dogs to detect *C. diff,* and early on we realized our control samples needed to be a close match at least in age.

"But here's my challenge," she told Platt. "I can take care of the dog handlers with protective gear, to reduce their risks of catching this virus. But how do I protect the dogs?"

"We have no evidence that dogs can catch the bird flu."

"You keep saying that," Creed told him. "Saying it over and over doesn't make it true. Is there any evidence to prove they *cannot* catch it?"

"Look, I understand the concern," Platt said, and he was addressing both of them as though this subject had already been discussed many times and he was impatiently telling them again. "I think we need to think of these dogs like we would military dogs."

Creed couldn't believe Platt was using Wurth's poorly conceived argument. "We send those dogs out first into combat," Platt said, "and into minefields knowing the risk that they'll take a bullet for us, so to speak. This is really no different."

Creed had to cross his arms and clench his jaw to keep quiet. He had already explained to Wurth and to Platt that this was *not* the same thing.

"I actually don't agree with that assessment, Colonel," Dr. Avelyn said. "There's a major difference. Military dogs are not trained with live ammo or live explosives. In this case you're asking us to train these dogs in an environment where they need to learn by sniffing and possibly inhaling these samples into their respiratory systems. They are at extreme risk during their training."

Platt shot Creed a look. And this was the same argument Creed had made. The man wasn't just frustrated and impatient but bordering on anger. Did he really think he might convince the veterinarian otherwise? Creed kept quiet.

"That's partly why Deputy Director Wurth suggested getting high-risk dogs from shelters," Platt told Dr. Avelyn. "He's paying a premium price for these dogs."

"That doesn't really matter," she said in a calm voice that made Creed proud to have her on his side. "Whether these dogs would have been euthanized anyway is hardly the point. If any of the dogs are infected with the virus during training, they're worthless to all of us. Have you thought of that?"

She waited for him to grasp what she was saying, then continued, "If the dogs become infected they won't be able to go out and work in airports. They won't be able to go anywhere. They'll be too sick. And they also might be contagious."

50

HARTSFIELD-JACKSON ATLANTA INTERNATIONAL AIRPORT GEORGIA

O'Dell waited for Platt or Wurth to return her phone calls. In the meantime she had her laptop out, searching for flights with available seats, not just for herself but for Rief as well. She was getting frustrated. The ticket agent had already told her the earliest flight from Atlanta to New York didn't leave until that night at 8:45 PM unless she wanted to be on a standby list. O'Dell put herself on the list, then started searching on her own.

Omaha to New York was equally difficult. There was a flight that left at 5:05 PM but with a connection in Chicago that would put Rief in New York later than O'Dell's 8:45 PM nonstop flight from Atlanta. She was beginning to believe that neither of them would be able to meet this woman any sooner than midnight.

Her panic had kicked up a notch just as Charlie Wurth called.

She tried to move to an area with fewer people until she realized that no one was paying attention to her. They were all on their own cell phones, engaged in their own conversations. She told Wurth everything that Rief had shared, but she didn't stop there.

"Charlie, if you suspect that DARPA is somehow involved in this, you need to tell me now or I swear I'm calling Kunze and having him take me off this case."

"Believe me, Maggie, if I knew that was a possibility I'd be back in D.C. and be up in Colonel Hess's business like he's never had anybody in his business. But here's the thing — Hess has actually been helping us."

"How has he been helping?"

"He's sent a couple of his DARPA scientists to the CDC to assist with a possible vaccine."

"What about Lawrence Tabor?"

"I have no idea who this Tabor guy is."

"He works for DARPA," O'Dell told him.

"So what if he does?"

That silenced her.

"Seriously," Wurth said. "Look, Maggie, I understand Hess is like a raw nerve for you ever since North Carolina. But Dr. Shaw escaped with property that belonged to his research facility. I wouldn't be surprised if the man's going to be overly sensitive to this whole thing. She took a virus that she created while she was under his employment.

"Come on, Maggie, the guy's a war hero. A living legend. Under his direction, DARPA's research and technology has saved hundreds, if not thousands, of soldiers' lives. If he's sending out his people to try to contain this outbreak, is that such a bad thing?"

"Without telling us. You're forgetting that part. And that's okay with you, Charlie?"

"No, it's not okay with me. I just have more important issues to take care of right now."

"He's done it before," she said. She parked her roller bag and sank into a seat at a boarding gate that was empty.

"Ben seems to trust the man."

"Ben is blinded by this guy," O'Dell told him. "He's some big important mentor and influence in his life. Hess took matters into his hands last time and almost got me killed, so forgive me if I don't trust the man."

"You're forgetting something, O'Dell. Hess is on our side. He wants Dr. Clare Shaw caught and stopped just as much as we do."

"I hope you're right, Charlie, because

these watchers that Christina Lomax claims are following her around New York remind me an awful lot of Lawrence Tabor and the other henchmen that Hess is used to sending out."

She could hear his deep sigh on the other end before he said, "Let me find some flights for you and Ms. Rief. I'll meet the two of you in New York. I'll see if I can get someone with the CDC to take care of Ms. Lomax."

"Ben isn't coming with you?"

"He'd probably rather be with me, but he's working with your dogman."

With all the emotions running their course, O'Dell wasn't sure how she felt about Benjamin Platt and Ryder Creed — the two men who confused her head as much as her heart — spending time together.

51

Creed left Platt and Dr. Avelyn to figure out the details.

He saw that Penelope Clemence was early. She'd already pulled up in front of the kennels and was talking to Jason.

He and Jason had spent about an hour sectioning off a space for the new recruits, a special holding area. After hearing that Platt couldn't guarantee the risk this virus posed to the dogs, Creed realized that he would need to figure out a way to keep these dogs away from his for their entire training.

He and Jason had already set up separate crates for each in the back room. The crates would protect them from one another and duplicate the shelter environment that they were used to. Hopefully the extra planning would reduce their stress from being moved.

Penelope was grinning at Creed when he got to the vehicle. He glanced at the crates in the back of her Jeep Wrangler.

"I have a friend bringing the others," she told him. "I could only fit three. She's bringing four more in her van."

He nodded. The conversation with Platt had unnerved Creed. He kept telling himself that in seven years of eating, sleeping, thinking dogs, he had never heard of any dog contracting the bird flu. But then the virus hadn't hit the United States until 2013. If there were any incidents of dogs being infected, they would have had to happen in China or other parts of Asia. He wondered if the Chinese would even care about reporting such a thing.

"This is a good thing you're doing," Penelope said when she noticed his reticence.

"I hope so." He didn't mean to sound so doubtful.

"You just saved seven dogs' lives. Actually, more than that." And she smiled again. Her southern drawl made the words sing. "It was such a pleasure telling the Alpaloose folks that they could change their status to a no-kill shelter. I can't wait to hear how you managed that, Ryder."

"I have another favor to ask, Penelope."

"You name it, sweetie." And she winked at Jason.

"I could sure use another dog handler. We only have three days to train these dogs and prepare them. It would be three tough days starting early tomorrow morning."

"Well, I can certainly ask around and see if there're any handlers available."

"Actually, I meant you."

The smile faded in her surprise.

"Ryder, I don't have any experience doing what you guys do."

"It's okay. I'll be walking everybody through it step by step. It helps if each dog has his or her own person, sometimes as much for moral support and confidence as for training." When he saw her still hesitating, he added, "I can't think of anyone else who cares more about dogs and is able to interact with even the most difficult and obstinate ones. If it doesn't work for your schedule, I certainly understand."

"So I'd be stuck working alongside this guy, too?" She smiled again and swung her thumb at Jason.

"Unfortunately there is that drawback," Creed said. He noticed the kid actually looked like he was enjoying the attention and ribbing. "Jason already has some expertise in this area."

"I do?" he asked as he came around the vehicle ready with leashes.

"The *C. diff* training is pretty close to what we'll be doing."

"Okay then," Penelope said. "I'll give it my best." Then she headed to the back of the Jeep. "Let me introduce you to your new recruits."

First out was a yellow Lab, bright-eyed and excited but cautious.

"This is Winifred," Penelope said. "I'm told she has an addiction to bread."

"Regular bread?" Jason asked.

"Yep. Will do just about anything for a slice."

"I don't usually use food as rewards, but I'm considering it for the health alert dogs. In other circumstances, especially cadaver searches, we can't have dogs eating what might be evidence."

"Well, thank you for that picture. That's disgusting."

"Sorry, but it's true. As much as we love them, dogs do love stinky stuff."

Creed squatted down to pet Winifred, letting her sniff his hand first before touching her. He was pleased to see the dog's nose giving him a once-over. She was definitely a sniffer. That was a good sign.

Jason helped carry out the next dog, a black-and-white cocker spaniel.

"This is Tillie," Penelope told him as she took a leash from Jason and put it on. The dog didn't flinch at having something put around her neck.

"She sure is pretty," Creed said as he reached his hand over to her, but she was more interested in sniffing Jason.

"The last one I have with me is named Dooley."

"As in Tom Dooley?"

Creed stood to look inside the last crate.

"He's a little shy at first," Penelope said.

That wasn't a good quality. Creed opened the door to the crate and let the dog come to him. Dooley had the blue-and-white coat of an Australian cattle dog. His left eye and left ear were solid brown. That ear stood up, the other flopped. Because of the lop-sided markings, Creed thought he looked like he was hanging his head to one side. But then the dog started to wag. His tail tap-tapped the back of the crate.

Cattle dogs could be tougher to train. It was instinctive for them to herd, not just cattle but other dogs. Creed had rescued a Border collie, a hit-and-run left for dead on the side of Highway 98. After Dr. Avelyn repaired her crushed pelvis, Hannah nursed the dog back to health and named her Lady. The dog was smart and wanted to please, but she was more interested in rounding up the other dogs and sometimes even people. She failed miserably as a scent detection dog but made a great companion for Hannah's two boys.

He hoped that wouldn't be the case with Dooley.

Creed looked up at Penelope. "It's a start. You did good." Then to Jason he said, "Let's get these dogs settled. Get them fed."

Jason took all three leashes and led the dogs with a confident stride. By the time he got to the back door of the kennel all three dogs were looking to him for direction and guidance.

"He's come a long way," Penelope said when Jason was out of earshot.

"Yes, he has."

"Can I ask you something?"

"Sure."

"Why aren't you using any of your own dogs for this assignment? Seems with such a tight deadline you'd want to work with dogs that were already experienced in scent detection than starting from scratch."

"I made a deal with Homeland Security to train a certain number of dogs each year. These three and the four that your friend brings will be the first in that program."

"That's how you're able to pay for Alpaloose to convert to a no-kill? The government's paying for it?"

He met her eyes trying to judge if she approved or would be offended. Finally she nodded and smiled.

"There's another reason," Creed said. He figured she deserved to know. "They can't tell me whether dogs can contract this virus."

The smile disappeared. Her eyes left his and she looked off toward the kennels. He caught a glimpse of her emotion. She crossed her arms over her chest and then she simply nodded again.

52

OUTSIDE ATLANTA, GEORGIA

Stephen Bishop stayed in the office even after the cleaning crew had shut off most of the lights inside the building. Except, of course, the areas they weren't allowed to access. This was when Bishop felt most comfortable. Alone with no one around to second-guess decisions. No one asking stupid questions.

There was a cabin in the woods for Bishop to retreat to, but this office was large enough to use as a makeshift apartment. The sofa made a comfortable bed. Someone had mentioned that the office had belonged to a scientist who had used a wheelchair for most of his tenure, so it came with an attached private bathroom including a handicap-accessible shower. Bishop had added a microwave and mini refrigerator. It was fortunate that many scientists were introverts or demandingly private. So although some might have suspected that

Bishop spent an unusual number of nights here, they would also find it unremarkable.

Tonight exhaustion had taken its toll. The plan that had been worked on for so long was finally being implemented. It was a milestone, a historic event that should be greeted with celebration. Instead, Bishop felt anxious and stressed.

Besides having a crew that couldn't be trusted and a life that had been uprooted, there was also the albatross of Colonel Hess. The only reason the man had agreed to be a part of any of this was his own self-preservation and his obsession with eliminating the enemy. Both things Bishop could understand and even appreciate. The man had done amazing things in his career.

Under Hess's leadership, DARPA had developed groundbreaking and revolutionary technology. The contribution of drones to modern warfare would appear minor compared to the biological weaponry that was being developed in Hess's research facilities throughout the country without the American public and most of the political class knowing about it. But if turning the bird flu into a biological weapon proved successful, it would dwarf all the other projects. Bishop would feel vindicated for decades of work.

The cell phone started ringing.

"What is it?"

"What the hell happened with those birds?"

Bishop winced. Nothing like cutting to the chase. Hess was brilliant but totally void of manners.

"It wasn't me. I gave Dr. Robins perfect instructions. *She* messed up." Bishop wanted to remind Hess that he had chosen Dr. Getz and Dr. Robins, but by now it didn't matter. "I've changed the formula. Another flock will be ready in several days."

"Your grandfather did amazing things with mosquitoes," Hess said, sounding suddenly nostalgic.

"What are the numbers in Chicago and New York?" Bishop wanted to change the subject.

"According to my sources at the CDC, two hundred sixty-seven people in the Chicago area. New York is reporting only seventy-five."

"Fatalities?"

"Only five," Hess said with disappointment. "But there could be many more that simply haven't gotten to a hospital. Or" — and he paused — "it could mean our health care providers are much more prepared than we expected. That's good news."

"But bad news for killing armies of ISIS soldiers."

"Yes," he admitted. "So using human virus carriers alone isn't a viable plan. What are the chances of using birds?"

"I believe I'm close."

"I don't know how many test runs you can make before people get suspicious," Hess said. "Too many lakes filled with dead birds and having them fall out of the sky . . ."

"The American people are used to mistakes," Bishop said. They had already talked about this. "Live anthrax spores accidentally sent through the mail. Cattle from university research facilities accidentally being taken for commercial slaughter. Freezers with smallpox virus malfunctioning." Those were just a few of the examples Bishop could throw at Hess. There were many more incidents, some that had shocked and frightened even the scientists who had been a part of them.

Hess was silent for a change.

Then finally he said, "We're on schedule for phase two?"

"Yes," Bishop said, and ended the call.

Christina pulled the second burner phone from her tote bag just to look at it again. She had done this compulsively almost every ten minutes for the last several hours. She needed to check to make sure it was turned on. That the battery had not died. If there were enough bars. If it was possible that she had missed a call. Each time everything checked out fine.

She had given the biologist all the information and details necessary of where to meet and what time. She had asked that she not try to contact her. And yet Christina was disappointed that she hadn't heard from the woman.

Maybe she needed confirmation that she didn't think Christina was a nutcase. Maybe she wanted reassurance that Rief hadn't contacted federal officials who were now tracking her by using this phone. Just that line of thinking should have convinced

Christina to shut the phone off, but she couldn't bring herself to do that. It felt like the only lifeline she had right now.

Speaking of tracking, her self-inflicted wound hardly ached at all despite how much she ended up digging to get the microchip out of her arm. The tiny glass capsule had fascinated her. Once she washed it off she could see the coils of threadlike wire. She had slipped it into the zippered pocket of her tote bag. For now it would continue to travel with her. She didn't want the watchers to panic when she did disappear from their radar.

The soldier who followed her had started to leave her for longer periods of time. It was easy for him to catch up with her as long as he could track her with whatever GPS technology must be contained in the microchip.

Now as the day grew late, Christina realized she might need to return to her hotel room and let them feel assured that she was tucked in for the night. She needed to rest if she was going to be back on the streets again at nine o'clock tonight.

What concerned her was that she wasn't sure her body would last much longer. She was burning up, her forehead slick with sweat. Her layers of clothes were damp against her skin. It hurt to breathe. The muscle aches made it difficult to move. This afternoon she sat on benches and inside cafés, moving only when her coughing fits drew too much attention.

She needed to lie down for just a few hours. But what if she wasn't able to get back out of bed?

This was something Christina didn't think the biologist had understood. How could you fully relay to a stranger that you knew you were dying and might already be too sick to even help yourself?

Reluctantly she started to trudge back to the hotel. By now she should have known the way by heart, but the fever was playing tricks on her mind and her eyesight. And worse, in the last hour the sky had darkened with storm clouds. All her confidence in being a survivor was already slipping away by the time the first raindrops started to fall.

Jason hadn't looked inside the box since the night he picked it up from Tony's mom. Creed wanted everyone to get a good night's sleep. He wanted them up early — fresh, rested, and ready to work long hours for the next three days. But he couldn't sleep. For some reason he needed to see what Tony had left for him — now, tonight.

He carried the box as carefully as if it were filled with glass Christmas ornaments. He couldn't imagine what Tony wanted him to have.

Couldn't imagine, or dreaded finding out?

Knowing Tony, maybe it was filled with some last prank. Jason found himself hoping that was exactly what it was.

Scout had followed him. The dog had paid more attention to the box since its arrival than Jason had. Thankfully he no longer looked to the door watching for Tony to come in and play fetch.

Jason put the box by the sofa and invited the dog to jump up and join him. In case there was something strange or illicit inside, he didn't want Scout grabbing it.

He opened the lid. The item sitting at the top took his breath away.

The leather was worn. An elastic band kept loose notes from falling out of the notebook. The cover was stained with greasy fingerprints and spilled beer. There was a small rusty splatter in the corner that Jason knew was blood. He knew it because he'd been there when it happened.

They'd been hunkered down for the night. Their unit had spent the day chasing Taliban fighters, pushing them back only to send them hiding in the hills waiting for nightfall so they could come back down and try again. Some days it felt ridiculous. They even laughed about it because if they considered the actual risk, they'd never be able to get through each day.

Tony had this small notebook. He was forever jotting things down, doodling in the corners, writing scraps of thoughts. He was doing just that when gunfire erupted. The assholes had found their courage in the dark, figuring they knew the terrain better than the American soldiers. And they were right.

The blood was from a fellow soldier, staff sergeant Timothy Garcia. Head shot. Probably wasn't just blood but some brains and bone, too.

Jason reached for the book, his fingers stopping inches from picking it up when he realized something.

Tony would never have left this behind. He had it with him everywhere. There was no way he would have gone to Chicago and not taken it with him. Unless he knew he wasn't coming back.

There was something sticking up out of the notebook. Curious, Jason gently started to tug on it to pull it out. He stopped himself. It was tucked into the last half of the book. What if it was marking a particular page?

Jason peeled the elastic band back and opened the notebook. The paper sticking out looked like a deposit slip. When he looked at the pages his pulse quickened and he felt a clammy chill. The entry on the right-hand page, written in Tony's familiar chicken-scratch, started with:

DEAR JASON.

55

Both Amee Rief and Charlie Wurth were waiting for O'Dell at JFK.

"I have a driver out front," Wurth said instead of a greeting. He grabbed her roller bag. He already had a duffel bag slung over his shoulder and another roller bag — what must have been Rief's — and started leading the way.

"Good to see you, too, Charlie," O'Dell said to his back, getting only a wave of his hand. He didn't slow down. She asked Rief, "How are you doing?"

"I'm okay. My ticket was in first class."

"Nice. I was on the aisle in the last row next to the bathroom."

"That's no fun. I'm glad you're here."

The black Escalade had two rows of leather captain's chairs. Wurth made sure Rief and O'Dell were comfortable in the second row before he climbed into the first, where he could give the driver instructions.

From their conversation, it was obvious the man had worked for Wurth before.

Turning back to the two women, Wurth explained that Roger Bix from CDC was on his way with a team.

"Bix wants both of you wearing surgical masks and latex gloves."

"Seriously?" O'Dell asked. "How are we supposed to not look suspicious on the streets of New York with surgical masks on?"

"Have you walked the streets of New York lately? You'll fit in just fine. Besides, it all needs to go down quickly. The place she's chosen makes it very difficult for a snatch-and-grab, but that's basically what we'll be doing."

"Wait a minute," Rief interrupted. "Snatch-and-grab? This isn't what I signed up for. She sounded really scared."

"If she has the bird flu she's going to be very sick," Wurth said. "And highly contagious. Didn't she even tell you that she was instructed to walk around and contaminate as many people as possible?"

"That's true, but I don't think she —"

"The fact that she arranged to meet you where there'll be crowds of people tells me that either she doesn't know how devastating this virus is, or she only cares about herself."

"Survival instinct kicks in," O'Dell said. "You know that, Charlie. You can't blame the woman for wanting to save herself. Sounds like she didn't know exactly what she was signing up for. If she did, they wouldn't need to send watchers. I think Amee has a valid point. This woman is frightened. By now she must be feeling like hell. If Roger's team comes in with hazmat suits and attempts to grab her off the street, she might run. She's decided to trust Amee. I think she'll be okay with me being there. Why can't Amee and I simply escort her to the CDC's vehicle?"

"And what about her watchers? You think they're going to let you just 'escort her' away? Didn't you say she described one of them as a soldier?"

"Can't you get *us* some soldiers, Charlie?" O'Dell told him. "Didn't it occur to you that we might need some protection? Some help in case these watchers try to prevent us from taking this woman."

"I thought about that, but this flash drive will be worthless to us if they know we've taken the woman. It might push them into acceleration mode. She has to come with us without her watchers seeing it happen."

"Are you sure you can pull that off?"

He gave her his wide grin and said, "You

really need to start trusting me, Maggie."

O'Dell and Wurth had worked together before. They'd tracked a terrorist mastermind after an attack at the Mall of America. A few years ago the Coast Guard had found a cooler with body parts stuffed inside just off the shores of Pensacola Beach, and O'Dell and Wurth went down to investigate despite a hurricane barreling up the Gulf. She wanted to remind him that she had trusted him before and bombs ended up exploding and he had left her stranded in the path of a hurricane. Several times she had trusted Wurth with her life. But now, even the deputy director of Homeland Security wouldn't be able to protect any of them if they contracted this virus.

56

Christina had fallen asleep. For the first time in weeks she dreamed instead of tossing and turning.

She was lying on a beach in a luxuriously comfortable lounger. The sun felt warm and soothing. Within her reach on the side table were iced beverages with tiny umbrellas and slices of fruit on the rims. She could hear the waves, a lovely soft rolling sound muffling the caws and squawks of the seagulls.

When she reached for one of the drinks her hand slipped and suddenly there was glass everywhere, including a chunk stabbing into the palm of her hand. She grabbed at it and pulled it out, but now she could see dozens of tiny glass capsules buried deep in her hand. Frantically she started plucking at them. She used one of the shards of glass to dig deeper. She didn't even notice the blood until it was everywhere, dripping down her arms and legs and into the sand.

The sun had turned into a heat lamp beating down on her. Now so hot that she was burning up. She wiped at her forehead with the back of her wrist and when she brought it back down she saw that instead of perspiration she was sweating blood.

When Christina finally startled herself awake, she was so relieved to find herself in the familiar hotel room that she didn't even mind that her muscles felt like rusted armor. She looked at her hands, and she breathed in a deep sigh that was immediately interrupted by coughing.

Again her sheets were drenched in sweat, but there was no blood. Actually that wasn't true. Her pillowcase was spattered with blood from her coughing fits. But nowhere else was she bleeding and, for now, that was a small victory.

She noticed the dark outside her window and her eyes darted to find the time.

Almost nine o'clock!

She needed to be there when the shows let out. She couldn't be late. She needed to hurry. But it hurt to move. She heard an annoying chuffing sound and realized it was coming from her. When had it become so difficult to breathe?

Somehow she managed to get herself to the bathroom and assess the damage.

Hollowed-out cheeks and dark-rimmed eyes. Her skin was so pale, as if life had already drained out of her. She ran warm water, cupped it in her hands, and brought it to her face over and over. She thought about a shower and dismissed the idea immediately. She had too little time but most of all she couldn't imagine how painful it would be to have the water hitting her aching body.

She made herself as presentable as possible and pulled on fresh clothes. She stuffed everything she'd need into the zippered tote bag, even going through her suitcase one last time and taking whatever she couldn't bear to part with. If the biologist didn't show up, Christina wanted to at least have the alternative of going somewhere else.

She had already checked out several other hotels. She had enough cash to pay for a week, maybe more. If she could lose the watchers even for a short time, she could take a train or a bus or a flight. But that was when it got trickier. Where would she go? She couldn't go back home to North Carolina. They'd find her.

It was exhausting just thinking about it. And although she hated to admit it, her hotel room at the Grand Hyatt had become a safe haven. Maybe it wouldn't be such a bad place to die.

Stop it! She scolded herself. *She was not sick enough to die.*

She couldn't start to think that way.

She chugged the last of her cough syrup and popped four Tylenol. She made herself eat a protein bar, though even chewing was becoming painful. She drank a bottle of water, gagging on the last sips.

Then she finished packing up her tote bag and checked to make sure the glass capsule — the microchip that helped track her — was still inside the zippered pocket and within easy reach.

Outside the hotel, down on the street Christina walked for several blocks, keeping an eye out for any watchers. They weren't accustomed to her going out this late, so it might take a little longer for them to follow. That was perfect.

She unzipped the pocket and carefully pinched the glass capsule, pulling it out and cupping it in the palm of her hand. She flagged down a taxicab. She climbed into the back but kept the door open. As she chatted with the driver she slipped the glass capsule down in between the seat and the back.

"You know what," she told the driver. "It

looks like the rain's stopped. I think I'm going to walk after all." And she handed him a twenty-dollar bill before he could complain.

She wondered how long it would take her watcher to figure out that she had tricked him. How much longer would it take to find her again? She had to believe she had bought herself at least an hour, maybe two.

She walked around the corner, continued for two blocks, then flagged down another cab. This time she told him where she needed to go. She sat back and prayed that the motion and car exhaust wouldn't burst open the panic that was already swarming inside her head and her stomach.

57

A phone started ringing and startled Christina. She was gripping the door handle of the cab and willing her stomach to not send up its contents. She checked the driver's eyes, but he wasn't paying any attention to her.

She dug in the tote bag and pulled out the phone. She'd completely forgotten about the burner, so much so that she hadn't shut it off. And now she held it like a live grenade.

What if it was her watcher? What if they'd already discovered that she had ditched the microchip? Could they have found a way to use the phone to track her?

No, it was a familiar phone number. It was the one she had committed to memory. Still, she answered apprehensively.

"Hello?"

"Christina, it's Amee Rief. I'm sorry, I know you said not to call, but I wanted to let you know I'm here."

"I'm on my way." She almost wanted to cry with relief.

"I brought my colleague with me," Rief said. "Maggie O'Dell. The woman who was on the television news report with me. I hope that's okay. I just don't know New York City very well."

"I have the item with me," Christina said.

She'd almost forgotten the reason for this meeting. For the last twenty-four hours all she cared about was getting away from the watchers and keeping strong enough to hide. But now she realized that wouldn't be enough.

"There's something else," she said, then was surprised at the catch in her voice.

She didn't know this woman, and yet she remembered her kind eyes during that newscast as she talked about all those poor dead birds. And her voice sounded sincere and kind.

"What is it?" Rief asked after Christina had let too much silence go in between.

"When I give you the item . . ." She wasn't sure how to say this. "I'm just so sick," she whispered though, again, the cabdriver didn't seem to be paying any attention to her. "When I give you the flash drive, can you take me with you?"

There was a hesitation, but before Christina could regret her decision, Rief said, "Absolutely. That's what we intend to do, Christina. But you need to listen to me carefully. You're going to need to do exactly what I tell you. And Christina —"

"Yes?"

"You're going to need to trust me."

58

O'Dell was already questioning Wurth's plan. The streets were jammed bumper to bumper, and in between the lines of vehicles, crowds of people spilled out of the theaters.

Wurth avoided glancing back at her. He was in the passenger seat of the white van, driven by one of his men. The guy actually looked like he belonged to the electrical company whose logo decorated the outside panels.

Rief and O'Dell sat in the windowless back on a bench seat that faced the sliding door. It was a bit claustrophobic with all the spools of cable and equipment. Wurth had actually arranged to borrow what looked to be a real company van. Instead of being impressed, O'Dell wanted to ask him how he thought they could make a quick getaway stuck in traffic that inched along.

They were all wearing white overalls and

latex gloves, and surgical masks dangled from their necks ready to be put in place. It was a slapped-together operation, but with major resources already in use, they would have to make do. O'Dell had been in tighter situations.

"She's going to need to find us," Wurth said over his shoulder to Rief. "Get her back on the phone. It's time to give her the description of our vehicle."

Rief did as told.

"Ask if she sees her watcher," Wurth said.

"Christina, do you know if you were followed?"

Rief listened, then shook her head. She asked what the woman was wearing. After a few seconds she said, "A gray hoodie with 'New York' on the back, blue jeans, and a black baseball cap."

"Great." Wurth cursed under his breath. "That narrows it down to about three dozen people."

"Wait," Rief said. "She sees us. She's up in front of us. Under the billboard for *Wicked.*"

O'Dell caught herself smiling. Somehow that seemed appropriate for a victim carrying a deadly virus and being stalked by a potential killer. Although as she looked at the crowd under the sign, it was still difficult to pinpoint Christina.

"Oh no," Rief suddenly said. "Are you sure?" Then to Wurth, the biologist said, "She sees the watcher."

"Where? And does he see her?"

"He's across the street."

"What does he look like?" O'Dell asked as she started to scan the crowd on that side. Her view was limited as she leaned forward to see through the windshield. She saw that Wurth's focus was still trying to pick out Christina.

"He's wearing a military fatigue jacket," Rief said. "Short cropped hair. Muscular. She doesn't think he's seen her yet. Said he's looking at the people on his side of the street."

"There!" O'Dell pointed. The guy's chin was up as he tried to look over the crowd. He was directly across the street from where Christina said she was.

"Tell her when we get in front of the sign she needs to approach the curb," Wurth instructed. "Slowly."

The biologist relayed the message.

"He's starting to look across the street," O'Dell warned. "Looks like he's thinking about crossing over."

"Crap!" Wurth muttered. To the driver he said, "Can't you edge up faster?"

"Not without drawing attention."

"He's coming across," O'Dell told them.

"She needs to come to the van. Now! Everyone put your face masks on."

O'Dell did so as she kept her eyes on the watcher. He was trying not to shove at the crowd as he made his way into the street. She glanced under the billboard and still didn't see a woman approaching the van.

"Where the hell is she?" Wurth asked. He turned around to Rief. "Did she get spooked? Did she bolt?"

Rief didn't lift her head. Her surgical mask still dangled around her neck. She plugged a finger into her ear and pressed her cell phone closer to the other.

"Okay," she was saying. "Just stay calm."

"He's halfway across the street," O'Dell reported, watching as the man weaved between the bumpers of vehicles.

"Open the door," Rief suddenly said. When no one moved, she said it more forcefully. "Open the doors. Right now."

O'Dell jumped up and grabbed the handle. The van had been inching along but came to a full stop. She pulled and the doors opened.

A woman with a cell phone still pressed to her ear appeared from behind the backside of the vehicle. O'Dell reached a gloved hand out. She took it and hopped in. Then O'Dell squeezed the door shut and the van started inching again. She glanced out the window to see the watcher cross in front of the vehicle ahead of them. He continued up the curb and started shouldering through the crowd, making his way up the sidewalk and walking away from the van.

"Christina Lomax," O'Dell finally said to the woman, who seemed small and frail inside the oversized hoodie. "You're safe now."

She couldn't, however, tell her that everything would be okay. She had no idea how sick the woman was or if she'd even survive. Dark circles made her eyes looked bruised, and her face was gaunt.

She nodded as tears streamed down her face. Her eyes hadn't left Rief's even though O'Dell had been the one helping her into the van. She was hugging her arms around her chest as she sat down — or rather collapsed — onto the floor of the van. O'Dell wrapped a blanket around her shoulders. Even as she shivered she pulled something out of her pocket and handed it to Rief.

It was the flash drive.

■ ■ ■ ■

THURSDAY

■ ■ ■ ■

59

OUTSIDE ATLANTA, GEORGIA

It was almost three o'clock in the morning. The ringing woke Stephen Bishop from an unusually deep sleep.

"The carrier in New York disappeared."

"How is this my problem? I thought the watchers were reporting to *your man.*" But this news brought panic to Bishop, enough to jump off the sofa and begin to pace. "What happened?"

"Her watcher lost her around nine o'clock last night. She went out again. Caught a cab. He said she never goes out that late."

"Is it possible she went to a hospital?"

"He doesn't think so. He thought he was following the right taxi but when he caught up with it the carrier wasn't inside."

"Wait a minute." Bishop rubbed at exhausted eyes. "The New York carrier has a microchip."

"There must have been a glitch."

"That's impossible."

It didn't make sense.

"He checked the area around Times Square," Hess continued. "He thought maybe that's where she may have gone — he'd followed her there before. Some people like the lights, the crowds, the excitement. He never found her. He returned to her hotel room and waited. She never showed."

Bishop's mind was reeling. If the woman bolted, where would she go? This was one of the problems with using human carriers. There was always the chance they would follow their survival instincts and seek out medical attention.

"Your people need to start checking hospitals and urgent care centers."

"We're already doing that," Hess said. "There's something else." And he paused long enough that Bishop started gripping the phone.

"What is it?"

"Did you know that Dr. Getz was in New York two days ago?"

"He claimed there was a family emergency."

"All of his family is in Oregon and northern California."

Bishop didn't need to ask how the colonel knew this. He was the one who had brought Howard Getz on this project. Of course he would know everything there was to know about the man.

When Hess took too long to respond, Bishop said, "I never trusted the man. He's always been too concerned with creating vaccines. I knew he didn't have the stomach for this."

"At the most, he might have contacted the girl, said something that scared her," Hess said, and his voice sounded almost too calm, as if Bishop had just reaffirmed what Hess had already been thinking about the scientist.

"Please don't tell me we need to delay phase two."

"No, absolutely not."

"But what if Getz —"

"Not to worry," Hess told Bishop. "I'll send Tabor to take care of him."

60

Creed could feel the tension banging in his chest despite the fact that the morning training session had gone well. The dogs and handlers were performing better than expected as Jason, Penelope, and Hannah took the new recruits through a crash course of basic obedience training.

Benjamin Platt had brought with him a couple of CDC scientists to work with Dr. Avelyn to create an acceptable way to protect the dogs from catching the virus. There was no way the dogs could learn the target scent without breathing it. And though Platt and his experts didn't mind sacrificing some dogs for the greater good, Platt had understood the consequences of the dogs getting sick. As Dr. Avelyn had pointed out, sick dogs would be of no use in detecting the virus. They actually would do more harm by contaminating more people if they were tracking through an airport.

In military terms, Creed would call this a major clusterfuck.

He took Dr. Avelyn aside, and when she saw his clenched jaw, she suggested they take a walk outside and out of earshot of the scientists.

"They still don't seem to get it," Creed told her. "Platt looks like he thinks it's a waste of time to figure out how to protect the dogs."

Dr. Avelyn put a hand on his arm and stopped. She waited until he met her eyes, then said, "What is it with you and Ben?"

"Oh, so now he has you calling him Ben?" He knew it was a mistake as soon as it came out of his mouth and even before she raised her eyebrow at him. "Sorry. I don't mean to bite your head off."

"You two worked together in North Carolina during the mudslide."

"Not really. He only showed up after everything was over."

She crossed her arms over her chest and cocked her head to the side, waiting for him to acknowledge the real reason.

Creed shrugged. "Okay, so the guy rubs me the wrong way."

"Because of Maggie?"

He shot her a look of surprise. Was he that

transparent?

"He kept information classified in North Carolina that almost got Maggie and me killed. Now he keeps saying over and over that dogs can't get this strain of the bird flu. I don't trust the guy. Push comes to shove, he's going to protect his own interests, and I get the feeling my dogs will be at the bottom of his list."

There. He said it. And now he watched for Dr. Avelyn's response.

Instead of arguing, she surprised him when she said, "I think you're right."

Creed found no comfort in that acknowledgment.

"I've been doing some research. I didn't want to share it with you until I knew more." She started walking again and he followed alongside. "There's a new canine flu. We haven't seen it much around here, but the Midwest had an outbreak last spring. About a thousand confirmed cases. The clinical symptoms are similar to the common flu in humans: a soft, moist cough, fever, lethargy, and reduced appetite along with nasal discharge."

"Is it fatal?"

"If untreated, it can lead to pneumonia and death. But most dogs have recovered. Still, there's a fatality rate of around ten percent. It sort of came up out of nowhere. Dogs aren't usually susceptible to the flu. I did some digging, and I mean real digging because very few are willing to admit it, but this virus strain is believed to be a result from a direct transfer of avian influenza."

Creed felt as if she had just injected ice into his veins. "Son of a bitch! So dogs are vulnerable to the bird flu." He waved a thumb over his shoulder and back at the clinic. "And those bastards knew it."

"Wait a minute. It's not all bad news. Last November the USDA approved and granted a conditional license for a vaccine. It's considered what they call a 'lifestyle' vaccine, meaning only dogs with a high risk of exposure are to be vaccinated."

"They said there was no vaccine."

"To be fair, the CDC and even Platt may not have known. They're used to dealing with people, not dogs."

"You're cutting them a lot of slack."

"It doesn't matter. I ordered enough vaccine for all our dogs. We'll have it before you start working with the virus."

He heaved a sigh of relief, evidently so pronounced that Dr. Avelyn laughed at him.

"You're amazing," he said.

"Well, if you think that's amazing, wait

until you hear my idea for a doggie surgical mask."

"You're kidding?"

"They won't wear it." She smiled, and then her face turned serious again as she explained about using a surgical mesh placed over the tubes that contained the virus. "It's made of the same fibers in surgical masks, only a bit heavier. The dogs will still be able to sniff the scent, but the mesh will protect them from inhaling the virus."

"And how long will it take to get this stuff?"

"They're delivering it with the vaccine. I thought I'd have our brainy CDC guys figure out how to secure it over the training tubes."

"Thank you." And this time Creed hugged her.

61

Finally Creed felt confident they could actually do this. He told his handlers to take the dogs and give them a break, feed them, play with them, and put them back in the kennel to rest. Then he wanted the handlers to report back for their training after they had lunch and some rest.

Creed didn't take a break for himself. He needed to keep busy. And he needed to stay away from the clinic to let Dr. Avelyn and Platt work without interruption. He was up to his elbows washing dog bowls when he heard someone come into the kennel.

"Hannah told me to bring you this," Jason said.

On the plate under tightly wrapped plastic wrap Creed could see a sandwich filled with layers of deli turkey and cheese. Beside it was Hannah's cucumber salad and a dill pickle. He couldn't help but smile. She always looked to make things better with food, and most of the time it worked.

He washed and dried his hands and gestured for Jason to pull up a chair to the small bistro table in the corner. He grabbed a couple of Pepsis from the refrigerator and offered one to Jason.

"It's not your fault," Jason said as he popped the tab on the soda. "These guys just aren't used to being questioned. Hell, I'm not sure they even think about the consequences." He raised his stump of an arm. "I'm a perfect example of them not thinking about their consequences."

Creed didn't say anything. He peeled back the plastic wrap and took a bite of the sandwich. He hadn't even realized until now how hungry he was. He had made sure the dogs and everyone else was fed, but he'd forgotten about himself.

"Tony's another example," Jason continued. "You think any of those top-brass bastards even consider what kind of a mess we are when we come home? Those of us who don't come back in boxes, that is."

"Can I ask you something? Why haven't you gotten fitted for a prosthetic yet?"

Jason shrugged like it was no big deal. "VA kept putting me off. Said I hadn't been back long enough. I guess I got tired of calling. Every time they'd refer me to somebody else and I'd have to tell my story all over again."

"Doesn't seem right," Creed told him.

"I've talked to guys who have them and they've said theirs rub them raw or they're forever having it refitted. Maybe I'm not missing much. Not like they're gonna be able to replace my hand, right?" He took a couple sips of his soda. "You gonna eat your pickle?"

"Yes," Creed said, and purposely took a bite. The kid was constantly homing in on his food.

Then out of the blue, Jason said, "You know that research facility in North Carolina? The one we searched for under the mud?"

"Yeah?"

"Turns out Tony was there last August."

Creed swallowed hard. "How do you know?"

"Tony's mom gave me a box of his stuff. He told her he wanted me to have it if anything happened to him. His journal was on top. I've never seen him without that little notebook. The fact that he left it behind . . ."

He didn't finish, and Creed knew what it meant.

"How do you know he was in North Carolina?"

"He talks about it in the journal. Left a receipt for the check he received. Three thousand dollars for two days. Some experiment where they injected him with something. He wasn't sure what."

Creed thought about Dr. Shaw. It couldn't be a coincidence. That must have been how Tony ended up with the bird flu. He kept from voicing his suspicions. He'd promised Maggie. Even Tony's family didn't know the young man had been infected. But Jason . . . he deserved to know.

"He left me a note," Jason said, and this clearly had affected him. "Basically he told me to not be a coward like he was." He met Creed's eyes, and it was the first time he'd seen tears there. "I guess he really did jump."

"No," Creed said. "No, he didn't, Jason."

And he told him everything he knew, everything that Maggie had shared about Tony being infected with the bird flu. He told him about the bruise on his back that didn't make sense, and Maggie's suspicion that someone might have pushed Tony over the railing.

Then Creed waited, and he was surprised when the tears still came, but odd as it seemed, he knew that now they were tears of relief.

■ ■ ■ ■

FRIDAY

■ ■ ■ ■

62

O'Dell was supposed to meet the others, but she had flown into Pensacola early enough that she decided to take a detour. She knew it was a long shot but something still nagged at her, and she needed to check it out.

One of the hardest lessons to learn in profiling killers was overlooking a killer's weakness. Killers made mistakes. They overcompensated. What kinds of things could trip them up? Was there something or someone they held dear to them? And if so, what was it?

It wasn't unusual for a killer's Achilles' heel to be much the same as an ordinary person's. Arrogance, greed, or a sentimental attachment could force them to make a simple, stupid mistake. Ted Bundy was caught as a result of a routine traffic stop.

The one thing that stuck in O'Dell's mind about Dr. Clare Shaw was the devotion the scientist seemed to have for her grandfather. He was the only person Shaw kept in touch with. The director at the man's long-term care facility had been anxious to answer questions when O'Dell told her that she was investigating the disappearance of Dr. Shaw. According to the director, Shaw had visited on a regular basis — at least once or twice a month. She sent packages and cards. All that stopped last fall. The staff believed the scientist had died in the mudslide that also took her research facility.

Panama City was about an hour and a half from Pensacola. O'Dell found the care center on the outskirts of the city. She had called ahead and asked if she could visit with Mr. Carl Shaw. She was told that was fine as long as Mr. Shaw had no objections. The director warned O'Dell that the old man did have dementia and there was a good chance he might be combative or simply refuse to talk to her. There was also a chance he might not even acknowledge her presence.

After O'Dell signed in, one of the staff members directed her to the small courtyard and told her, "Call him Carl. He doesn't always respond to Mr. Shaw."

He sat across from a row of azaleas and seemed mesmerized by them, leaning forward and patting at the brilliant pink blossoms. O'Dell approached slowly and sat down next to him without announcing herself or asking permission. Then she simply waited until he was ready to notice her. It took longer than she expected.

He sat back and swiped his feathery white hair from his forehead with blue-veined hands. She noticed that his shirt matched his trousers, but his vest was misbuttoned, off by two, and he was wearing bedroom slippers. He crossed his legs, then crossed his arms over his chest. All this while O'Dell sat quietly by his side.

Finally there was a glance over at her. Only a second or two. Then he was distracted again as a staff member brought another resident out into the courtyard, staying beside her as she navigated her walker.

He pointed at the old woman and said, "She never finishes her juice."

"It's a shame to waste it," O'Dell said without missing a beat.

"I like milk better anyway."

"Chocolate milk?" she asked.

This time he turned to look at her, and there was a sparkle in his eyes.

"I haven't had chocolate milk in ages."

"You should ask for it tonight."

He was still staring at her, and she knew he was trying to decide if he should know who she was. He surprised her when he cocked his head to the side and asked, "Clare? Is that you?"

Before she could respond he added, "I like this disguise better than that beard."

O'Dell's mind swirled trying to think of questions to ask the old man. She knew very little about dementia. Was it possible that his granddaughter had visited using a disguise? Or could it be only a figment of his confusion?

He was watching the old woman again, no longer paying attention to O'Dell. Only a minute had passed.

"Carl," she said.

He looked at her and this time there was a bleary-eyed gaze void of recognition. She waited, hoping he might offer something more about Clare while she wondered what to ask.

"Is it time for dinner?" he asked her, then shook his head. "I don't want to go in just yet." He stared at the azaleas again.

"You can stay right here," she told him.

She sat with him for another fifteen minutes, then got up and left as unceremoniously as she had come over. Inside, she stopped at the director's office, but the young staff member who O'Dell had talked to earlier told her the director was gone for the day.

"I was wondering" — O'Dell tried to sound friendly and casual and not like an FBI agent — "does Carl have many visitors?"

"I've only been here for three months and I haven't seen any family stop by."

"So no one?"

"It's always sad when that happens. His doctor drops by once in a while."

"His doctor?"

"He was here a few weeks ago. They sat out in the courtyard for about an hour."

"Does his doctor happen to have a beard?"

"Yeah, he does. How did you know?"

63

PENSACOLA, FLORIDA

This time Creed met them at the Fish
House overlooking Pensacola Bay. It was
warm enough to sit outside, so he got a
table far from the entrance and close to the
water. It was still early. They'd have plenty
of privacy. He was expecting Wurth and
Platt but was surprised when he saw Maggie walking between the two men. He had
talked to her last night about Jason's discovery that Tony was connected with Dr. Shaw,
but she hadn't said anything about coming
to Pensacola. To be fair, she sounded completely exhausted.

Instinctively he stood up from the table,
then realized maybe it made him look too
anxious. They hadn't seen each other since
North Carolina, and yet when her eyes met
his, they held him the entire trek down the
wooden platform.

He reminded himself that this was business. He'd let her take the lead. But when she hugged him he held her for a beat longer. It felt good. *She* felt good, and he wondered how he had forgotten how good she felt. He didn't even care that Platt was frowning at him. Wurth, however, had a huge grin.

It appeared Wurth knew this restaurant, too. Well enough that he took the liberty of ordering them all beers and appetizers, rattling off a list of his favorites. Then the deputy director sat back and looked out at the water.

"This is beautiful." He waved his hand at the view. "And unfortunately I won't get to enjoy it." Then he glanced at Maggie and said, "Maggie and I were in New York City. We actually went to Broadway. Didn't get to see one damned show. But we did get one of Dr. Clare Shaw's guinea pigs."

"I talked to Roger Bix this morning," Platt said. "Christina Lomax is responding well to treatment. He was impressed that she kept herself hydrated. I guess she was downing vitamin C and protein bars, too."

"I thought you said there is no treatment for this strain of bird flu," Creed said.

"There's no vaccine to prevent getting it," Platt told him. "Once you get it, your body tends to be your worst enemy. Oftentimes there's more damage done from your immune system — friendly fire, so to speak — than the virus. Roger and his team are using an aggressive approach with a couple of antivirals. The method seems to be working with about a seventy-five percent success rate."

Creed couldn't help thinking that once again, Platt sounded like a research doctor more concerned with statistics. At the same time, he knew that wasn't a fair assessment. Even before he admitted it to Dr. Avelyn, he knew he had a prejudice against this guy, and yes, all of it was due to Platt's hold on Maggie O'Dell. But Creed needed to focus on more important things right now.

"You said everything's changed," Creed said. "Maggie told me this woman had some classified information."

Wurth raised his eyebrows as he glanced at Platt to see if he knew about this. "You two talked recently?"

"Jason Seaver found a connection between Tony Briggs and Dr. Shaw," Maggie said.

Creed was glad to see that she wasn't defensive about their conversation.

"Agent Alonzo has been deciphering the flash drive that Christina Lomax gave us," she said. "There's a ton of information. Some of it still doesn't make sense. One was a list of names and addresses. Christina's and Tony's names were both on the list. And there was another familiar one."

She looked at Creed and said, "Izzy Donner had been to the North Carolina research facility, too. It appears Shaw and her accomplices approached those individuals who were already in their database. Those who had already volunteered and been paid to take part in other experiments at the facility."

"Do you have any idea who killed Tony and Izzy?" Creed wanted to know.

"Not yet. Christina talked about watchers. She said the guy who handed off the flash drive made her believe she wasn't supposed to survive the virus and that her watchers would make sure of that. She wasn't sure whether she believed him. She said she'd done other experiments and always been okay and also been paid very well."

"Any idea who this guy was?" Platt asked.

Wurth shook his head. "She didn't get to look at him. But she did take a look at what was on the flash drive and got freaked out by it. They'd warned her against going to law enforcement, but she saw Amee Rief — the U.S. Fish and Wildlife biologist — on TV. The documents on the flash drive talked about dead birds. She took a chance and contacted Rief."

"Is that what Tabor was? A watcher?" Creed thought about Sheriff Wylie and wondered if he was a victim, too.

The mention of Tabor brought a sour expression to Wurth's face as he exchanged a look with Platt and Maggie. It was Maggie who answered.

"Lawrence Tabor works for DARPA."

"You're kidding."

"I've confirmed that he works for Colonel Abraham Hess," Wurth told him.

"Let me guess," Creed said. "Colonel Hess had no idea his guy had gone rogue."

"Colonel Hess said that Tabor had been assigned to check on some things but that he had, quote, gone beyond the boundaries of his assignment, end quote. He assured me that Tabor is no longer on this assignment." Wurth said this last part as he looked to Platt.

"The colonel means well," Platt told them.

Creed thought Platt still sounded defensive and Wurth looked like he might not totally agree with the assessment that Hess meant well. Creed watched as Wurth shot Platt a look before he continued. "We don't need to worry about Tabor, but we do still need to worry about Shaw. She obviously has a whole crew at her disposal beyond the

346

list of guinea pigs. I've already put every single one of those names on the no-fly list."

"So does this solve your problem?" Creed asked. "You don't need my dogs if you have a list of names. Tony didn't use a fake ID. Did this Christina use her real name?"

Creed glanced at Maggie. But now her eyes were watching the water. Her attention and her mind seemed to have strayed from the table as well. It was Platt who answered this time.

"Yes, Christina used her real name. And so did Izzy Donner when she booked a flight for Atlanta. We don't know yet if there were others. So far, the CDC hasn't had any reports of the virus in cities other than Chicago and New York."

"But documents on this flash drive allude to a 'second wave' and a 'third,' " Charlie Wurth said. "We can't assume they'll be drawing from this list only. There's a lot of information on the flash drive for Agent Alonzo and his team to siphon through, but getting this is really a lucky break for us. It appears to have come from an insider. Maybe someone who's having second thoughts about being a part of the plan.

"There are specific flights marked on specific dates. All of them have Atlanta as a common denominator either for flights outbound, inbound, or connecting. It's possible they've already purchased airline tickets for these. They're going through the flight manifests, but there's really no way for us to tell who on those passenger lists might be a virus carrier or which flights may have been chosen."

"Can you just cancel all the flights?"

This time Wurth stared at Creed until a slow smile relaxed his face like he had finally recognized the joke. Then he said, "There must be at least a hundred and twenty flights over the course of two days. I have not been granted the authority to disrupt air traffic at the busiest airport in the world. At least not until and unless your dogs give an alert."

"Why do you suppose Shaw chose Atlanta?" Platt asked.

"People coming and going from places all over the world," Wurth said. "There's about twenty-five hundred flights a day. Eighty percent of Americans live within a two-hour flight of Atlanta. If you want to infect a whole lot of people all over the country, I'd say Hartsfield would be a great start. Think about it.

"Let's say they only use three virus carriers. Let's say each one is on a flight with a hundred and fifty people. Those hundred and fifty people land at another airport. For some of them, that city will be their destination, but for others, they'll board connecting flights and travel to yet another city. Then some of them will get in cars or taxis or they might take buses or subways and travel another hour to get home from the airport.

"Those hundred and fifty people not only have contaminated hundreds of others, but they will have also spread the virus over hundreds, maybe thousands of miles. They don't need to have an army of original volunteers or paid virus carriers. The first date on their schedule is in two days."

They were all quiet for a moment. Creed watched Maggie, who still seemed to be only half listening as she sipped her Diet Pepsi.

"But I'm still wondering," Platt said. "Why not O'Hare? Or Denver? There are other airports that would accomplish the same end results. Why choose Atlanta? Is it possible Shaw is somewhere close by?"

He glanced over at Maggie, who remained quiet. "When Charlie and I met you in the parking lot, you said you had some new information."

It seemed to take her a minute to realize he was talking to her.

"I think I discovered why we haven't been able to find Dr. Clare Shaw," Maggie said, sitting up and finally pulling her attention away from the water view and back to the table. "I think she's been disguising herself as a man."

64

O'Dell had been waiting to hear from Agent Alonzo before she shared any of her suspicions with the others. She had hoped to have something more to present as evidence than the mumblings of a lonely old man who was losing his mind along with his memories.

The care facility did have a mandatory sign-in for each guest, but only a name was required. No ID needed to be checked. No visitor badge given out. In fact, the guest book was in the lobby at the front door, casually displayed so anyone could flip the pages to see who had been there in the days before.

O'Dell knew the director had probably informed the staff that O'Dell was looking into the disappearance of Mr. Shaw's granddaughter. The staff member remembered Carl Shaw's doctor and had been eager to help with a description.

"He isn't very tall," she'd said. "About five eight. A little pudgy around the waist. Always well dressed — suit and tie. Heavy-framed glasses. Dark hair — a little long over his collar. His beard is short with a few streaks of gray, but I'd guess he's in his forties. Oh, and his hands are so neatly manicured. I notice hands," the woman had told O'Dell with a trace of embarrassment. "Mine are always so dry. I don't take care of them very well."

Unfortunately there was no record of where Dr. Stephen Bishop lived or practiced. He wasn't "local," the woman had told her. Then suddenly she brightened at another memory.

"The car he drove had Georgia license plates," she'd told O'Dell. "I was leaving once when he was arriving."

Maggie repeated the conversation to her colleagues.

"Georgia," Platt said now with elbows planted on the table. "That narrows it down."

Wurth rolled his eyes at him. "You have any idea how big-ass Georgia is?"

"I already have Agent Alonzo trying to find any research labs in the area," O'Dell said.

Wurth still shook his head. "Needle in a

haystack. Too bad that staff member didn't remember the license plate number." He laughed at that and sipped his beer.

"Security cameras," O'Dell said, the idea suddenly hitting her. "Excuse me."

She was digging out her cell phone as she shoved away from the table and headed for a quieter spot. She had asked about the camera at the front door of the care facility and the one in the courtyard, but unfortunately they didn't film anything. Both were monitors used only for staff to check on the residents. However, O'Dell remembered a preschool next door. Its parking lot ran alongside the care facility's lot with a patch of grass in between. She thought she had seen a security camera in the corner of that parking lot. Was it possible it captured both lots?

Agent Alonzo answered on the second ring. She explained it all to him and he listened quietly. She knew what she was asking was a long shot. Even if there was film available for the last day Stephen Bishop visited the facility, it could be so grainy there'd be no way to pick out the car, let alone its license plate.

When O'Dell returned to the table the three men were waiting for her. Platt looked exhausted. Wurth looked doubtful. But Ryder Creed simply smiled at her.

■ ■ ■ ■

MONDAY

■ ■ ■ ■

65

HARTSFIELD-JACKSON ATLANTA
INTERNATIONAL AIRPORT
GEORGIA

Jason had nicknamed the yellow Lab Winnie — short for Winifred. She was smart and sweet. Maybe a little preoccupied with wanting to please him, but Creed said that wasn't a bad thing.

She had slept in Jason's trailer last night. Whenever it was possible — especially in the early stages and especially with shelter dogs — Creed encouraged the handlers to spend as many "off-training" hours as they could with their dogs. Winnie was such a good-natured dog Jason couldn't imagine why anyone would give her up to a shelter.

Last night she didn't even mind Scout bossing her around, telling her which toys were his. The only problem Jason encountered was catching the dog with a loaf of bread she had managed to grab from the corner of his kitchen counter. She had ripped into it and devoured several slices before Jason caught her. Actually Scout had caught her and barked frantically, tattling on her.

It was a funny story to share with the other handlers that morning on the long drive to Atlanta. Penelope Clemence reminded him the shelter had told her the Lab had an odd addiction to bread. Jason realized they had no idea about Winifred's previous life, but he hoped she didn't devour bread because it had been the only thing she was fed in her life before the shelter.

They had all arrived at the airport early, before the first flights took off. Jason wasn't sure how Deputy Director Wurth and Agent Alonzo had figured out where they should be stationed and which flights they'd be covering. Actually he was glad to not be involved in that part. He had seen the toll it was taking on Ryder Creed, and Jason was glad to just follow instructions.

Each handler and dog had a separate terminal with a list of gates and flights with times. They were supposed to work their dogs up and down their terminal. When a flight arrived that was on the list, they were to stand off to the side at the gate as the passengers came in. When it got close to boarding time for each of the designated outbound flights, the dogs would need to work their way through the passengers waiting to board at the gate.

Wurth had warned them that there could be dozens of virus carriers or there might be none. However, if their dog alerted, they needed to activate a special app on their phone that sent an alarm to DHS with their location. The handlers were not to apprehend or attempt to detain. They were supposed to wait for a DHS agent. They could follow the suspect, but not engage. It all seemed a bit tame compared to what Jason had experienced in Afghanistan, but not that different. Many of those missions included a lot of hours of waiting, watching, looking for danger, followed by a burst of excitement.

For Jason this still seemed all too fantastic that the dogs could pick out the carrier of that scent from a crowd. He reminded himself that Grace and Molly had done just that at his grandfather's care facility. And thanks to the dogs, Gus Seaver's *C. diff* infection had been caught early enough that he was already recovering.

But Grace and Molly had been in training for months. Grace was a seasoned detection dog who could find just about anything Creed wanted her to find. Winnie had only days to learn. And after three hours and clearing every flight on their list without a single alert, Jason was beginning to wonder if the dog might be missing something.

She went through the drill, just as she had during training, working the air with her nose. Her whiskers twitched. Her eyes were intent, although they strayed once in a while when there were children close by.

Jason tried to remember what Creed always told him. "Listen to your dog. Pay attention. Your dog is your number-one priority. Assist your dog, don't try to influence her."

He also reminded himself that the dogs could smell their handler's anxiety, fear — probably even apprehension. He didn't want Winnie to sense that he didn't believe she could do this.

Jason led Winnie to an empty corner. He had set the timer on his cell phone to make sure he gave the dog regular breaks. She was getting used to these and sat down, waiting for him to pull out the collapsible bowl and fill it with water for her.

Their next gate on the list was diagonal from where they rested. He saw Winnie's head go up and turn toward it. She sniffed the air and her nose started twitching. Jason felt a pinprick of excitement until he saw what had drawn Winnie's attention. A little boy, about five or six years old, waved and pointed at the dog from across the aisle.

Was the dog distracted by yet another kid, or was she actually getting a whiff of the virus?

"Is it possible this place won't show up on my GPS?" Creed asked.

The last turn had put them on an old two-lane blacktop that seemed to wind and loop with no purpose. They hadn't passed a house or any sign of civilization in over ten miles.

"I couldn't find it on the satellite either," O'Dell answered from the passenger seat. "The place is supposedly off the grid. But these are the coordinates Agent Alonzo provided."

Creed shot her a look. "Any chance he got it wrong?"

"He hasn't been wrong yet."

Creed still wasn't sure how Alonzo had managed to get the license plate number. Maggie had explained about the security cameras next door to the care facility where Carl Shaw lived. On the last day that Dr. Stephen Bishop visited, there had been only one vehicle with a Georgia license plate. Using enhanced technology, Alonzo had been able to pull the number.

The black sedan was registered to the National Bio and Agro-Defense Facility, a sprawling campus outside Atlanta located at the foot of the Smoky Mountains and conveniently hidden in the forest. It coincidentally worked closely with DARPA and housed Level 4 laboratories. And it also housed agricultural projects. Several scientists at the facility had been instrumental in working with the USDA during the recent bird flu when millions of commercial poultry were infected.

"Was this place ever on your radar?" Creed asked.

"No, it wasn't. There was no evidence that they had Level 4 pathogens here since 2011, so we didn't know about the labs until Ben made some phone calls."

He knew that Maggie and Platt had worked together for the last twenty-four hours running down information on the facility. Platt had somehow even managed to get them access, gaining security clearance for Creed, Maggie, and Grace.

Platt had wanted to come along. Having him and his credentials would certainly make this visit easier. But Maggie insisted that if Colonel Abraham Hess was involved, they couldn't risk the DARPA director finding out and possibly tipping off Shaw. And Platt's name on the visitors list could actually do just that. There would be many more questions about why the director of USAMRIID would suddenly choose to go to this particular facility.

Instead, Grace would be the focal point. She had an appointment with a scientist at the facility who was working on a device that could duplicate canine scent capabilities. Creed knew there were programs across the country trying to build what they called "an iron nose." Hannah had received phone calls from several asking for their dogs to participate in the research, but Creed had always declined. He was skeptical. A dog's nose was amazing and complicated. He didn't believe science would ever be able to duplicate it effectively.

Creed glanced in the rearview mirror. Grace was in her usual spot. She was watching between the front seats, staring out the windshield, already anxious to get to work.

Maggie had brought an evidence bag with unwashed personal belongings from Dr. Clare Shaw's North Carolina apartment. The bag had been sealed five months ago and had been sitting on a shelf since then.

He knew that enough of the scientist's scent would have been preserved with the belongings, absorbed by the clothing's fabrics. He had asked for at least one pair of well-worn shoes to be included, and if possible a pair of dirty socks.

People often wondered why dogs chewed up their shoes and loved their socks, especially when they left the dogs alone. Sometimes it was just a bored dog, but most of the time what the dog wanted was the scent of the owner — they found comfort in having those items. Also, shoes rarely got laundered. And no matter what Clare Shaw's new disguise was, she probably hadn't changed much about her feet. The scent would be the same.

Their plan was to find the Biosafety Level 4 laboratories and catch Shaw off guard — that is, if she was actually at this facility. Creed was hoping Grace would then be able to identify her no matter what Shaw's new disguise. He had faith the little dog could certainly accomplish the task. However, he'd warned Maggie that Shaw's new identity would include new scents. Some of them would replace old ones. If she was dressing like a man she might also be using more masculine-scented soap, shampoo, deodorant.

But there were other natural scents attributed to each individual, and some of those would be difficult to mask even with new skin and hair care products. Creed knew that a dog could smell fingerprints left on a wall the week before. He had seen Grace sniff out his footprints on a wood floor after others had walked over his tracks. An average person sheds about thirty to forty thousand skin cells per hour. Though weathered and dry, these still held scent. Scent that Grace could separate and identify. Or at least, Creed hoped she could.

"Up ahead," Maggie told him as she pointed.

Through the trees Creed could finally see slivers of redbrick buildings.

67

HARTSFIELD-JACKSON ATLANTA INTERNATIONAL AIRPORT GEORGIA

This was it. Or so Jason thought as he watched Winnie.

Her nose was in the air and her breathing was getting more and more rapid. She strained at the end of the leash. She had led him across the aisle to the boarding gate they were supposed to check out next. But the crowd was thick here. It was obviously a larger plane with many more passengers than their last several searches. They couldn't just walk up and down through the seated and standing passengers. In some places they couldn't get through at all.

A few people saw Winnie's vest with WORKING DOG on the side, and they helped make a path for her and Jason. Others ignored them. He had to ask them to please move. Not an ideal situation. He wasn't supposed to draw attention to himself or to his dog. It pissed him off when people wouldn't move for Winnie, but then they'd glance at his empty shirtsleeve and move back. He didn't care if they were being polite or if they were disgusted, he just didn't want to be treated any differently.

To make things more complicated, Winnie was still paying way too much attention to the little boy. The kid now wrestled with his mother, who was trying to keep him from running toward Winnie. At one point the young mother asked Jason if her son could pet the dog. He shook his head and pointed to Winnie's vest. Under the word WORKING DOG it read in smaller letters DO NOT PET.

Jason still couldn't figure out who Winnie was zeroing in on. The dog slowed at times, even stopping once in front of a group of teenagers. He had already activated the phone app and signaled that he might have a virus carrier. He didn't care if Winnie ended up with a false alert. He wanted DHS here. He'd let them decide what to do with the person, if and when the dog lay down at someone's feet.

She kept circling back to the little boy. What was it about little kids? Had the dog been taken away from one who was important to her? Maybe she hadn't seen too many before and they fascinated her. Or was it that this boy made so much noise? Whatever the reason, Jason started to get impatient.

He tried to shut out all the noises and concentrate only on Winnie. He needed to calm himself, to slow down his own breathing so that the dog didn't smell his anxiety. She had already looked up at him twice with her head cocked to the side as if asking if he was okay. Once again, he forced himself to remember all the things Creed had taught him.

His phone started to vibrate. Jason ordered Winnie to sit so he could hold her leash and answer the phone.

"This is Charlie," Wurth said. "I'm headed your way. Just wanted to warn you. Keep your distance from the target. Hannah and Tillie tracked one about twenty minutes ago and the girl freaked and tried to get away. Started shoving and punching passengers around her."

"Son of a bitch," Jason muttered.

"I'll see you in five."

Wurth ended the call before Jason could tell him that he hadn't located the carrier yet. Or if there even was one. Winnie stared hard at the little boy and the whole time her nose was working the air.

Then Jason saw the guy.

He was standing behind the little boy and

the mother. The man was pretending to not
be interested in Winnie, and yet he was
watching her every move from beneath the
brim of his ball cap. From twenty feet away,
Jason could see that the man was sweating . . . a lot.

68

Jason took Winnie around to the far side of the row of filled seats. It was difficult to navigate over waiting passengers' feet and their luggage sprawled between the rows. He wanted to come at the man from a different angle just to make sure this was Winnie's target.

He saw the emblem on the man's ball cap, and at first Jason thought he'd misjudged the guy. The black cap had 22KILL embroidered in red on the crown. The 22KILL represented the twenty-two veterans who were killed by suicide every day on a yearly average.

That's how they worded it: "killed by suicide" not "committed suicide." The idea being that many of these veterans would not have chosen suicide if they had not been suffering from PTSD or other mental and physical disorders caused by their service. The organization hoped to raise awareness to the epidemic.

Jason knew all this because Tony had talked about joining. Now he glanced at the man's right hand and he could see the black band — the honor ring — that members wore symbolically on their trigger finger. It was meant to be a silent salute to all vets.

Maybe the guy had been watching Jason, not Winnie. If he was a veteran, Jason's amputated arm might have brought back memories of his own combat service.

Jason was just about to dismiss him and start examining the surrounding passengers, but then Winnie began shoving her way through the maze of luggage. Jason gave her a longer lead so he could stay back. From his position, the man in the black ball cap would be able to see Jason through the crowd, but he couldn't see Winnie down below, hidden by legs and bags and seats.

For a second or two even Jason couldn't see the dog, but he held the retractable leash tight then felt it stop before it reached its limit.

Winnie had stopped.

Jason felt a kick of panic in his gut. He tried to see her through the crowded mass. There was no way he could just reel the dog back. He glanced over heads and around bodies. Another dozen seconds went by and now Jason couldn't see the man in the black ball cap.

69

THE NATIONAL BIO AND AGRO-DEFENSE
FACILITY
GEORGIA

O'Dell and Creed had gotten through the security checkpoint. They were on the visitors list just as Platt had promised. O'Dell tried to shake the heated argument the two of them had about whether Platt should come along. She knew he just wanted to help, but his name on a visitors list would have drawn too much attention. The truth was Platt still trusted Colonel Hess even after what happened in North Carolina. And because of that, O'Dell didn't trust Platt's judgment when it came to Hess.

The guard didn't even seem interested in Grace or their reason to be here. When Creed asked directions to the scientist they were meeting, the guard circled the building on a map of the campus and handed it to Creed.

Because the man was so lax, O'Dell decided to risk pushing the envelope and asked, "I'd like to drop by and say hello to an old friend who just started here. Can you tell us which building Dr. Stephen Bishop works in?"

He stared at her. Then he picked up a small spiral-bound book and started flipping through it. The whole time O'Dell was holding her breath. What if he was looking up Bishop's phone number instead of the building? What if he picked up his phone and called?

She saw Creed give her a sideways glance like he was looking for direction because she had gone off script. She noticed that his right hand gripped the gearshift as if ready to shove it into reverse if necessary. O'Dell could even see Grace impatiently shuffling her front paws. And suddenly she started to inch her hand inside her jacket, fingering her weapon where it was tucked into her shoulder holster.

The guard put his hand out to Creed, surprising both of them.

"The map," he said when Creed didn't understand. "I'll circle Dr. Bishop's building. That one's easy to find. It's right next door to the aviary."

Neither of them said a word until Creed parked in a shaded space in the corner of the lot, far away from the only security camera.

"Did that just seem too easy?" Creed asked.

"Maybe a bit reckless," O'Dell admitted. "But I don't think we have very much time. If and when the dogs catch the first virus carriers, their watchers will be alerting Shaw about what's happening at the airport. And if she gets spooked she'll disappear again. I've been looking for her for over five months. I don't want to lose her."

O'Dell looked over her shoulder at Grace and said to the dog, "Let's go find her, Grace."

"Where's the target?" someone whispered next to Jason, startling him.

It was Charlie Wurth.

Jason was trying to figure out a way to get to Winnie without pushing and shoving. His heart pounded out the seconds. That Wurth was here beside him was not a relief. He wanted to get his dog. That he could no longer see the man in the black cap made Jason's gut twist into a knot.

"He was on the other side of this row of seats. I think Winnie stopped in front of him. You said I shouldn't approach. You said I needed to keep my distance."

He held up his end of the retractable leash. He clutched the case, holding it tight, when suddenly he felt the tension slack. Then came the dreaded sound of the retractable leash whizzing back through the legs of passengers, snagging temporarily on a luggage strap before it clamored noisily back into the plastic case still clutched in Jason's hand.

Someone had unclipped it from Winnie's collar.

"Son of a bitch," Jason said.

Wurth did a double take at the case, and then his eyes followed where the cord had come from. Suddenly the calm, cool deputy director started grabbing shoulders and pushing open a path into the crowd. He flashed a badge when a couple of men shoved back at him. They immediately held up their hands and stood back. Jason followed, sick to his stomach that he had put his dog in jeopardy. What the hell had happened?

Wurth continued to wave his badge, and now he was yelling for passengers to move. People started getting out of the way of the crazy black man waving something in the air. Then they parted enough for Jason to see Winnie. She was lying on the floor, between two rows of seats. The man with the black ball cap kneeled beside her with his hands on her neck. Jason rushed him but Wurth held him back.

The man looked up at Wurth and Jason. This close it was easy to see that his eyes were watery and his cheeks hollow. He was drenched in sweat. But now Jason could see that the man wasn't hurting Winnie. He was petting her with both hands, over and over again.

"She's such a good dog," the man told them. "She reminds me of my Abby." Then he wiped at his runny nose and said, "I can't do this. I can't get on that plane. I'm just feeling so sick. I just wanna go home to my dog."

Wurth had his cell phone to his ear even as he said to the man, "Don't worry, buddy. You just stay put. We're going to take care of you. We'll get you back home to your dog."

71

THE NATIONAL BIO AND AGRO-DEFENSE FACILITY
GEORGIA

Stephen Bishop swiped the security card and shoved open the door to the lab. Only the three scientists had access. Dr. Sheila Robins had left for the day, and Getz hadn't shown up this morning. Perhaps Hess had already done something with him . . . or to him. Bishop couldn't be bothered. There were many more pressing issues. Besides, Howard Getz was the colonel's responsibility.

One of the burner phones started to vibrate. The old man couldn't possibly be expecting an update on phase two this soon.

"What is it?"

"We just heard from one of the watchers at the airport," Hess said in a tone edged with hysteria. "They've taken one of the carriers into custody."

"Impossible," Bishop said.

"They have dogs. Several watchers have now reported seeing them."

"But how? The canine patrols at airports are trained for explosives and drugs."

"You tell me how. You're the scientist."

"We need to abort the plan," Bishop finally told Hess.

"How can we do that? Some are boarding planes as we speak."

"Pull them off. Have their watchers get them out of there. Do you want more of them caught and risk what they might tell officials? You still haven't even found the New York girl. I tell you, if any of them are caught they'll be able to lead the authorities to this lab." Bishop stopped at that realization. It wasn't safe here. How much time before they discovered where the carriers were injected?

"You need to scrub everything," Hess said. "I'll send Tabor to take care of you and Dr. Robins."

"Okay." Bishop ended the call with a sense of relief, then suddenly remembered that was the same thing Hess had said about Dr. Howard Getz. That he'd send Tabor to take care of him. What did that mean?

Hess was only concerned about his own self-preservation. He had chosen the other scientists and arranged for them to use the labs and offices at this facility. He took over the watchers and even provided the new list to be used for virus carriers. What started out as Bishop's lifelong project had slowly and manipulatively been taken over by Hess. Bishop saw that now and remembered how the colonel had "scrubbed" other projects that had gone wrong.

Bishop started packing a small case, adding several bags and syringes filled with the virus. There were always ways to replicate it and start over. These syringes would be for security and if necessary serve as the only weapon available right now.

The scientist started to open the lab door and get what was needed from the corner office but stopped at the sound of someone approaching. It was a strange click-clack gait on the tile floor. Bishop pulled the door closed and sneaked a glance out of the small window at the top of the door.

Coming down the hallway were a man, a woman, and a small dog.

72

Creed kept his eyes on both Maggie and Grace. He'd seen Maggie take risks before. Maybe they were alike in that respect. They were willing to risk their own well-being when they believed what they were doing was the right thing. Yes, sometimes it was reckless and dangerous. But there was one major difference — Creed wasn't willing to risk his dog's welfare. So he didn't like this idea of walking directly up to the office of Dr. Stephen Bishop alias Dr. Clare Shaw and knocking on the door.

He'd seen what Shaw was capable of doing. In North Carolina he'd helped recover the bodies that had ended up buried in the mudslide. All of them had been shot in the head. But the bodies of Shaw's test subjects were covered with red angry welts from experiments she had put them through. There were indentations on their scalps from where electrodes had been placed. The lone survivor, Daniel Tate, was plagued with hallucinations.

Yes, these men had volunteered and were paid just like Tony Briggs and Christina Lomax and Izzy Donner, but Shaw had gone way beyond ethical bounds. She had no regard for her test subjects.

Creed watched Maggie as they continued to the corner office at the end of the hallway. She kept her right hand tucked into her jacket, and he knew being armed gave her confidence. But he had a feeling bullets couldn't compete with what Shaw was capable of using in order to escape.

Maggie must have noticed his apprehension.

"Just identify her," she said in a low voice, almost a whisper. "Then both you and Grace need to move to safety."

"I'm not going —"

"Please, Ryder, just promise me."

He nodded and tightened his grip on Grace's leash. He had purposely left off any special vests that might draw attention to her. Back at the Jeep, he had poured all of Shaw's belongings out of the sealed evidence bag and into the cargo area. Then he let Grace take her time with them, pawing through some and sticking her nose far into the toe of one of the shoes. There would be a bunch of scents, but she would be able to pick out the overwhelming common ones and separate them out. She had done this before. She knew the routine. When she was ready she sat back and looked up at him.

Now almost to the corner office, Creed saw that Grace's nose was skimming the floor tiles. Then her head reared back and her nose nodded up and down like she was tapping the air with it. He could see her chest rising and falling as her breath increased. They walked by one door and Grace skidded to a halt. There was a keypad. No other signs or notices that it was a secured area.

Grace hesitated there, sniffing the floor and door frame. Maggie had continued walking to the corner office, expecting Grace and Creed to follow. She turned and stopped. Her eyes flashed to the keypad right at the same time that Grace started back up again. The dog walked slowly, passed Maggie, stopped and considered the secure door again, and then started for the corner office.

Maggie knocked on the door as she waved Creed and Grace to step aside. When there was no answer, she pulled out her Glock and tried the doorknob. Creed could see that it turned easily in her hand. He pulled

Grace to the wall as Maggie shouldered the door open, entering with her weapon stretched out in front her.

She was in the room for only a few minutes when an alarm from up the hall began to screech. He could see red lights flashing over the exits. Doors all along the walls began to open and scientists, some in casual attire, others in white lab coats, spilled into the hallway. Some of them asked each other questions that couldn't be heard over the loud screech.

Maggie came out.

"She's not here," she yelled to Creed. "What the hell's going on?"

A man came out of the office next to them and said, "Fire alarm. In these labs it's best to get out and not even guess whether it's a false alarm." And he followed the others.

Creed reached down to lift up Grace, but she bolted away. She was so quick he almost lost hold of her leash. He hurried to keep up, glancing over his shoulder and mouthing to Maggie, *Shaw!*

73

Clare Shaw used what little time she had to rid herself of Stephen Bishop. In no time she pulled off the jacket, tie, shirt, and trousers. It took a bit longer to unzip and peel away the elastic body suit that flattened her breasts and added extra girth to her otherwise slim figure. She discarded the heavy-framed eyeglasses and peeled away the beard, scrubbing her fingers over her smooth face to wipe away any remaining glue.

Thankfully Dr. Sheila Robins always left extra clothing in her locker. Without the pudginess that belonged to Bishop, Shaw and Robins were about the same size. The only thing that didn't fit quite right was the shoes. Rather than try to stuff her feet into too-small slippers, Shaw kept on Bishop's loafers. If she were to escape, she'd need to be able to run. She had a long trek through the woods before she'd get to the old cabin where she had already stashed everything she'd need if this day ever came.

Last, she pulled on one of Dr. Robins's long white lab coats, then stared at herself in the mirror. She ruffled her fingers through her short hair, leaving some of it to stand on end, looking more chic than tousled. Even without makeup, the tight-knit sweater and smooth-lined jeans defined her as female without a doubt. The loafers were the last thing anyone would notice about her.

Still, she felt like she needed a distraction. That was when she decided to pull the fire alarm.

She waited until some of her colleagues were already outside their offices and labs before she opened the door. She hurried up the hallway, passing others, and took the first exit. Before that door closed behind her, she caught a look at the man and the dog in front of Bishop's office. Though the dog squirmed, the man didn't seem to notice her.

Shaw headed down the steps. There was one place she needed to stop before she disappeared into the woods.

74

O'Dell searched for anyone fitting Bishop's description. When Grace bounded off, O'Dell thought the dog must have been spooked by the alarm. Her toenails clicked and skidded on the tiles as she pulled faster than Creed wanted to allow. He kept telling the dog to slow down and Grace wouldn't have any of it.

Then Creed turned to make sure O'Dell was following and she thought he mouthed the word *Shaw*.

Was it possible that Shaw had pulled the alarm and managed to sneak out?

Grace certainly thought so.

By now the hallway was filled with staff and scientists spilling from the labs and offices. And because of the screeching alarm they couldn't hear O'Dell yelling at them to move aside. Creed tried to keep Grace close to the wall. The dog was straining at the end of the leash, but Creed couldn't squeeze through the crowd fast enough to let her pick up the pace. When the scientists pushed through the first exit door and started down the steps, it was almost impossible to get by them.

She could see Grace pulling, going down step by step, her collar practically choking her because Creed was left behind nearly three or four steps up.

O'Dell shoved her way to catch up. At the top of the stairs she tapped shoulders and started showing them her weapon. That startled them and moved them out of the way. When she reached Creed's back she continued reaching around him and touching the shoulders of those clogging the stairs. At the sight of the weapon, eyes widened, faces paled, and a couple of people almost tripped, but at least they moved out of the way.

Grace waited impatiently at the exit door and Creed shoved it open. The dog hesitated only for a second or two, sniffing the air. When O'Dell squeezed out the door she noticed lines of people pouring out of other exits. They all filed toward the parking lots. Grace took off, but she was headed in the other direction. Creed kept pace, jogging behind her. But O'Dell waited.

This didn't seem right. If Shaw knew they

390

were here, if she was the one who pulled the alarm, why wouldn't she be racing for the parking lot, getting her vehicle, and making her escape?

Creed and Grace were running to an odd-shaped structure surrounded by chain-link fence. They were almost to the gate when there was a loud swoosh. A large wave of netting flew loose from the top of the structure, and through it came hundreds of birds, wings flapping, and a crescendo of chirps. For a brief moment the sky turned black with birds.

Creed stopped and watched, holding tightly to Grace's leash. The little dog appeared annoyed with the pause and paid little attention to the flocks overhead.

O'Dell caught up with them. Neither she nor Creed said a word, but when they went through the gate they were now walking instead of running.

Grace led them into the open aviary where the birds had just exited. O'Dell couldn't help thinking that Shaw had set loose one last batch of infected migratory birds, one last attempt to wreak havoc. The space was as large as a football field. It was an open-air warehouse with netting instead of a roof. The netting was attached in sections to the metal beams, and in the middle O'Dell could see where it had been purposely opened, the latches set free by some mechanism. Shaw was probably able to operate it with a remote of some sort.

The birds were gone. Lone feathers fluttered in the air. But Grace's nose was still twitching. Only she wasn't in a hurry now. She twirled, scratching at the dirt floor, and just then O'Dell realized the three of them were standing on the droppings and breathing in the residue air of what were most likely birds infected with Shaw's strain of the bird flu.

Grace spun around and started back to where they had just come from. O'Dell saw the flash of white.

"Stop!" she yelled, and she fired a shot into the wood above the doorway. To her surprise, the figure stopped.

The woman's hair was chopped short and darker, but O'Dell recognized Shaw. She was shocked to see that she had shed her male disguise, but of course Shaw knew they'd be looking for Stephen Bishop and so the perfect trick was to morph back into her old self.

"Was it the birds that gave me away?" Shaw asked as she approached them.

"Stay where you are and take your hands out of your pockets," O'Dell commanded, but Shaw kept walking toward them.

"It was Grace," Creed told the woman.

He scooped up the little dog. Out of the corner of her eye O'Dell could see him quietly pull the pink elephant from his shoulder bag and hand it to Grace. Her reward. Grace took it and started squeaking it, wanting to get back down, but Creed held her firmly against his side, protecting her from the bird droppings.

"The dogs at the airport," Shaw said calmly, nodding at Grace like she finally understood. "You trained them to detect the virus." She stopped now in front of them and still seemed undeterred by O'Dell's weapon pointing directly at her chest.

"Take your hands out of your pockets," O'Dell said again.

They came out slowly but halfway out, O'Dell could see that Shaw had something in both. Neither was a gun or knife. They were small plastic bags, what looked like harmless everyday Ziplocs, and they confused O'Dell enough to hesitate as Shaw flung both directly at them. The open bags hit O'Dell and Creed at the same time, and though both had put up their arms instinctively, the contents had already begun splattering them in midair. It looked like blood.

Shaw used those few seconds to turn and

run. This time O'Dell didn't hesitate. She would not let this woman get away a second time. While wiping blood from her face, she aimed, took a deep breath, and squeezed the trigger twice.

■ ■ ■ ■

TUESDAY

■ ■ ■ ■

Jason had just finished the kennel chores. It was the first time he'd done all of them alone without Creed. From the sounds of it, he'd need to get used to it. His shoulder ached. He had gotten into the habit of gripping bags of dog food and pinning them under his arm. He carried them against his body with his amputated arm, so he could leave his hand free to open gates and doors. He had actually gotten pretty good at it, but his body was still trying to adjust.

He was heading to the house for coffee with Hannah and Dr. Avelyn when he saw a shiny black SUV winding its way through the trees. It reminded him of Tabor, and immediately he felt a knot in his stomach.

Jason came in the back door just as the SUV took the last curve in the long driveway.

"We've got company," he told the two women.

Hannah didn't look surprised. Instead she went to the cupboard and took out another coffee mug.

"I baked a batch of pecan rolls," she said, pointing to the kitchen table, where a plate of pastries sat in the middle of the paperwork she and Dr. Avelyn had been working on.

The scent of fresh bread, sugar, and cinnamon made Jason's mouth water, and already he had forgotten the knot in his stomach. He was slathering a roll with butter when Hannah opened the back door and called to their visitor.

The last time Jason had seen Charlie Wurth he had been shoving and yelling at passengers to get out of the way. Now the man greeted them with a wide smile. He wore dark trousers, a light blue shirt, and a striped tie to match. His shirtsleeves were rolled up and his sunglasses were pushed up on top of his head. Jason started to stand up, but Wurth waved at him to sit back down.

"Sure does smell good in here," he told Hannah. "You are definitely not the typical contractor I'm used to working with."

Jason glanced at Hannah. He'd never seen that look on her face. She was actually flustered by Wurth's praise.

"How's Rye doing?" she asked him as she gestured for him to sit. She poured coffee for the two men and offered to top off Dr. Avelyn's.

"They're still running tests." Wurth dropped a manila envelope on the table but stayed standing until Hannah came around to her seat.

"When I talked to him he sounded like a long-tailed cat in a room full of rocking chairs. He won't admit it, but I think he's a bit claustrophobic after being buried under that mudslide."

"Do they know if the blood Shaw threw at them was contaminated?" Dr. Avelyn asked.

"Colonel Platt didn't believe it was, but they're being extra cautious."

Wurth picked up the envelope and tapped it against his open palm. Jason thought the man looked impatient and ready to talk about why he was really here.

"I wanted to thank all of you again. As you know, Mr. Creed drove a hard bargain to make this all happen, and it was certainly worth every cent. I look forward to working with all of you in the future. But there was one piece of the agreement that I still need to deliver."

Wurth surprised Jason by handing him the

envelope.

Jason looked from Wurth to Hannah and Dr. Avelyn, then back to Wurth before he set his coffee mug down. He hesitated as he took the envelope.

"What's this?" he asked.

"Something your boss insisted we include in the agreement."

Jason looked at Hannah again, and she said, "Go ahead and open it."

He pulled out a folder and opened it, but he still didn't understand what he was looking at. On one side was official paperwork from Johns Hopkins University with instructions including dates and times. Tucked in the other side of the folder were several brochures. One of them had DARPA printed at the top. He pulled it out. The graphic on the front was a robotic hand. A quick scan and he picked out phrases: "Revolutionizing Prosthetics Program," "touch sensations," "mind-controlled," "dexterous hand capabilities."

"I don't understand," Jason finally said.

"It's state-of-the-art technology," Wurth told him. "I'm told it just passed a thirty-five-volunteer test study with flying colors." Wurth reached across the table and tapped a business card that was stapled to the document on the other side. "You're all scheduled, but if you need to change dates, you call me. It'll be about a week for the fitting and adjusting, as well as some time for you to get used to using it. That paperwork includes hotel reservations for you and your dog."

"My dog?"

"I was told you have a dog you'd probably want to bring with you."

Jason looked at Hannah. He couldn't believe this. He thought of Tony and his upcoming funeral, of all they had been through together. He had followed in Tony's footsteps almost all his life, and over the last several days he struggled to imagine how to go on without his friend. Maybe this was a good start.

"I don't know what to say," he told Hannah.

She took his hand and squeezed it, fighting back her own emotion as she smiled.

Creed was already tired of wearing the hospital gown. No one would tell him how much longer he'd be stuck in here. He was worried about Grace. They would only tell him that the dog was fine, but they wouldn't let him see her.

They had allowed him to talk to Hannah on the phone last night. He knew she'd be worried, especially if she'd heard about the two of them being splattered with blood. He had been told that the blood wasn't infected with the virus. Supposedly they were taking extra precautions because of the bird droppings and being in the aviary, breathing in the air contaminated by what they believed were birds infected with the bird flu.

Hannah told him about Tillie tracking the first virus carrier. And he told her about Grace sniffing out Dr. Shaw. She also told him how well Jason had done with Winnie.

All in all, they'd managed to help apprehend three virus carriers. They had no way of knowing if those three were the only ones.

Creed kept the television on. It was the only thing that kept him from climbing the white walls of the isolation unit. Charlie Wurth and Benjamin Platt were able to keep secret the reason for the commotion and arrests at the Atlanta airport. But there were rumors and suspicion about a new flu sickening hundreds in the Chicago and New York areas. The CDC reported nine deaths despite their claim that the strain was not as strong as they had initially suspected.

There was, however, no mention of the bird flu, and no journalists seemed to make the connection even after several reports of birds falling from the sky. On one of the channels Amee Rief, the biologist with the U.S. Fish and Wildlife Service, was being interviewed about the strange occurrence. Creed listened for a while until he realized that Charlie Wurth had managed to control this story line, too.

Of course, most of the 24/7 news cycle was concentrated on Washington, D.C., where Colonel Abraham Hess, the legendary director of DARPA, was stepping down. The official word was that the man was finally retiring, but there was speculation that his resignation had been forced. This news came after a DARPA field agent named Lawrence Tabor had been arrested for the murder of Sheriff Wylie. Tabor was also being investigated in the suspicious death of a scientist named Dr. Howard Getz, whose vehicle had been found in a ravine not far from his research facility.

Creed shook his head at the politics of it all. None of it surprised him, and he thought about how Hess's attempt at cover-up wasn't really much different than what Charlie Wurth, Benjamin Platt, and the CDC were doing. They were all so good at it.

The fact that the colonel was resigning and not being led away in handcuffs spoke more about his skills of survival than the cover-up. He claimed Tabor had gone rogue, and he insisted the agent had not been acting on any orders given or implied. Of course, all that might change once Dr. Clare Shaw recovered from her gunshot wounds and began telling tales of Hess's involvement. It probably depended on how much the federal government wanted to admit about what DARPA and its research facilities were actually working on.

There was a knock at the window. Creed wanted to wave the person away. Certainly they had already taken enough of his blood and saliva for the day. But when he looked up he saw Maggie standing in the neutral zone at the thick window that separated his room. She was wearing a matching hospital gown and under her arm was Grace. Behind her Creed recognized Benjamin Platt, though he was dressed in one of the blue space suits.

Platt gestured for Creed to stand back away from the door. He could feel the air exchange as the seal disengaged and the door opened. Maggie came in with a wiggling Grace. She put the dog down on the floor and in seconds Grace was jumping into Creed's arms.

"You have two hours," Platt said, his voice muffled through his glass shield. And he closed the door.

"I talked him into it," Maggie told him. "He knows how much I hate being in an isolation unit."

Creed just stared at her.

"You don't mind, do you?" she asked, suddenly concerned that she might have stepped over some line.

"You are cramping my style as a loner."

"I also talked him into bringing us a pizza."

He smiled at that and said, "He's a good man."

"Yes, he is," she said, but there was something sad and mournful in her voice.

He watched Maggie go to sit down on the sofa in the corner with Grace prancing alongside. A gentleman would tell her that her gown needed to be tied up better in the back. Maybe he'd mention it when she was leaving.

AUTHOR'S NOTE

Most of you know I love doing research for my novels. At times it's difficult to stop and make myself sit down and write the book. But, as fascinating as the research was for this book, I must confess it was unsettling in a way that I've never experienced before and in a way I certainly didn't expect.

I've had the idea of using virus-sniffing dogs in one of my Creed novels ever since I discovered the In Situ Foundation. This organization has been dedicated to scientifically training dogs to detect early-stage cancer in humans for more than twelve years. (See more at dogsdetectcancer.org.) Their published findings have been impressive. In many cases, dogs are able to detect certain types of cancer — lung, breast, and prostate, to name a few — sooner and with more accuracy than some of the leading medical equipment and lab tests currently available.

Dogs are already being used to detect epileptic seizures before they occur and insulin imbalances in diabetics. They have been able to detect *C. diff* in patients before there are symptoms. The applications seem limited only to the trainers and their abilities to communicate what they want the dogs to detect. It's very exciting.

TSA is gearing up to add hundreds more dogs at airports to help get us through those long security lines quicker, but it may be just a matter of time before they use dogs to also detect Ebola, tuberculosis, and other dangerous pathogens coming into the country. In fact, there are speculations that our next terrorist attack could be a biological weapon in the form of virus carriers. And if that doesn't scare you enough, the CDC has all but admitted that they may not be ready. It's been said that Hurricane Katrina was a hard lesson on how to evacuate an entire city. But the CDC has suggested that it might take an actual outbreak of a deadly virus to teach us how to quarantine an entire city.

So how likely is it that the bird flu could be one of those deadly viruses? The strains we've seen here in the United States are different than the Asian and Eurasian strains, which seems to further prove that the virus mutates often and rapidly. Scientists say it's only a matter of time before the bird flu becomes airborne. In fact, scientists have already created in laboratories a strain that can spread easily to humans and be transmitted airborne. They've done this in the hopes of creating a vaccine, but if the virus changes so quickly, how can we stockpile vaccine?

The bird flu actually hadn't been seen since the 1950s. It's believed that the H1N1 flu strain that caused a pandemic in 1977 and continued to mutate and circulate, now for over twenty years, was accidentally released from a lab in Russia or China. Who's to say that couldn't happen again? In the past few years, U.S. research labs have made the news by mistakenly sending out live anthrax spores and live samples of the plague. In 2014 a Belgian vaccine plant accidentally released live infectious polio virus into waterways. Those are only a few examples, but there are many more and even some that might not have been reported.

So you see this idea that I had brewing in the back of my mind about Ryder Creed training and using virus-sniffing dogs took a twisted turn from scary make-believe fiction into scarier real-life fact. I didn't realize how close my fabricated story could be to the truth — that we actually could be only a few steps away from a pandemic of the bird flu, whether through a planned bioterror attack or a simple laboratory accident.

Now, here's the kicker — about a third of the way through writing the book, something else hit me. Dogs can sniff and detect cancer and diabetes and *C. diff* without getting cancer or diabetes or *C. diff.* But can they sniff and detect the bird flu without becoming infected by the bird flu?

Suddenly, Creed's panic became my own. And that one question literally sent me scrambling back to my research and digging for the answer. I'm still not sure I found it.

ACKNOWLEDGMENTS

As with each of my novels, I have a whole lot of people to thank and acknowledge.

Thanks go to:

First and foremost, Deb Carlin and the rest of the pack: Duncan, Boomer, Maggie, and Huck. You guys are my inspiration, my heart, and my soul.

My friends and family, who put up with my long absences and still manage to love me and keep me grounded: Marlene Haney, Sandy Rockwood, Patti and Martin Bremmer, Patricia Sierra, Sharon Kator, Maricela and Jose Barajas, Patti El-Kachouti, Diane Prohaska, Dr. Elvira Rios, Linda and Doug Buck, Leigh Ann Retelsdorf and Pat Heng, Annie Belatti, Cari Conine, Lisa Munk, Luann Causey, Christy Cotton, and Patti Carlin.

Amee Rief, my friend and biologist extraordinaire, for allowing me to use her name and expertise for my fictional biologist. When I asked Amee if I could use her name, the character played a small role in the story, but before I knew it, she ended up entangled in a major way. So if I got any facts wrong, please remember it's on me and not Amee.

My fellow authors and friends, who make this business a bit less crazy: Sharon Car, Erica Spindler, and J.T. Ellison.

R.J. Russell for her amazing talent and insight in creating and bringing us a cinematic vision of Ryder, Grace, and Maggie's world.

Ray Kunze, once again, for lending his name to Maggie O'Dell's boss.

Penelope Wilson and Penny Clemence for combining their names to become Creed's dog rescuer, Penelope Clemence.

My pack depends on some amazing veterinarians, and now they've become friends as well as invaluable resources for writing this series. Special thanks to: Dr. Enita Larson and her crew at Tender Care Animal Hospital and Dr. Tonya McIlnay and the team at Veterinary Eye Specialists of Nebraska.

Again, an extra thank-you to Dr. Larson, not only for patiently answering some of my crazy questions about dogs but also for allowing me to name my fictional veterinarian after her children: Avelyn Faye and

Ayden Parker. Dr. Avelyn Parker has quickly become an integral part of the Creed novels. And she definitely saves the day . . . and the dogs, this time.

Speaking of dogs — there are some special tributes this time: Tillie is named for my friends and neighbors Dan and Paula Nielsen's seventeen-year-old black-and-white cocker spaniel who passed away earlier this year. Tillie used to love to run the fence line with my pack. We all miss her dearly. And Winifred (Winnie) is named in memory of reader Patricia Lauer's beloved yellow Lab. Of course, Jason's black Lab puppy, Scout, is named for my Westie, Scout, whom I lost in 2014.

Thanks also to my publishing teams: my agent, Scott Miller, and his colleague Claire Roberts at Trident Media Group. At Putnam: Ivan Held, Sara Minnich, Christine Ball, Alexis Welby, Lauren Lopinto, and Elena Hershey. And at Little, Brown/Sphere: David Shelley, Catherine Burke, Jade Chandler, and Katherine Armstrong.

As always, thank you to all the booksellers, librarians, book clubs, and book bloggers for mentioning and recommending my novels.

A big thank-you to all of my VIR Club members, Facebook friends, and faithful readers. With so many wonderful novels available, I'm honored that you continue to choose mine. Without you, I wouldn't have the opportunity to share my twisted tales.

Last but certainly not least — a humble and special thanks to all those past and present who have served in our military, including all the four-legged heroes.

ABOUT THE AUTHOR

Alex Kava is the *New York Times* best-selling author of the critically acclaimed Maggie O'Dell series and a series featuring former marine, Ryder Creed and his K9 dogs. Her stand-alone novel, *One False Move*, was chosen for the 2006 One Book One Nebraska and her political thriller, *Whitewash*, was one of *January Magazine*'s best thrillers of the year. Published in over thirty countries, Alex's novels have made the bestseller lists in the UK, Australia, Germany, Japan, Italy, and Poland. She is also a co-author of the novellas *Slices of Night* and *Storm Season* with Erica Spindler and J.T. Ellison. Her novel *Stranded* was awarded both a Florida Book Award and the Nebraska Book Award. She is a member of the Nebraska Writers Guild and a founding member of International Thriller

Writers. Alex divides her time between Omaha, Nebraska and Pensacola, Florida.